WILDFLOWER WORDS

T0125855

"It's full of exciting adventure and the promise of romance. It's sweet, fresh and hopeful. It takes me back to my teenage years, the good parts of those years at least. I read this in a few hours, only stopped long enough to have lunch. I hope I won't have to wait too long for the sequel—I have high hopes for Jastyn, Aurelia, their friend Coran, Eegit the hedgewitch and Rigo the elf."—*Jude in the Stars*

"A fantasy book with MCs in their very early twenties, this book presents a well thought out world of Kingdom of Venostes (shades of The Lord of the Rings here)."—*Best Lesfic Reviews*

"Sam Ledel has definitely set up an epic adventure of star-crossed lovers. This book one of a trilogy doesn't leave you with a cliffhanger but you are definitely going to be left ready for the next book…As a non-fantasy lover, I adored this book and am ready to read where Ledel takes us next. This book is quality writing, great pacing, and top-notch characters. You cannot go wrong with this one!"—*Romantic Reader Blog*

"If you're a huge fan of fantasy novels, especially if you love stories like this one that contains a host of supernatural beings, quirky characters coupled with action and excitement around every tree, winding path or humble abode, then this is definitely the story for you! This compelling story also deals with poverty, isolation and the huge chasm between the royal family and the low-class villagers. Well, fellow book lovers, it really looks like you've just received a winning ticket to a literary lottery."—*Lesbian Review*

By the Author

Rocks and Stars

Wildflower Words

The Odium Trilogy

Daughter of No One

Broken Reign

The Princess and the Odium

WILDFLOWER WORDS

by
Sam Ledel

2022

ISBN 13: 978-1-63679-055-8

THIS TRADE PAPERBACK ORIGINAL IS PUBLISHED BY
BOLD STROKES BOOKS, INC.
P.O. BOX 249
VALLEY FALLS, NY 12185

FIRST EDITION: JANUARY 2022

CREDITS
EDITOR: BARBARA ANN WRIGHT
PRODUCTION DESIGN: STACIA SEAMAN
COVER DESIGN BY TAMMY SEIDICK

Acknowledgments

Thank you to Sandy Lowe, Radclyffe, and the entire Bold Strokes Books team. Thanks to my editor, Barbara Ann Wright, who always manages to make the terrifying prospect of editing an enlightening and entertaining experience.

A special thank you to Lisa, who handed me *The Book Woman of Troublesome Creek* by Kim Michelle Richardson a couple of years ago. While the seed had already been planted to tell a story featuring one of the daring, adventurous "book women" of the Pack Horse Library, reading that fueled the flames of creativity and provided great insight. For anyone interested in another fictional account of a Pack Horse librarian, please give that excellent book a read.

For my family, including the woman whose spirit, grace, and generosity inspired the character of Clara Thompson: my mother. The enthusiasm you all share in this writing dream means the world to me. Thank you.

CHAPTER ONE

L ida Jones stepped off the passenger car and onto the crowded platform of the Pine City, Utah, train station. Narrowly dodging a harried-looking porter as the train whistle confirmed their arrival, she inhaled deeply.

"Smell that, Pa?" she asked, turning as her father, Yaromir Jones, helped a well-dressed red-haired woman down from the train. "Smells like burning coal and tired people, like all train stations," he replied. Lida noticed the redhead eye her father upon hearing the deep timbre and thick Russian accent from his tall but otherwise unassuming frame. As her father took his duffel from a passing porter, the same woman glanced at Lida, who smiled the way she knew people interpreted as "I won't bite. I'm only new here." She found a smile went a long way in America.

Lida gripped the handle of her suitcase as they moved across the platform toward the station, a two-story brick building sitting between them and their latest destination.

"I was referring to the fresh air, Pa." Lida followed him through the passersby. Many of the men donned flat caps or wide-brimmed ones like Lida's, as well as heavy coats to keep the crisp spring air at bay. She glanced up at the clear sky. It seemed so much bigger, at least compared to the choking city streets of Cincinnati. "We can actually breathe here."

"You enjoy. Tell me about it when I come up for air."

"You won't be in the mountain every day, Pa."

He grunted. "I'll see the inside of the earth more than that blue," he countered, pointing skyward.

She laughed. "Where did you say we're to meet Mr. Havish?"

Holding the door for her, he said, "At the Canyon Café." Inside the station, they wove through a series of benches where young and middle-aged men in suits sat, most reading newspapers outdated by a week. Lida briefly caught the headline next to last Wednesday's date, May 1, 1935. "Canada Begins Circulation of Silver Dollar." Meanwhile, her father fished out a scrap of paper from the pocket of his worn brown wool coat. Lida reminded herself to rework the stitching of the bottom button. It dangled sadly by an old thread. "Yes, Canyon Café. Three o'clock."

They made it through the station, both sighing in relief to be out of the crowd. Outside, Lida found what she presumed was the main street of Pine City. It looked like all the other main streets she'd ever visited: a single, roughly paved road ran between lines of one- and two-story buildings, some brick, others wood and painted in blues, reds, or greens with gold or white lettering declaring the purpose.

Puddles of slush from a recent snowfall littered the street where a mixture of vehicles gathered. Several mule wagons sat haphazardly in front of a market, while another—brimming with long beams of lumber—idled near a drugstore. Near them, horses stood patiently tied to long wooden posts, waiting for their riders to return. Lida was pleased to see less congestion on this road than where she and her father had been before. A few cars were parked on the street, their wheels dirty with old snow, but their metal sides gleaming. Lida had ridden in a car one time before; she'd found the experience rather terrifying as she and a friend had flown down an old lake road in Ohio.

As they crossed the street, stepping up onto the opposite sidewalk, they paused under a green awning attached to what looked to be a wagon parts store. Lida set her suitcase down. It felt good to walk after the long train ride. She stretched, twisting her torso to ease the crick in her lower back. Doing so drew the attention of several nearby children. A few of them stopped their game—something involving hopping around a rock—to gawk at her.

Lida was used to this. Ever since she was a child, newly immigrated to America, people looked at her like the children were now. Their wide, light eyes roved over her. Perhaps they noticed the similarities in the new strangers: how she shared her father's bushy dark hair, which she kept in a braid that ran down her back. Like her father, she had deep-set, dark brown eyes, with perpetual shadows that sat beneath them.

Adjusting her coat, she pulled out a handful of candy from her pocket. One of the kids, a young boy of maybe seven, looked from the yellow foil-wrapped sweets to her.

She smiled, extending her hand. The boy grinned before sprinting forward, the cuffs of his shorts as dirty as his knees. Right before he could snatch the candy up, she pulled back her hand. "First," she said, kneeling to meet his gaze, "promise me you'll share with everyone."

The boy glanced over his shoulder to where his friends all tittered anxiously, watching. "I will."

"Then here you go."

Standing, Lida watched as the boy handed out the treats.

"You will give them cavities," her father said. He seemed focused on the glass of a shop window, though, and ran a comb from his pocket through his thick black hair.

She shook her head, then waved as the children hollered their thanks and resumed playing. Turning to him, she said, "Pa, your tie."

He brushed his mustache and harrumphed. She turned him around and swiftly redid the disheveled knot.

"You know what to say?" she asked.

Her father nodded. "I already have job. It's a formality, this meeting."

"I know," she said, remembering the telegram they'd received a month ago about an opportunity for work in the iron mines of southwestern Utah. Her father had sent a letter to the address listed, a mining company owned partly by one Mr. Walter Havish of Pine

City. "Still, we want to make a good impression." She hesitated before adding, "We want to show him we're reliable."

Her father's gaze flickered to the awning flapping in the breeze. "That's enough now." He brushed her hand away from his tie and stepped back to stare at his reflection once again. Beside him, Lida fixed a stray piece of hair that refused to stay behind her ear. She'd always been told they looked alike, though while Lida possessed his coloring, her wide jaw, heart-shaped face, and broad cheekbones came from her mother. At five foot seven, she was several inches shorter than her father, whose towering, nearly six-foot frame always drew curious eyes. He continued, "They don't care if my tie is straight, but they do care if I am on time."

Lida grimaced. That was what she'd been trying to tell him. "You're right, Pa." Stepping closer, she brushed the coarse material of his coat near his shoulders, searching for lingering soot from the train. He pulled out an old pocket watch. A breeze blew by, and she caught the faint whisp of alcohol on his breath when he cleared his throat. She frowned, supposing he must have found a fellow passenger willing to share while she slept last night. "Here." She handed him the last lemon drop candy. When he raised his bushy brows, she placed it in his hand. "For good luck. Not cavities."

He gave a reluctant smile. "Come, then." Together, they wandered up the main street where a sign pitched fifty yards ahead on the damp sidewalk read in bold, burgundy letters Canyon Café, with a finger pointing the way.

Lida took another deep breath. She tried to let the new, unfamiliar mountain air quell her nerves. On either side of them, the tall mountains loomed in greeting like the gates of a great, ancient city. Maybe this time, she thought, things will work out.

CHAPTER TWO

One fried chicken with a side of potatoes and greens." Hazel slid the plate in front of Jerry Spector, one of the many regulars at Wednesday's lunch hour.

"Thank you kindly," he said, running an eager hand down his soot-smudged cheeks.

"Gosh, that looks good." Mike Evans sat across from Jerry wearing a matching pair of dirty blue overalls over an undershirt that might've been white once upon a time.

"Tastes good, too," Hazel replied before handing Mike his own full plate.

"See what you been missin' working on that land of yours?" Jerry said through a mouthful of chicken smothered in white gravy. He leaned back and gestured to the plate of food. "Now that he's a miner, he gets the perks. I told him this place has got the best fried chicken this side of the Rockies."

"Darn right, Jerry." Hazel brushed aside a lock of hair that fell across her eyes as she refilled their water cups. "Eat up now, boys."

They thanked her as Hazel collected three plates from another table, the only thing left on them a few cornbread crumbs. She glanced over at Mike on her way back to the kitchen and smiled at his bug-eyed satisfaction as he spooned more potatoes into his mouth.

"Table two's clear, Momma," Hazel said as she passed from the Old Lodge's dining room into the kitchen. The warmth of the room enveloped her as she placed the dishes in a basin already nearly full with remnants of the busy lunch hour.

"Pass me that rolling pin, will ya, honey?" her mother, Clara Thompson, asked from behind a cluttered counter in the middle of the modest-sized room framed by a wood-burning stove, a perpetually burning fireplace hosting a large cauldron full of cooking oil, and an imposing cast-iron range where three pies baked and several pots emitted lazy steam.

Handing over the wooden pin, Hazel did a sweep of the kitchen, mentally running through how long she had before Hank Cavill and Stephen Akers at table five would need a refill. Their routines were predictable, like most days at the Old Lodge. Hazel knew every customer, knew what each person would order, and how long they'd stay to talk after. Like the steady hum of conversation in the dining room, her days were constant, familiar. Every day nearly the same, save for what kind of pie her mother had baked.

"Give those birds a turn, Hazel, honey."

"Yes, Momma." Standing before the blazing fireplace, Hazel squinted into the bright flames. The seasoned fat inside the cavernous black cauldron crackled. With practiced ease, Hazel turned the spit where two pairs of chicken breasts and four wings spun inside the hot liquid.

"That boy out there, Mike Evans," she said, tossing a glance back through the doorway into the open floor of the Lodge. "He can't be more than sixteen."

"Mike is fifteen. I remember. Born nearly one year after your brother."

Hazel frowned at the image of her brother Nicholas forced to don coveralls and a mining helmet like Mike. The image made her shiver. "He's not old enough, Momma."

"Old enough to work," her mother replied, her strong hands rolling out a new piecrust like Hazel had seen her do thousands of times.

"But in the mine? That's no place for a boy that young."

Her mother made a noise like a grunt. "Ain't nowhere else for him to go, honey. Bank took half his family's land."

Hazel sighed, turning back to watch her mother work. The apron she wore over the lavender-checked dress was tight on her sturdy frame and was covered in flour and plum preserves. The cross-stitching of primrose near the top was Hazel's touch. It matched the pattern on her own apron tied around a dress similar to her mother's, only a soft periwinkle blue instead. Her mother shifted her weight in her low-heeled clogs, making Hazel's ankles seem to remember how tired they were in a matching, hand-me-down pair. They'd been up with the sun, like most days, and Hazel worked hard as her mother's right hand. She felt a distant tiredness, but like everything else, it was simply a part of life, an unshakable aspect of her routine she'd grown accustomed to.

For a time, they worked in silence, only the sound of the meat crackling as it fried and the soft hum of conversation from the diners in the main room.

"Afternoon, Mrs. Thompson."

Hazel looked up to find Arthur Davis standing in the back, his broad figure framed in the open doorway, which allowed the crisp spring breeze to cool the warm room. He removed his hat, revealing a receding hairline of short black hair.

"Why, Mr. Davis, is it two o'clock already?" Her mother quickly and perfectly set the dough atop a peach pie.

Arthur ducked as he passed into the kitchen. He carried a white sack propped on his left shoulder. "How are ya, Miss Hazel?"

"I'm fine, Mr. Davis, thank you." Hazel didn't miss how her mother subtly adjusted the stray wisps of light blond hair back into the collection of pins atop her head. Since Arthur began delivering goods from Pine City for them two years ago, Hazel had noticed that her mother's eyes brightened in his presence. When she'd brought it up six months ago, though, her mother had quickly dismissed the idea that she was fond of Arthur in any way, calling Hazel's inquiry "utter gossip."

"That must be the cornmeal we ordered," her mother said, moving to open the door opposite the big stove that led to the pantry.

"Right you are, Mrs. Thompson."

"Well, go ahead, and I'll just find my purse."

Arthur disappeared into the storage room, again ducking so as not to hit his head. He called from inside, "You know this here delivery is the best part of my week, Mrs. Thompson."

Hazel grinned and looked pointedly at her mother, who made a shooing motion at Hazel and dipped her chin in a failed attempt to hide her blush. "Don't be silly, Arthur. We ain't nobody but cooks in a crowded kitchen."

Arthur closed the pantry door behind him. He straightened his coat, a light beige color over dark blue coveralls that had a tear on one knee. The cuffs were frayed, the strings hanging over tall, brown leather boots. He seemed to ponder how to respond to her mother's comment and ran a large hand over his hair and forehead, the dark skin around his eyes pulling into crow's feet when he grinned.

"You know I'd be perfectly happy with a plate of that fried chicken. It smells mighty good today."

Her mother looked at Arthur a moment as she wiped her hands on a rag before reaching beneath the waistband of her apron. Hazel caught the flash of a coin between her fingers.

Arthur smiled wider. "Don't wanna leave a man hungry now, do ya?"

Hazel and her mother laughed. "Certainly not." Then her mother reached out, smoothly placing the coin in Arthur's palm. "Go on, then. Table by the fire's open."

"There's a slice of apple pie saved just for you, too," Hazel called after him.

"Thank you, Miss Hazel," he said but kept his playful brown eyes on her mother.

"Go on, then. Hazel will bring your plate out in a jiffy."

He was two steps into the main room when he turned back. "Oh, by the way, I reckon you'd wanna know I saw your boy Nicholas on my way here."

Hazel paused shelling a pile of green beans. Her mother kept peeling potatoes but raised her gaze to listen.

"Saw him on the Boley property, just outside the fence. Was up in a tree. No idea what he was doin' but thought you outta know."

The tiredness in Hazel's body gathered in her gut, a squirming agitation taking its place. Her brother wandering was another part of her routine, and the older he got, the more brazen he seemed to get with where he ventured. Sighing, she shook her head.

"Thank you, Arthur," her mother said, smiling still. Hazel could see her eyes grow worried.

When they were alone, Hazel dropped the beans into a bowl and removed her apron. "I'll go, Momma."

"Of all the properties, that boy has to go there."

"I know. I'll fetch him. Can only hope no one else has seen him."

Her mother rolled up a sleeve, grabbed a large fork, and started mashing the potatoes. Hazel could see the extra oomph in her movements, her agitated grip in the whites of her knuckles, and the general shift in her demeanor whenever she worried about Nicholas.

"I'll be back soon," Hazel said, placing a quick kiss on her cheek.

"Thanks, sweetheart." As Hazel grabbed her coat from a chair in the corner, her mother added, "Those dishes won't wash themselves. Hurry back now."

Waving, Hazel hurried out the back door of the Old Lodge. She could only hope this time, like all the other times, Nicholas hadn't gotten himself into anything she couldn't handle.

She raced down the stone steps, hopped onto the seat of her family's wagon, and started up the mountain.

CHAPTER THREE

Inside the Canyon Café, a brunette woman wearing a red blouse tucked into a pair of trousers greeted them from behind a tall desk.

"I have meeting with Mr. Havish. Three o'clock," Lida's father said, removing his tattered bowler hat.

The woman's smile faltered at his wording. "And who should I say you are?"

"Mr. Jones. Yaromir Jones."

Lida matched her father's smile. The woman lifted one thin brow but told them to wait there a moment. Lida exchanged looks with her father before sweeping her gaze over the large restaurant. Behind the desk where the woman had greeted them was a long room that held thirty low, circular tables draped in fine white tablecloths, each surrounded by four polished chairs. The room was warm, but a constant breeze blew in through the back, where Lida guessed the kitchen had a back door propped open.

"Follow me, please."

They followed the woman between several tables hosting well-dressed men and women, some of whom held their teacups still as Lida and her father wound their way to a side table adorned with a wildflower centerpiece next to a lone, dull candle.

"Mr. Jones!" The man seated behind a plate of half-eaten steak and scalloped potatoes lathered in butter nearly tipped over his wineglass as he stood to extend a hand. "Thank you, Mayra," he said to the hostess, and she hurried away. "Walter Havish. It's good to meet you, Mr. Jones. How was the train ride in?"

"Fine, fine," her father said, turning his hat in his hands.

Next to him, Lida shuffled awkwardly. She met the gaze of the woman next to Mr. Havish. She looked ten years older than Lida, at least, and wore a lovely blue dress that reminded her of one she'd seen in a film back in New York. Faint lines surrounded her kind, light brown eyes that, to Lida's surprise, roved up and down her figure.

"Please, sit." Mr. Havish gestured with pudgy fingers to the two open seats. They both did, and Lida was conscious of the dirt that trailed off her boots. "And this must be your daughter," Mr. Havish was saying. He lowered his chin to sip his wine, which made his nearly nonexistent neck disappear into the high collar of his starched shirt.

"Yes," she replied, fidgeting on the chair cushion. "I'm Lida. How do you do?"

The woman next to him cleared her throat, adjusting the large, jewel-encrusted brooch near the neck of her fine dress.

"Forgive me," Mr. Havish said. His bald head glistened in the daylight that poured in through a nearby window. "I'm always a little scattered. This is my wife, Mrs. Cynthia Havish."

"I'm charmed to meet your acquaintance, Mr. Jones. And it is a delight to meet your daughter." The way she spoke was like the movies, too. Each word seemed to be carefully enunciated through her red lips.

Lida glanced between the Havishes, wondering how they could have met. Maybe, she imagined, in a bigger city, like Salt Lake. She wondered how often they traveled. They looked like they had the means.

"Well." Mr. Havish swiped his napkin over his mouth and freshly shaved chin, then dabbed his perspiring forehead. "This will be brief." Lida sat back in her chair, pressing her right foot against the base of her suitcase. "I wanted to formally welcome you, Mr. Jones, to Utah. We're glad to have you. Not everyone is up for the mine, you know."

"I have no trouble with it," her father replied, lifting his chin.

"Very good, yes. Well, you'll start Monday at eight a.m. sharp. There, the site manager, Mr. Williams, will meet you at the lower mine entrance to show you the ropes."

Her father nodded. He was still turning his hat below the table.

"Pardon me, Mr. Havish," Lida said, "the telegram made no mention of starting pay."

"Lida." Her father frowned, and Mr. Havish looked startled but smiled.

"I think it's fair we know how much my father will be making. We know all about your expectations. Six days a week, eight a.m. to five p.m. One hour for lunch. We're happy to be here for this work, Mr. Havish. My father is eager to start, but what will he earn in return for this labor?"

While a smile seemed to get her far in the company of strangers, speaking on behalf of her father tended to have the opposite effect. Most men laughed, the foreman or factory-line workers guffawing at her assertive requests. If she had her way, Lida wouldn't be the one saying these things. She wished her father still had the backbone he once did, when she was younger. But they'd left New York a long time ago, and ever since the first incident in the Yonkers hay mill, her father had turned inward. She'd had to take command.

Her eyes held Mr. Havish's. He folded his napkin, glanced at his wife—who looked positively entertained—then smiled. "Your daughter is quite savvy, Mr. Jones."

Her father cleared his throat. "We have moved a lot. Lida has worked, too." He straightened. "It's a good skill, to talk in business."

"Absolutely." Mr. Havish finished his wine. "To answer your question, Miss Jones, starting pay is seventy cents an hour. There's a chance for a three-cent increase after six months, so long as there are no problems." He pushed his plate forward. Next to him, Mrs. Havish finished the last of her potatoes while Lida did the math in her head. That'd be over one hundred dollars a week, which was more than the steel mill in Ohio. Her father seemed to come to the same conclusion as he gave a small smile that peeked out from below his mustache.

Eventually, he said, "That's very good, Mr. Havish. Thank you."

"Thank you, Mr. Jones. It's getting harder and harder to find miners these days. But it's good work, yes, solid work. And, Miss Jones"—he met her gaze across the table—"thank you for venturing out to our little corner of frontier. I do hope you'll like Cedar Springs. That's where you'll find your lodgings. It's closer to the mine. Makes more sense to stay there. I'm sure you understand." He pulled a pocket watch from his silk vest. "There's a man who will be outside at half-past four to drive you up there."

"Up?" Lida asked. She hadn't expected to stay in Pine City, of course. The city and its people looked like they'd never seen a pickax, much less a mine. Still, the prospect of climbing to their destination left her nervous.

"Yes. Up the mountain. It's a five-mile trek just around the peak to Cedar Springs."

"Very good," her father said.

"Indeed." Mr. Havish stood. "If you'll excuse me just a moment, I've got to send a telegram, I just remembered."

"Go on, darling," Mrs. Havish said with a wave of her hand, each nail perfectly polished to match her dress. He placed a kiss on her rouged cheek.

"I'll be back in a jiffy to see you off. Pardon me."

When he left, Mrs. Havish turned to Lida. "Your English is quite good, dear."

"Lida has been in America since she was a girl," her father answered. "She's had long time to learn. She's better now than me," he added. They all chuckled.

"And, Mrs. Jones," Mrs. Havish said, "will she be joining you all later?"

It was Lida's turn to answer. "My mother died seven years ago."

Mrs. Havish's face fell, and she clutched her long necklace. "Oh my, I am so sorry to hear that. Pneumonia?" she asked, her voice a whisper.

"Tuberculosis."

Mrs. Havish shook her head. "That's dreadful. You know, they say the air out here is better for you than anything back east. That's why we moved fourteen years ago from Baltimore. So many people out there, so close together. Why, it's impossible to breathe." She flinched at her own words and seemed to realize Lida did, too. Her gaze turned apologetic. "I am so sorry."

"Thank you," Lida replied. She liked Mrs. Havish. She wasn't like a lot of the people they'd met east of the Great Lakes. She spoke quickly, like they did, but there was a lightness, a softness to her demeanor that was a welcome change.

Mr. Havish returned and stood next to his chair. "Well, I do hope you find Cedar Springs to your liking."

Lida and her father stood, shuffling to gather their things.

"What's that, dear?" Mrs. Havish pointed at Lida's coat. She glanced down to find her copy of *A Doll's House* poking out of her pocket.

"Oh, I always have a book on hand. Well, this is a play. It helps pass the time. You know, for the long train ride. Or anytime, really."

Mrs. Havish reached out. "You know, I actually know this one. Henrick Ibsen. He was Norwegian, was he not?" Mr. Havish frowned in confusion while Lida's father seemed surprised. Lida, too, had to admit that most Americans typically only recognized stories by their own authors, with the exception of Dickens or Shakespeare. She didn't blame them; literature took a long time to circulate, and not everybody could afford the luxury of the written word. Most of her books were found by happy accident, picked up underneath factory shelves or given to her by a friend along her journey across the United States. Some, like the one she handed to Mrs. Havish to look at, were from Europe and had journeyed alongside her most of her life.

As she read the back cover, Mrs. Havish gasped and looked up.

"Good Lord, Cynthia," Mr. Havish said, starting back. "Whatever is the matter?"

"I nearly forgot." A silk handbag appeared, and Mrs. Havish dug through it furiously. She unfolded a piece of paper. "She'd be perfect, don't you think?" she asked her husband before passing him the note.

Lida and her father exchanged glances. A flare of worry struck in her chest, but a sense of intrigue quickly overran it. The way Mrs. Havish's face lit up had to be a good sign.

Mr. Havish held the paper at arm's length as if to read the fine print. "Oh yes. This. Quite right."

"I'm afraid I'm curious now," Lida said, sitting back down.

Mrs. Havish was practically bouncing in her seat. Her long, shimmering earrings dangled against her cheek as she faced Lida. "It's the Pack Horse Library. Do you know it?"

Lida shook her head. Mrs. Havish beamed, taking a quick breath. "It's a brand-new program within the WPA," she said, and at Lida's blank look, explained, "the Works Progress Administration, created by President Franklin Delano Roosevelt himself."

"You speak as if you know him, sweetheart," Mr. Havish said behind a teasing grin.

"Hush now," she continued. "They've had great success with it out in Appalachia. I've got a cousin whose sister is a part of it out there. It's simply marvelous, the entire endeavor. A genius idea for these times."

Lida tried to hide her smile. Meanwhile, Mr. Havish had gotten distracted by another note he found in his pocket and motioned for her father to follow him to the front desk. When Mrs. Havish paused in her adoration of the president, Lida asked, "What exactly *is* the Pack Horse Library?"

"Oh, yes, well, it's a program, dear. I've told Walter a dozen times we need this out here." She patted the table for emphasis. "We're no Salt Lake City, you know." Lida nodded, though she didn't really know. "Books. Books, my dear, are a lifeblood the people here need." She held up Lida's copy of *A Doll's House* for emphasis. "The Pack Horse Library is a way to bring books to the people of Cedar Springs."

Lida listened, enthralled by Mrs. Havish's enthusiasm, who continued passionately. "I've been trying to find people to help get it started, but all the young ladies here have their eyes set on moving north. You would be perfect." Mrs. Havish leaned back to scrutinize Lida, who now understood the woman's initial gaze. She was sure that, even under the coat, sweater, and thin shirt Lida wore, Mrs. Havish sensed her strong shoulders, her athletic build forged in the factories of a burgeoning industrial mecca. "And," she said, pausing dramatically, "it pays."

Lida let her smile spread across her face. She glanced at her father. He had high hopes for this job. He'd picked them up from the shared housing in Cincinnati the moment he'd received the telegram about this opportunity. He had to have high hopes because they'd lost all of it, again, when he'd missed a week of work at the steel mill and was fired. Just like in Raleigh and Pittsburgh and Columbus. Like the conveyor belt in those ear-splitting, chaotic factories, it continued over and over again. Each time, each new town was a fresh start. But even Lida's hope had begun to wane. Maybe, she thought, as she looked from her father to Mrs. Havish, then down at the paperback in her hands, maybe if she eased her father's burden, if she pulled her weight more than she had at the clothing mill or the glass factory, they'd make it longer here than anywhere else. At least long enough to have more than a dollar in their pockets when they left.

Lida tucked her book away and smoothed her coat. "Where do I sign up?"

CHAPTER FOUR

Hazel tugged her horse's reins to the right, directing the wagon up the drive of the expansive Boley Ranch. She spotted her younger brother up a massive ginkgo tree, perched contentedly on one of its lowest branches.

"Lord, what is it this time?" she muttered, her breath warm against her face as the chilly wind blew by on the clear spring day. She scanned the stretch of grassland beyond the wooden fence that ran five miles in each direction. In the distance sat the sprawling Boley house, a long home that seemed to grow each passing year, claiming more of the earth beneath its fine walls. The Boleys had become the most prosperous family in Cedar Springs and the most successful cattle ranchers in Iron County. Hazel gave a silent thank you at the sight of the empty front porch.

"Nicholas," she called, bringing the wagon to a stop under her brother. "You should be at home. What about Grandpa?"

"Grandpa is napping," he replied without tearing his gaze away from something Hazel couldn't see in the thick branches overhead. "Twelve thirty-five. Grandpa's naptime."

"Right." She rubbed her hands together as the reins rested in her lap. Their horse, Sasha, shook her head as if she was as eager as Hazel to get back to the Lodge. "Well, you're comin' with me. Gonna help Momma with the dishes."

Nicholas's willowy frame swayed in the wind. Hazel bit back the urge to holler at him to get down; she and everyone else in town had learned hollerin' only made Nicholas dig in his heels. And she didn't much care for his heels to be dug so high up in that tree. "Besides," she added, keeping her tone light, "we saved a slice of cobbler just for you."

This made him look down. With one hand holding a branch for balance, he grinned. His light brown hair flew every which way over his forehead. "Really?"

"Peach, too. Your favorite."

"Yum."

"What're you lookin' at, anyway?"

"Birds."

She snorted. "Had to come all the way out here to see some birds? We got birds at home."

"We don't have these." He pointed to the thick leaves coating each branch.

"And what, pray tell, are 'these'?"

"Merlins."

"I see." The distant chug of a car motor made her turn, the boards of her seat creaking beneath her. Coming up the same road she'd taken was a big blue Chevy Roadster, its white roof gleaming in the sunlight. "Well, you'll have to tell me all about the merlins at the Lodge. It's time to go."

He looked from her, up into the branches, then back again.

"Nicholas." The car drew closer. "It's time to go."

His blue-green eyes looked past her, and he crouched when Hazel turned again as the car motored up the road only fifty yards away. "Mr. Paul is back."

"Yes."

Nicholas's brow furrowed in a scowl, a look that reminded Hazel of her father, as he jumped from the branch onto the bed of the wagon. He landed easily next to a few bags of chicken feed. Hazel was about to turn the wagon around when the car pulled up, blocking the road and her path.

"Well, if it isn't Miss Hazel Thompson. Paying me a surprise visit?"

She forced a smile as Paul Boley leaned out the window. His slicked-back hair lay flat against his head, and his high brow jutted out over steely blue eyes that roved from her bosom to her exposed ankles.

"Just collecting my brother, Mr. Boley. We'll be on our way now."

"Please, Hazel," he said, turning to smile at the empty passenger seat as if it was amused by their interaction, "Just 'cause I wear a tie now don't mean you can't call me Paul. How long we known each other? Since we were babes born, what, twenty-five years ago?"

"Only twenty-five? My, it feels so much longer."

"Hello, Nicholas," Paul said, raising his voice over the motor. Glancing over her shoulder, she caught Nicholas give a meek wave. His eyes were back on the tree. Paul looked skeptically skyward, then refocused on Hazel. Running his fingers over the shining steering wheel, he said, "My sister Mary was recently hitched, if you'll recall. She nabbed herself an oil baron from Texas. Those Texans are a rowdy bunch." He chuckled. "I'm just coming from town. Got a telegram from her. They're livin' outside of some place called Lubbock."

"How lovely." Hazel was only half listening. The Boleys were a large clan: four daughters and one son, all of whom Hazel couldn't stand. They'd all gone to school together until she and Paul were twelve. That was when the school had shut down because the teacher left for a better-paying gig, and no one else in town would take the job. Each Boley sister seemed more intolerable than the last. Fortunately, each had been married off to different parts of the country to wealthy men, leaving Paul, who Hazel likened to a fruit fly. No matter how many times she swatted away his advances, he never seemed to disappear.

"Pop and I are heading to Pine City next month for negotiations on a deal with a company up north." He pressed back in the seat as if blown away by the news. "I'd love to show you the city sometime."

She pitched her voice higher, hoping her irritation wasn't obvious. "I've seen it. Gone to town once or twice for supplies." She glanced at the front of his vehicle, wondering if they could dart out from under this conversation if she snapped the reins.

"I know that. I mean, really see the city. See it at night. Dine at the café."

She fought to keep the smile on her face, though her cheeks were starting to hurt. "Sounds lovely. But you know how hard it is for me to get away. Between the Lodge and helpin' Momma. Plus, there's Grandpa and Nicholas."

Paul tapped the exterior of the driver's door, drawing Hazel's gaze to the fine leather watch below the cuff of his coat sleeve. "I won't wait forever, you know," he said. His wide smile made her shiver.

"I hope not," she mumbled. Nicholas gave a satisfied laugh.

"What was that?" Paul asked over the motor.

"I said, we really must be gettin' back now." She motioned for Nicholas to join her up front. His spindly legs led him over the seat to plop down beside her. She brushed invisible dirt off his brown pants and red sweater to avoid looking at Paul.

"Well," Paul said finally, pointing at them both, "take care now, Hazel." He drove on down the gravel road, and Hazel exhaled before she and Nicholas were consumed by a cloud of exhaust.

When they were out of sight of the ranch on their way back, Nicholas said, "He smelled sharp."

Hazel chuckled. "He was wearin' cologne. Surprised we could smell it over the smog that hunk of metal was spewin'."

"Why does he wear it?"

"Well." Hazel thought a moment, listening to the steady *clop* of their horse's hooves as they bounced lightly in their seats. "You know how the male robin has that bright red chest?"

Nicholas nodded.

"Cologne is kinda like that. Men wear it to…attract women."

"Like a mating signal?"

"Yes. Like that."

He was quiet a moment. Glancing sideways, she could see his eyes flitting side to side, the way they always did when he was running through his collection of facts. Ever since he learned how to read, he had showcased an astonishing ability to recall certain things, mostly concerning numbers, dates, and facts about his favorite animals. Finally, he asked, "Did it work?"

"What?"

"Paul's cologne. Did it work on you?"

Hazel's mouth opened, but a response halted in her throat. She should be used to her brother's candid questions. It had always been how he was. Most people in town knew to expect up-front and often personal inquiries in Nicholas's company. "Boy don't know how to keep that trap of his closed," their grandpa always said.

Over the years, Hazel and her mother had come to learn it wasn't that Nicholas wouldn't keep his questions to himself; it was that he truly struggled to know how. "He's got a mind like that river in summer. Ain't nothin' gonna stop it gettin' to where it wants to go," their mother had said when they were young. "Because of that, he ain't afraid to ask things the rest of us never would."

Of course, this also made for rocky encounters with people in town. And like today, Nicholas had a habit of wandering off to fulfill his inquisitive mind.

Hazel pulled herself from her thoughts, returning to her brother's question. "I can happily say it did not work on me."

"Why?"

She looked at him. He kept his gaze on the world around them: the tall grass on either side of the road—slush from old snow and dirt rather than gravel—where cows grazed lazily, the sloping gorge at the side of the mountains ahead of them, and the blue sky that wrapped itself over patches of wildflowers sprinkled like confetti along the hills.

Hazel considered telling him the truth, that no man had ever stirred anything inside her. Especially not Paul. She'd known for a long time that her leanings were toward women but had never acted on anything she'd ever felt for a school friend or a woman passing through the Lodge. Even those attractions had been merely fleeting flourishes she could easily ignore. Besides, she was too busy for love.

"I reckon it's because I don't fancy any kind of sharp-smelling robin. No matter how shiny and rich they may be."

"If you don't like robins, what do you like?"

She shook her head, clucking her tongue to signal their horse, who whinnied and turned right at the crossroad, pulling them back to the Old Lodge. Hazel wrapped an arm around her brother. "I'll let you know when I find it."

CHAPTER FIVE

"We'll get out here, thank you."

"Here?" Lida hurried to grab her suitcase as her father leapt from the back of the mule cart.

"Why not?" he replied, his voice pitched higher as he gathered his hat from the grass and straightened. The glint in his eyes matched the glee in the corners of his smile. He turned to their driver. "You say it's only a quarter mile more?"

The elderly man Mr. Havish had arranged to drive them nodded, a chunk of tobacco thick inside his grizzled cheek. "Seager house is around the next curve. Can't miss it."

After hopping down, Lida thanked the man, who tipped his hat and returned the way they came.

Lida's legs felt shaky from the bumpy ride, but it was better than the lingering swaying feeling that the train had left her with. As they readjusted their coats and brushed off their pants, Lida said, "I thought the mountain air was too clean for you, Pa."

He harrumphed. "Nonsense. Away from station, it's nice. Much better than Ohio."

"Sky's bigger," she said, craning her neck to take in the wide stretch of blue that reminded her of a sheet of fabric she'd once unfurled in a factory in New York, before she and ten other young women cut patterns for things like pillows and tablecloths.

Her father pulled her from her thoughts, his voice light. "The pay is better, too."

She eyed him. Wherever they went, her father's moods always started this way: bright and boisterous. He knelt to find a rock, rubbed it with his thumb, then tossed it over a low fence where it disappeared into the thick grass lining the road. Maybe this time, she thought as they walked up the slight incline, it'll last.

Sure enough, half a mile later, Lida spotted the low wooden fence that marked the property of Mr. and Mrs. Seager, their landlords. She smoothed the front of her coat, then brushed grass from her father's shoulders. Smoke unfurled from a thin, crooked chimney poking out of the tin roof. From inside the small house, a baby cried. Nearly a minute after her father knocked, the door opened.

A young woman around twenty-three—four years younger than Lida—stood with a wailing baby on her hip. Her dark brown eyes looked surprised. The rickety boards of their front porch creaked beneath Lida's feet.

"Mrs. Seager? I'm Lida Jones. This is my father, Yaromir." She spoke loudly in an attempt to be heard over the baby. It's entire face, from scrunched eyes to balled fists, seemed puckered in frustration. The baby's blue sleep dress had stains on the neck and front that matched ones on a cloth over the woman's left shoulder.

"Is it Wednesday already? Lord, I know it doesn't look it, but we were expecting you." She bounced the baby as she spoke. In between sobs, it opened its eyes, revealing brown irises that matched the woman's. It reached for her black hair that was parted down the middle and woven into two long braids, but missed. "Please," she said stepping aside, "come in."

Lida smiled. "Thank you, Mrs. Seager."

"Please, call me Martha. Mrs. Seager makes me sound old. And it's still so new." She smiled shyly, closing the door behind them.

"Newly married?" her father asked, waving goofily at the baby, who stopped crying to gawk at the strangers.

"Almost a year," she replied. "We were married back in Pittsburgh last June. Then we moved out here when I was four months along." She gave her baby another bounce against her hip. "My husband's out back. I'll fetch him. Sit, make yourselves at home."

"Cute baby," her father said once she was gone. He took a seat in a rickety wooden chair near a low table. Lida joined him. The house was modest in every sense. No, modest was the foreman's office at the factory in New York. This was sparse. They sat in two of three chairs. A soft fire glowed from a hearth to their right. It gave the room a warm blanket from the cool air outside as dusk approached. A single kerosene lamp sat in the middle of the table between them. A calendar and an oval mirror, barely bigger than her hand, hung on a far wall. To their left, a doorway was open, and a smell like fresh linens floated out to greet them.

When Martha returned, walking quickly from a back door that sat only twenty feet away, she was followed by a strong-looking blond man with a wide smile set in his strong jaw.

"Mr. Jones," he said, wiping his hands on his overalls before reaching out. "Welcome. How was your trip?"

"Fine."

"Good." He looked at Lida. "Hi, Miss. I'm William Seager. It's a pleasure to meet you both."

Lida shook his hand before he turned to Martha, who was offering various pieces of mushy fruit to the baby.

"I presume you met the man of the house, Little Thomas?" William asked, beaming. Handing him over, Martha smiled as he situated Thomas against his broad chest.

"We have," Lida replied.

Her father added, "Strong lungs."

William gave them a knowing look. "Must be milk time." He stepped over to the woodburning stovetop where an old pot sat on one of the burners. "Martha—"

"I got it, honey." She adjusted the material of her yellow dress and motioned for them to follow. "Your place is out back."

Fifty paces from the back door, past a trio of chickens and one sleeping pig, they approached a tiny log house. "It ain't much," Martha said, stepping over mud. Her worn brown shoes were coming untied.

"It's wonderful," Lida said, taking in the low roof, the chestnut planks of the walls hammered together, any gaps between them filled with mud and grass. Windows framed the green front door. Several paint chips lay scattered before it. She counted three steps up to the front porch, same as the Seager house.

"William had this built for his momma when she got sick. Wanted her to live here when it got too hard to look after herself. She was here until this past winter. Still, it fits two people fine."

Lida tried to sound encouraging. "It's really great, thank you." She noticed the way Martha glanced at the brass buttons on their coats and the shine on their boots. Lida wanted to tell her all of it was from a donation bin they'd found before taking the train from Cincinnati.

Once inside, her father made a circle of the main room. "Much bigger than New York," her father said, nodding approvingly.

"Well." Martha ran a hand up and down her forearm, her dark skin dotted with goose bumps as she stood near the open window. "I'll let you get settled." She hesitated. "I guess you've discussed rent through Mr. Havish."

"We have," her father replied.

Martha said, "I'll be sure William confirms with him." She glanced around. "Well, I do hope it's all right. Outhouse is thirty paces that way." She pointed northwest, toward the back door. "Supper's at six. Breakfast is at seven. Of course, you're welcome to find your own."

Like her father, Lida walked a circle of the small room, her steps making the uneven boards creak. Dirt and dust fell between them to the ground several feet below. A skittering, like a mouse running, rushed by under her feet.

"Thank you," she said again, meeting Martha's gaze after she lit the kerosene lamp for them that hung on a nail inside the door.

"Holler if y'all need anything."

When Martha had gone, Lida set her suitcase in one of two wooden chairs near a table that looked the same as the Seagers'. She imagined much of the furniture was built from the nearby cedar trees. Everything smelled like the tall, towering pines outside. The scent mixed with mustiness, and Lida opened the second window to let more air in. Scanning the room, she noticed nearly everything was identical to the Seager home: the single kerosene lamp, the fireplace with old logs, the stovetop equipped with a single pot. Beside it was a wooden cabinet, its doors half-open. Inside, she found a pile of dishes and utensils that looked thirty years old.

Her father returned from the only other room. "You take in here," he said, pitching his thumb over his shoulder.

"Pa, you should have it."

"Nonsense." She smiled at one of his favorite English words. "You're a young woman. You should have the room."

Lida frowned but didn't protest. They'd been sharing cramped, one-room places for years. Sometimes, it was only part of a room they'd packed into with two or three other people. New York, she recalled as she stared at the beams of the ceiling layered by sheets of tin to form the roof, had been particularly claustrophobic. "Now I know how sardine feels," her father had said when they'd slept elbow-to-elbow with other factory workers in the city overflowing with immigrants hoping for work and a way to a new life.

"A whole room," she said now, more to herself than her father. It was small, but that didn't matter. She turned in the doorway, one hand on the jamb. "I wouldn't know what to do with it."

"Place for those books," her father said, examining the stove. "When do they come?"

"Mrs. Havish said they'll be delivered to their house in three days. I'll pick them up on Sunday, then start my route Monday morning."

He grunted. "You haven't ridden a horse since you were girl."

She laughed. "Maybe it's like riding a bike." She pictured the nine months spent in Pittsburgh, when she'd learned to ride after borrowing a neighbor's bike to get to work at the factory. The handlebar always skewed right, but it saved her half an hour each way. She replayed her conversation with Mrs. Havish, when she'd explained Lida's responsibilities as a member of the Pack Horse Library:

"It's quite ingenious. He's brilliant, truly, he is, FDR. What a mind he has for ideas."

Mrs. Havish patted the edge of her mouth with a napkin.

"How often will the books come in?" Lida asked.

"Every month. You'll deliver to these families once every two weeks." She handed Lida a slip of paper. "I don't think you'll have any trouble finding them. Cedar Springs is no Pine City." She laughed at her own remark as the waiter refilled her wine. Lida smiled. "I'm afraid you'll have to find a horse, but there's plenty out there." Lida had a feeling, despite Mrs. Havish's confident claims, that her actual knowledge of the number of horses in Cedar Springs was as reliable as the watch Lida's grandfather had given her before their journey to America when she was seven. The minute hand always fell behind.

"It will be grand, Miss Jones, simply grand. All those families gifted the written word. It is a shame the school closed, but this is the next best thing, really."

Lida put away her copy of A Doll's House. "I'm looking forward to it. Thank you for the opportunity."

Mrs. Havish motioned for the waiter when she met Lida's gaze. "Oh yes. The last Friday of the month is when you'll collect your payment. It won't be a problem returning to town, will it?"

Lida didn't see why it would. Cedar Springs was only five miles away. She shook her head.

"Excellent." Mrs. Havish shook Lida's hand. "Welcome to the Pack Horse Library, my dear."

The low, wood-framed bed in her new room featured the least lumpy mattress she'd ever slept on. Lida rearranged the bed so it was flush against the wall opposite the door. This way, she thought as she stood with her hands on her hips, starting to perspire in the tight quarters, when she lay down, she could see out the window. Satisfied, she removed her coat so that she wore only two layers now—her white button-down that had once been her father's and a brown sweater—and returned to the main room.

Her father had started a fire. "Great pile of logs out back," he said, answering her silent question as he knelt, stoking the wood.

Another low wooden bed, one of the legs clearly shorter than the rest, was shoved in a far corner behind him.

"You're sure you don't want the room?" she asked.

He'd also removed his coat, the sleeves of his red wool sweater pushed up to his elbows.

"Lida, this is a grand place. More space inside and out."

She glanced out the open back door. The rest of the Seager property stretched more than fifty yards until it met the dense forest of tall alpines. A dirt path disappeared into the waving grass, which reminded her of the ocean. Vague memories lingered at the edges of her mind of the passage she, her father, and mother had taken twenty years prior from a port in southern Italy that docked twelve days later at Ellis Island.

"Everything does seem bigger here," she agreed. Lida moved a kitchen chair to sit by the fire. Her father searched through his luggage, a khaki rucksack nearly as long as he was tall, then pulled out a glass bottle. Lida rubbed her hands to warm them, adjusting the sleeves of her sweater as her father found two cups from the cabinet. As he poured, she said, "Now, Pa?"

"It's important to acknowledge our new start," he replied, dark eyes focused on his hand around the bottle. "Here." He handed her a cup.

Lida looked from it to him. She'd enjoyed the version of her father that had accompanied her on the trek west from Cincinnati to Pine City. They'd been so busy preparing to arrive in a new place, there'd been no time for her father to even look at his latest bottle. Her jaw clenched as she stared into the clear liquid, then back up at her father. His eyes were bright and clear. By the end of their eight months in Ohio, they'd grown clouded, overrun by the effects of liquor and sadness that clung to his every movement since it had slithered into the cracks of their lives seven years ago.

In Russian he said, "To success," and raised his cup.

Slowly, Lida brought her cup to his. "To success."

He downed the vodka, and Lida set hers aside to gaze out the back door where the distant, towering trees stood as if watching.

Between their fragrant scent and the land beyond dotted with lilac and columbine, a sense of hope stirred in Lida's chest. She forced the smells and the air of the mountain to chase away the sharp odor of the liquor now circling the room.

Maybe here, her father would do well. Mining was a new type of labor for him, one she imagined he might actually succeed at. And she had the Pack Horse Library. Perhaps Utah would deal them a better hand. They'd closed so many chapters, been forced to turn over pages in Cleveland, Cincinnati, Pittsburgh, and New York. Oftentimes, Lida had barely cracked the first page before they'd moved on.

The west seemed different. Bigger. Maybe they'd find the push they needed to get to California. Her father was convinced, ever since her mother had died, that the land of gold and glory held the answer for them. Lida had read about the West Coast in magazines and books. It certainly sounded like a beautiful place, full of opportunity, but she wasn't sure it held the answers her father sought. She wasn't even sure what the question was. Maybe it was finding a place where their belongings weren't always half-packed, ready to be picked up to flee at a moment's notice. Maybe it was a place where her father didn't have days where he clung to tear-soaked blankets, drops of vodka mingled with his desperate cries on a dirty pillow. Maybe it was a place where Lida could be her own person and live a life she'd only read about in books.

Her father stood and stretched in the doorway as if he could see the potential in this new land and what it held for him. She watched him, hoping this attempt to start new wouldn't end in a firing, an eviction, or an angry manager chasing them out of town. She stared at the sky etched like a painting around her father's tall frame. She willed this time to be different, to not amount to nothing.

Lida's gaze slid to the bedroom door. *My own room.*

That, she decided, was something.

CHAPTER SIX

W as wonderin' when you'd get back. I woke up to an empty house and an emptier belly." Hazel's grandfather, Henry Criley, patted his protruding stomach as he leaned back in an old rocking chair, a stitchwork quilt of periwinkle blue and rose red across his lap.

"Hi, Grandpa." Nicholas bounded past their grandfather, heading for the back door.

Hazel called after him, "Bring that laundry in quick, it'll be dark soon. Then come on back to help me with the dinner prep."

Nicholas waved before disappearing outside. In front of the long-dead fire, their grandfather rocked, his wrinkled face settled into a frown. His stubbly, pale cheeks billowed as he exhaled loudly.

"I see you, Grandpa," Hazel said, moving to light the kerosene lamps.

"I'm old, don't mean I gotta be invisible," he replied.

"Don't mean you gotta hem and haw like those old goats out there, neither." She leaned over the back of his rocking chair, giving his shoulders a squeeze. "Besides, how could we forget you? I don't know who makes more of a fuss when they miss a meal, you or those chickens out back."

"My own flesh and blood treatin' me so." He yawned, continuing to rock.

Hazel fetched him a roll she'd brought back from the Lodge,

then slipped into the next room, calling over her shoulder, "Hush now, Grandpa. Ain't nobody sayin' nothin' that isn't well-earned."

"Gonna have to have a word with your mother. Where is she, anyway?"

"At the Lodge," she called, quickly changing out of her blue dress and into another, this one with white lace on the wrists and neck. She fiddled with the frayed pieces in a foggy mirror atop a wooden table. How old was this one, four, five years? She glanced at the jewelry box below the mirror. Aside from one pair of pearl earrings, a necklace she'd bought cheap from a catalog, and one brooch that had been her mother's, the tin box also hosted her earnings from the Lodge. Hazel wondered how much she'd have to save to buy a new dress.

Her grandpa's voice interjected into her thoughts. "Busy today?"

"A little. Momma wanted to get ahead with the dinner menu. I'm headin' back up in a bit. Had to fetch Nicholas."

In the main room, she folded a pair of patchwork quilts that sat atop an old chest next to her grandpa's chair. He gathered a pipe and tobacco from a dusty side table, stuffing the open mouth methodically. "Where'd he get to today?"

"The Boley Ranch."

He brought a lit match to the pipe's opening and puffed on the end. The familiar, comforting scent Hazel had always associated with her grandpa filled the room with the curls of smoke. "That Paul is a good young man."

Hazel turned to hide her eye-roll.

"He's got a good head on his shoulders."

"It's as big as his ego."

Her grandpa puffed in silence as she relit the fire for him. He pushed his left foot against the old floor to keep the rocking movement going. "He's keen on you, Hazel."

She kept her eyes on the logs. Everyone knew Paul was keen on her. She'd done her best since they were teenagers to avoid his attempts at courtship. Everyone else being interested in their getting hitched, though, only made matters difficult.

"What kinda pie you want me to bring home tonight?" she asked, changing the subject. "Momma's got a plum one bakin'. Mr. Davis brought some more peaches, so we could make one of those."

Her grandpa grumbled. "Mr. Davis was by again?"

She turned to face him, smiling at the memory of his interactions with her mother. "He's a kind man. Especially to Momma."

Her grandpa spoke from the side of his mouth. "I bet he is."

"What do ya have against him?"

"I ain't got no quarrels with him. Your momma should respect her vows is all."

Hands on her hips, Hazel glanced out a window to make sure Nicholas was still busy. She turned. "You of all people should know what it's like to lose a spouse, Grandpa."

"Exactly." He held his pipe to his mouth. The tarnished bronze of his wedding band caught the firelight. "Your grandmomma, God rest her soul, wouldn't stand for none of your momma's... socializin'."

"Grandpa, Daddy's been gone nearly ten years. I see no harm in her talkin' to Mr. Davis when he comes by."

Another grumble and her grandpa fell into a quiet contemplation that told Hazel he was done with their conversation.

Nicholas returned with a woven basket of precisely folded clothes stacked neatly inside.

"Thank you, Nicholas," she said, taking the plate of crumbs that sat next to her grandfather's tobacco box. She scrubbed it over the washbasin.

Her brother blinked his acknowledgment. His cheeks, rosy from the cool air, reminded her of Mike Evans, the young boy at the Lodge today.

"You know the Evans family?" she asked her grandpa. "Young Mike is startin' in the mine. Can you believe it?" She shook her head.

"I reckon he's old enough."

"He's fifteen, Grandpa."

"I was seven when I started work on my daddy's farm."

"That was a hundred years ago, Grandpa," she said wryly, turning to catch his offended look.

He snorted. "Young folk gotta help as much as anyone."

"Maybe," she said, washing her hands after setting the plate aside to dry. "But in the mine?"

"What else he gonna do, Hazel?"

She considered this as she dried her hands on a rag. He had a point. The mine was the only means to make a decent living in Cedar Springs. At least in the last twenty years. Unless you were the Boleys or happened to have a good crop, the money was in the mine. And even then, it wasn't much.

"Ain't like when my daddy first broke ground here. I can still see him poundin' that sign into the top of that hill." He pointed at the eastern wall of their log cabin. If she followed it all the way down the road, past the Old Lodge and to the mouth of the woods at the eastern ridge, she'd find the sign stating the marker of Cedar Springs, incorporated as a town in Iron County in 1871. The sign hung from a white post that, last time she'd seen it, was in need of a paint job.

When her great-grandfather had joined four other men to sign a land charter, they'd imagined Cedar Springs as a bustling mountain town, not unlike its sister city nearby. Unfortunately, Pine City flourished with a friendly passage for trains at the base of the mountains. A boom in coal had lifted Cedar Springs up for a time, but that dwindled in the late twenties and seemed to be stagnant the last year or so. Lately, people left Cedar Springs when they could afford to. Otherwise, most were forced to take jobs in the mine, which Hazel had seen crush people with its relentless, unforgiving ways.

"Times change, Grandpa." She turned to face him. Nicholas worked quietly at the table, separating everyone's laundry into respective piles.

Her grandpa held her gaze. "What else would that boy do?"

She took a deep breath. "Continue his learnin', for one."

"In what school, honey? Cost half a month of his mine wages just to get to Pine City to go to their school. Ain't practical."

"If we could get enough people interested in reviving the school here, we could—"

"It's like you said, times are changin'. Ain't no use harpin' on a school that ain't there no more. If Cedar Springs is gonna be around after I'm gone, everyone will have to earn their keep." His voice softened. "It's how it's gotta be."

Hazel ran the back of her wrist over her forehead. She'd gotten hot in the conversation, agitated by the circumstances of Mike and every other young person like him. She also reminded herself she didn't need to start another argument. Generally, she and her grandpa got on fine. Henry Criley was a caring man, if a proud and traditional one. He'd worked hard to keep up his daddy's reputation as one of the founders of their small mining town. In his old age, he rode the coattails of that reputation, living off the meager savings he'd been left with when his parents died. "He's stuck in his ways, that's all," Hazel's mother would say when he ranted about the changes happening around them. He'd spent an entire month complaining when the post office in Pine City put in a telephone.

Cars were a forbidden topic. "Those horseless carriages are deadlier than bein' five hundred meters underground," Grandpa had said when Paul had driven up six months before to show off his new Chevy.

Hazel was of the mind that some changes couldn't come fast enough to their tiny, rural corner of the world. Still, he had a point. She hated to admit it, but Cedar Springs wasn't prospering like it once had. Change was good, but it seemed to be workin' backward here, leaving her hometown behind. Cedar Springs wasn't hanging on by a thread, but it certainly was beginning to unravel.

"Learnin'," her grandpa mumbled from his chair. "Ain't a luxury no one can afford."

Hazel pictured the school, two and a half miles around the mountainside, up beyond the Lodge toward the northwest side of Cedar Breaks. She tried to imagine it how it was when she was a kid: packed tight with eager children clambering over one another to listen to their teacher read a chapter of their newest book. Right after the school closed was when she'd started going to the Lodge with her mother. Once her daddy died, she spent the entire week there, losing herself in the hum of conversation in the dining hall or in the lively banjo music each Friday night. Home had become unbearable and strange without her father. So she and baby Nicholas would sit in the kitchen of the Lodge, watching their mother bake and fry and whip up an astounding number of meals to feed the hardworking men of Cedar Springs.

Was that why she sometimes felt stuck, stagnant like the water of the lake that sat on the other side of the hills? Ever since the school closed, her life had shifted. Granted, Hazel had never imagined leaving Cedar Springs. Still, she'd hoped to at least continue her schooling until she was sixteen. Then she could start to find work. Maybe open her own grocery store or supply wagon for the folks around town. Something to keep their mountain village afloat.

Hazel shook herself out of her dreaming. "Once you put your clothes away, go grab me two dozen apples from Mrs. Ashley's orchard next door, will ya, Nicholas? Meet me at the wagon once you're done." Any wishes she'd had for herself had died with the school and her father. Her future was here, was this. She gathered her handbag and headed for the front door. "We'll bring you that pie, Grandpa. See you after dinner. Don't go gettin' into any trouble, now."

"Don't be too late, Hazel," her grandpa called, now a hazy figure behind his cloud of pipe smoke. "The fire won't keep itself lit."

She waved and hurried out the door.

CHAPTER SEVEN

Lida stared at the high cedar beams where she stood inside the doorway of the Old Lodge. She'd ended up here after taking a wrong turn back to the Seagers' and was intrigued by the commotion she could hear from half a mile away. She removed her hat as a cacophony of conversation filled the vast and crowded room. It carried over the patrons' heads, drawing her gaze to a staircase to her left where antlers and furs adorned the wall above each step. She was about to place her hat on one of a dozen nails in the wall when something collided with her, hard.

She noticed three things simultaneously. First, two dozen glistening bread rolls scattered like mice across the floorboards. Second, the room seemed to halt as Lida found the third and most dazzling part of the last ten seconds: a petite blond woman in a blue-checked dress letting out a string of words so quickly, Lida wondered how she had time to breathe.

"Gosh darn it all to tarnation. The entire dinner basket, gone. I swear, Momma's gonna have my head for this. Dadgum."

Lida stared at the perfect way this woman's hair resembled the golden fields she'd seen waving on the train ride west. Pulling herself from her daze, though the shine in the woman's hair lingered like sunlight in the back of her mind, Lida stooped to help. "I'm so sorry."

As she reached for a roll now covered in bits of fallen cedar and dirt, the woman kept her head down and said, "I've got it."

Lida frowned as the woman graciously accepted assistance from a trio of older, grubby-looking men who'd swooped from their chairs with fearful looks on their faces.

"Oh, Hank, you're too nice," she said to one. "Thank you kindly." The woman smiled at everyone else until the rolls were recovered. Lida noticed one tucked behind the leg of a table.

The woman had turned to go, bread basket firmly against her hip when Lida called, "Wait. You missed one."

Finally, their eyes met, and Lida stepped back at the blaze from the blue irises. She swallowed. The woman was several inches shorter, even in a pair of low clogs that seemed to echo in the hushed Lodge when she stepped closer. She reached out, holding her hand open expectantly. When Lida handed her the roll, the woman's fingers held hers in place for a moment.

Her lips were set in a tight smile when she said, "Why don't you take your seat? Someone will be over to help you shortly."

Then she was gone. Lida glanced around the room. Many had returned to plates piled high with chicken and potatoes. At the only table boasting an empty chair, three men smiled knowingly. Too embarrassed to remove her coat, Lida shrank into the empty seat to join them.

For a time, the men seemed to be having a conversation by way of the clink of their forks and the way their brows raised. When she couldn't take their silence anymore, Lida asked, "Was it something I said?"

Like pulling a stopper from a barrel, this loosened the men's voices.

"You must be new," a heavy-set man in a pair of coveralls said.

"Ah, that's just Miss Hazel," the man next to him added. His lean frame reminded Lida of a ferret.

"Best thing to do once you at the Lodge is sit, lest you wanna be caught in a twister." This advice was given by the third member of the table, a man with tanned skin and several scars on his hands. His dark hair was tousled, but his brown eyes met hers with kindness.

"Jerry," said the lean-framed man, "ain't no twisters in Utah."

"Hell, I know that. Shoot."

"Then what you mean?"

"I was speaking figuratively."

Lida chuckled. "I take it she's the twister?"

The burly man took another bite of chicken as he hunched over his plate. "Only during the dinner rush. Most of the time, she's the kindest soul in all of Cedar Springs."

"Prettiest one, too," the leaner man added. Jerry slapped him in the back of the head.

Lida relaxed, unbuttoning her coat. "Suppose I learned my lesson."

They all nodded solemnly. Lida accepted a cup of water from a woman who seemed to appear from nowhere. She was older, her matronly figure wrapped snugly in an apron over a dress that complemented her fair complexion. Lida noticed she looked a lot like the younger woman Lida had just run into.

"Thank you," she said, taking a drink.

The woman asked, "You here for the dinner special?"

Lida looked from her to the men. One gave her a small nod. "Yes, ma'am."

She caught that same man frowning at her sweater and trousers. He leaned forward, pointing. "Say, ain't those men's clothes?"

Lida glanced down, her shoulder twitching at his scrutiny. She was about to respond when the woman stopped mid-pour of his cup and said, "Now, when did my establishment become some high-end shop?" Though she was smiling, her eyes turned hard as she lowered her voice near his ear, though Lida could still hear her. "It's probably all the girl's got. Now leave it be."

He grumbled an apology as the woman turned to Lida and said, "The special will be right out." She turned to the rest of the table. "How the rest of you boys doin'?"

A chorus of "Oh fine, Mrs. Thompson," rang out before she refilled their cups and was gone. After Lida hung her coat up and returned to the table, everyone introduced themselves. The burly man was Willard, the leaner man named George. They ate for a few more minutes, then Jerry asked, "You a tourist?"

"No." Lida leaned back, taking in the large fireplace, the

kerosene lamps lining the walls, and the staircase on the opposite end of the room. "I just moved here with my father."

"He must be that new worker they been talkin' 'bout," George said. The other two muttered their agreement.

"He starts on Monday." Why was it so easy to share things with these men she'd just met? People in the factories back east often kept their personal lives to themselves. Then again, she found her mind went numb after eight hours next to a deafening machine on an assembly line. It was never the ideal place for conversation.

"What's his name, your father? We'll be sure to make him feel welcome, won't we, boys?" Jerry said behind a spoonful of gravy.

Lida glanced between them. "Yaromir. His name is Yaromir Jones."

All three men exchanged glances. Willard, who had finished his food, leaned forward, his large elbows weighing down the table. "Where'd you say y'all moved here from?"

"Cincinnati."

"I mean, before that."

"Columbus. Before that we were in Pittsburgh."

She noticed George and Willard looking at her hair, which was pulled into a messy braid. They studied her eyes and tall figure. The skin around her knuckles seemed to catch the shadows thrown by the firelight.

Jerry cleared his throat, seemingly aware of the new tension at their table. "Well, we'll welcome him just like we did William Seager, won't we, boys?"

"Of course, Jerry. Any help we can get down in that mine is music to my ears."

"You wouldn't know good music if it hit you with a pan. That fiddle of yours been outta tune since last summer."

"It ain't outta tune. You just got no ear for it."

The men fell into an argument, and Lida exhaled. A familiar unease had risen in her as they had begun to realize she and her father weren't born in America. Even though she'd lived here most of her life, when people learned they immigrated from Eastern

Europe, it only raised questions and, for some reason, helped form opinions of her before they even knew her.

Though she found herself guilty of the same thing. Glancing toward the kitchen, Lida wondered about the woman, Hazel, she'd run into minutes before. Lida figured she was just another presumptuous blond American. Somebody who saw Lida's dark eyes, thick eyebrows, and men's boots and decided she wasn't worth the time. Though, Lida had to admit, she sure was pretty.

While conversation washed over her, Lida let herself wonder about the whirlwind of a woman in the kitchen of the Old Lodge.

CHAPTER EIGHT

The entire dinner basket, Momma, gone."

"Save one for Hank. He never did mind a bit of cedar with his food."

"Momma."

"Oh, honey, it's fine. We're bound to have a box of crackers in the cupboard back there. Don't make no difference to those boys so long as they're fed."

Hazel huffed as she stared at the dirt, mud, and cedar coating the two dozen rolls she'd dumped on the counter. The gleaming sheen of butter looked like it was suffocating under the ugly mix of browns. "It was a perfect batch, Momma."

"Ain't no such thing. Go on now, don't just stand there. Set 'em aside. We can crush 'em up and toss 'em to the chickens tomorrow. Put that bread to use, at least." Her mother stirred a pot of gravy, her cheeks flushed from the heat of the kitchen as every stove was in use during the Friday dinner hour. The crackle of frying chicken came from one side of the room while the savory scent of apple pie wafted from the other. "I kept tellin' you, we need to just bite the bullet and buy those baskets they been using at the café in town. They put one basket on each table. Keepin' the whole batch together was askin' for trouble."

Her mother glided over to the chicken to give it a turn, and Hazel pulled up her sleeves to take over the stirring. She didn't bother keeping the bitterness from her voice when she said, "That woman's the one askin' for trouble."

Her mother inspected the crisp exterior of the meat. "Wasn't nothin' but an accident."

"Tourists think they own wherever they go. She ruined the rolls, Momma." The sense of pride Hazel felt for her hometown reared in her chest, and she took a breath to quell her frustration.

"Quit your carryin' on. You wanna know what a real tragedy is? You remember when the bank man, I don't remember his name, came through these parts? The one from Salt Lake?" She deftly pulled the chicken from the oil, slid the bird off the iron skewer and onto a clean plate. "Remember how he was sittin' right there at table three, best seat in the house? I asked your brother to be in charge of the gravy. Lord bless him. You remember?"

Hazel did and tried not to smile as she listened to the story she'd heard dozens of times.

"Nicholas, he was eight. He walked out into that dining room, concentrating so hard on carrying that gravy boat. Gets all the way to the bank man. Bank man says, 'What you got there, son?' Nicholas says, 'Gravy for the chicken, sir.' Bank man says, 'Well, lay it on me, then.'" Laughter shook Hazel's shoulders as her mother continued. "Your brother tips the gravy boat over, right into the bank man's lap."

A few patrons from the dining room leaned over to glance through the kitchen doorway as Hazel's laughter grew. "That fine suit of his was ruined. I knew it. Too much grease in that batch of gravy." Her mother wiped her hands clean on her apron and met her gaze. "That, honey, was somethin' worth carryin' on about."

Hazel wiped tears from her eyes. "Oh, Momma. I guess you're right." She glanced back through the doorway and caught the eye of the woman she'd run into. Admittedly, it had been partially her own fault. She'd been in such a hurry to get the bread out, she hadn't noticed the woman in the dark coat and hat, whose hair and eyes were even darker. Those eyes were watching her now with a strange look Hazel wasn't sure what to make of.

She turned her back on the doorway. Straightening her shoulders, she concentrated on the gravy. Perhaps if that woman hadn't been standing in the middle of the entryway, the bread could've been saved.

"Quit thinkin' about those rolls," her mother said before bringing down a butcher knife that sliced a new, naked slab of chicken in half.

Hazel frowned at her mother's ability to follow her train of thought. With another glance toward the doorway, she gave a final sigh, then let herself fall into the rhythm of the Lodge. More diners came in, all of whom she knew by name, nearly all men, with their skin coated in a layer of black from a day underground, digging for something they'd never keep. She served them plates of chicken, collards, and potatoes. Mike Evans never showed. She imagined he was at home, collapsed from exhaustion from his first week of work in a place not meant for men, let alone boys.

When she cleared Jerry's table, she could feel the woman's eyes on her. Hazel kept hers on the cups and plates, surprised at how much she wanted to find out just how dark the brown was in the woman's irises. As she scrubbed the dishes once all the customers had gone home, and it was only her, Nicholas, and Momma, Hazel said, "I still don't know how I feel about those tourists comin' through."

"So long as they're comin' through here willing to pay for a meal, I don't see the trouble." Her mother dried the dish Hazel handed her. They stood shoulder to shoulder in front of the deep sink. Nicholas perched on a stool at the end of the counter. He munched on a pie crust as he separated the silverware.

Hazel blew a piece of hair aside before saying, "Momma, most of them are East Coast snobs. They come through with no manners, no grace. You remember that pair last month, the ones who said they were from New Jersey? He asked for Polynesian sauce to go with the chicken. Polynesian! Like somethin' was wrong with our gravy." Sprays of water flew up from the sink as she worked to clean a piece of meat from a plate. "And his wife sat on his coat like the chairs we got were gonna bite her backside."

Nicholas held up a spoon, breathed on it, then rubbed it with a rag. "Chairs don't bite."

"Exactly." Hazel tossed him an appreciative look.

Her mother shook her head. "Tourists are revenue, honey. Money comin' in is a good thing."

"Most stay in Pine City," Hazel countered. "*That's* where their money goes."

"Not when they drive up to see that monument."

"Cedar Breaks National Monument," Nicholas said, his tone flat. "Established 1933."

"Ain't you glad folks are comin' to see our town?" her mother asked, quickly sealing a jar of peach preserves while Hazel slowed her cleaning to talk.

"Of course I am," she said. She wasn't exactly sure why tourists bothered her so much. No, it wasn't that she didn't know why; it was that there were so many little things about them. They all had haughty attitudes. Not that she spoke to many, but she could tell. They came drivin' up in their fancy automobiles, wearin' their fine furs and frocks, wide-eyed when they stepped into the Old Lodge like they hadn't never seen a log cabin before.

Yes, Hazel was glad people wanted to see for themselves how beautiful this slice of Iron County was. She had always believed she'd been lucky to be born in a place full of rugged majesty, the mountains giving way to stunning gorges hosting dramatic cuts and patterns in the bedrock. The colors in the stone that made up Cedar Breaks seemed otherworldly at times. Like the sky reached down and used the wildflowers to paint the landscape with warm hues of lavender, scarlet, and silver. When they'd learned the government was dubbing Cedar Breaks a national monument, putting them officially on the map, she'd swelled with pride.

But as the world expanded, opening up to great bustle and bringing with it the acknowledgment she'd craved for her hometown, Cedar Springs seemed to float adrift. People from all over the country came to visit, to take in the glorious scenery and breathtaking views. All the while, her town and its people seemed to turn away. Like the spotlight cast upon them revealed its residents' harsh and dirt-stained realities. Miners, struggling farmers, mothers with too many babies to feed; these were the people of the acclaimed, esteemed land heralded as honorable on a national scale.

Hazel loved Cedar Springs. She loved its people. It was in her blood to love it, but even if it hadn't been, she'd love it still. She only wished that fierce love could help raise its people up, help secure them to a future where they would flourish like they once had. Times were hard for many people, but they seemed particularly tough for the people of Cedar Springs.

They'd fallen quiet, the steady *plop* of water, the *clink* of silverware, the low crackle of the fire the only sounds filling the room. Hazel glanced at Nicholas. What was his future? What did hers have, for that matter? She loved the Old Lodge, and she loved serving the townsfolk their meals, giving them something warm in their bellies when the nights were cold, and nothing would grow in their dry, hard plots of land. She loved being there for Momma, who'd seen more hours here than at home since her father's passing. This place was as much a staple of their lives as the cedar that fell from the trees, encasing them in a state of evergreen.

Maybe, she thought, these tourists—like the woman she ran into earlier—weren't the worst thing to ever happen. It wasn't them that drove boys like Mike Evans into the mine.

Hazel drained the sink after handing her mother the last dish, then faced her. "Momma, you think the money those tourists will bring in might help reopen the school?"

Her mother was busy pouring handfuls of leftover flour from the day into a large clay jar. She kept her eyes on the white powder as she spoke. "I reckon the fee those people pay to drive up here goes somewhere. They told us about that, didn't they? Five years ago, when them folks came tellin' us they were gonna open the park."

Both Hazel and her mother looked to Nicholas. He met their gazes, his eyes moving between them as he seemed to recall. "The fees for the park are used to enhance the visitor experience in the future."

Her mother snorted. "That's right. They use that tourist money to improve the parks."

Hazel frowned. "I guess that's a good thing."

"It is, honey. Just means that money fixes up Mother Nature but not the mothers of Iron County."

"But if more people come here, that's more money."

"Which is good for businesses to host those people."

"But," Hazel said, picturing the influx of strangers while the residents of Cedar Springs stayed in their homes, walked into the suffocating tunnels of the mine, and watched as their land was invaded by people who didn't care enough to stay. "We need somethin' else, Momma. We need a reason for people to want to do more than visit. Or…" She struggled to articulate her feelings. "We need something for our young people. Just the other day I heard Mr. Ashley sayin' his son was moving up to Salt Lake for work. And all the Boley sisters are gone."

Her mother shot her a look. "I didn't think you minded that much, honey."

Hazel grimaced. "That's not the point."

"What is, then? Our young folk have work. They have the mine."

Hazel placed her hands on her hips. "Momma, we talked about this. The mine is no place for people like Mike. A boy like that needs to finish his learning."

Her mother wore a sad smile. They'd had this conversation already. They'd had it several times, actually, since the school closed. But what could possibly happen to make people excited about things like learning and reading when there were so many other things to worry about, like how to put food on the table?

As they finished up their nightly chores, turning off the gas lamps and grabbing their coats, Hazel watched her brother. What if Nicholas wanted to do something else? He'd had one year of school before it closed. He was smart, had practically taught himself how to read when she had been busy with the Lodge. But eventually, he'd have to try to work. What if he wanted to go down into the mine, too? She could hardly stand the thought of him down there, surrounded by nothing but choking air and never-ending dark.

Outside, as the cool air hit her face, Hazel turned her gaze to the mountains. She gave a silent prayer to the peaks, wishing for a way to remind Cedar Springs of its own possibilities.

CHAPTER NINE

On Monday, Lida had breakfast with Martha and Little Thomas, sharing three boiled eggs among them. Martha told her about William's time in the mine. That morning, he'd left with her father before dawn, both men making the two-and-a-half-mile trek to the site manager's, Mr. Williams, office, where her father was to pick up his helmet, gloves, and other equipment.

When Lida mentioned she needed to go to Pine City to pick up her Pack Horse Library materials, Martha asked, "You got a horse?"

Lida paused, holding the crumbling bite of egg an inch from her chin. "I...no, I don't."

"Well, how do you expect to get places deliverin' those books?"

Lida recalled her conversation with Mrs. Havish. "I imagine I need to find one." She finished her egg, leaning back in her chair. "I probably should have thought about that over the weekend." She'd been so concerned about making sure her father was ready for work this morning, she'd forgotten about the library until he'd left for the mine. The last forty-eight hours had been spent unpacking and keeping an eye on the bottle of vodka, now placed next to her father's duffel bag beneath a chair, the lid firmly closed.

Martha was nodding, seemingly pleased that she'd been able to remind her of such a thing. "Old Man Coffer up the hill has a slew of mounts folks rent when they need one." She cleaned Thomas's face where a stream of milk ran from his lip. Lida noticed the way her eyes held the crumpled cloth in her hand as she said, "Ain't the nicest fella, Old Man Coffer. William rented from him last spring, had to bargain half an hour for a horse to ride into town to fetch a doctor for me. 'Caught in his ways' is the expression I reckon best fits Coffer." She seemed to study Lida's eyes, then her thick hair tucked into an unruly braid that fell halfway down her back. A flash of something filled Martha's gaze; was that a warning in it?

Lida nodded, beginning to understand. She'd met plenty of folks like Mr. Coffer. Despite New York being overrun by immigrants, people from all over the world seeking a better life, everyone ended up herding into the same groups they'd left. Many ended up clinging desperately to what they knew in this new place and struck out against what was different. As Lida and her father migrated west, the groups became fewer and far between, and there were fewer people who spoke Russian, fewer people who bore a resemblance to them. "I appreciate your advice. I won't forget it," she finally said. Martha smiled, and Lida excused herself to fetch her coat.

Later, when she stood on Mr. Coffer's porch, she prepared herself for the inevitable scrutiny from the short, bald man with dark eyes surrounded by wrinkles that ran down his cheeks in deep, sinking lines. His watery gaze looked up at her from his open door.

"What?" he asked, his voice louder than it needed to be. She jumped at the sound as it broke through the quiet morning.

"I'm here to see about renting a horse." She pointed beyond his one-room cabin, much like many she'd seen along the mountainside. The roof was in one piece, unlike some, but there were visible cracks in the windows on either side of his door, and she felt the slope of the uneven porch where she stood.

Mr. Coffer rubbed his face, blinking quickly and staring at her. Had she woken him? In the small space where the door was cracked behind him, a faint light from a lamp glowed alone in the dark room.

"I don't know you."

"My name is Lida Jones. I just moved here with my father." She tugged her coat tighter as his gaze roved up and down her. He frowned at her hat, then coughed at the sight of her boots that came up just below her knees over a pair of riding pants. "He started work in the mine."

This got his attention. "I worked that mine for twenty years." She couldn't discern his tone, though the way he lifted his chin implied he was proud of that fact.

She smiled. "I was told you're the man to see about renting a horse."

"Your father needs one?"

"No, sir. It's for me."

He raised his scraggly brows, merely tufts of gray below more wrinkles on his forehead. "What for?"

"I'm working for the Pack Horse Library, sir." She'd learned in years of work at factories that old men seemed to appreciate being addressed so. "I need to get to Pine City to pick up my materials. Then I'll deliver books and magazines to the people of Cedar Springs. People like you." She widened her smile as he coughed, some spit flying toward her.

"That one of them government programs?" he asked, scratching his chest. The white undershirt he wore was faded under old suspenders holding up a loose pair of brown pants. He wore a pair of leather loafers, their edges tattered.

"Yes, sir. From Mr. Roosevelt," she added, recalling Mrs. Havish's enthusiasm. Unfortunately, Mr. Coffer didn't seem to share in this.

"Nothin' but a government handout is what that is."

Lida hesitated. "Well, if you change your mind, I'd be happy to make a delivery here. They've got a list, but I'm sure adding another stop wouldn't be too much to ask. Especially if you're providing my transportation."

He squinted, seeming to weigh her words. Then he coughed again and pulled the door closed behind him. "This way." He gestured for her to follow. She hurried after him down the porch steps and around the back of the house. Fifty yards away, they came to the backside of a barn and half a dozen horse pens. Several troughs lined the edges of the pens. A pair of cows stood lazily in a pasture that looked more like a patchwork quilt than a blanket of green, more dirt than anything.

"How long you need one for?" he asked, hacking then spitting.

"Well." Lida thought for a moment. "Until the weather turns, probably. November, maybe."

He guffawed. "You really ain't from 'round here. Ain't nobody goin' nowhere by late September. October if we're lucky. Roads packed tight with snow by then."

"Oh. Right." Back east, the roads were cleared fairly quickly in the winter. She recalled trudging through gray slush mixed with the salt that had been dumped on the roads on her way to the factory in Pennsylvania. She'd forgotten how isolated Cedar Springs was, its people and its places without the means to do things like clear roads as easily.

They stood between a pair of horses, each taller than both of them with black manes and strong sturdy builds. Lida reached out to one, a chestnut-colored mare. The horse snorted, blinking at her.

"You got a place to keep her?" Coffer asked.

Lida said, "I'm staying with the Seagers. They have an old barn that's not being used."

"The Seagers, eh?" He turned to her, again looking her up and down. "Didn't know they was rentin' out a room." He added after a second, "Didn't know they could."

Confused, Lida said, "Why not?"

"Well, his wife's a colored. Ain't legal, them livin' together."

"They're married."

He grunted. "Not in the eyes of the state of Utah."

Lida's confusion grew. She didn't like the disdain growing in Coffer's eyes, so she said, "How much for this one?" patting the nose of the horse. It pressed gently into her hand, the smooth coat soft against her palm.

He stared at the horse, chewing his lips and throwing a glance to the shining buttons on her coat. "Twenty cents a week."

Lida did the math in her head, weighing the cost against her earnings. It was a lot, but she hadn't seen any other options, and something in her didn't want to give Coffer the satisfaction of knowing she could hardly afford such a rate.

"You've got a deal." She stuck out her hand.

He eyed it but only nodded. "I'll get her stuff ready. Meet me out front."

After she'd set up the saddle and reins, Coffer, seemingly amused, chuckled as she climbed atop the horse. "You know what you're doin', don't ya?"

Lida was surprised by the mild concern in his tone, though it was probably for the horse, not her. "Yes, sir." Her hand caught, and she accidentally pulled too hard on the reins. The horse whinnied. "Sorry," she whispered, leaning forward to pat her neck apologetically.

"She'll need brushing, and don't forget to mind her hooves. There'll be a charge if she comes back in worse condition."

Lida swallowed. She'd never cared for a horse but remembered part of a conversation she'd had with the Seagers the week before. "William Seager kept horses a few years ago. He'll make sure she's taken care of."

Coffer watched her another minute, then disappeared inside his home without another word. Lida imagined he was satisfied with the sixty cents she'd handed him, enough to cover her for a few weeks. Once she managed to steer the horse down the muddy drive and out onto a gravel path that led to town, she took a deep breath, relishing for the first time all morning the clean mountain air. Her shoulders relaxed.

"You need a name." The horse's ears twitched as if in recognition, then flicked its head to one side as they trotted along. Lida combed her mind, flipping through pages of books she'd read over the years, all the while contemplating the sweet black eyes that blinked back at her when they turned at a bend in the road. "Beth," she said definitively. Her horse brayed, then snorted. Lida smiled. "I'm glad you like it." A crow flew overhead, cawing and drawing her gaze. "We better get a move on. You ever see Pine City, Beth?" Her horse shook its head, and Lida tugged her rein, turning them slightly. "Well, then, this will be a great adventure."

Town was a whirlwind. Lida found the old church Mrs. Havish had instructed her to find, the chapel playing host to the library donations. A trio of women, each with their long, flaxen hair pinned beneath stylish hats, flocked to her when she entered.

"You must be the woman Cynthia told us about," one of them exclaimed from behind the pulpit. They all wore gloves, despite the warm air inside the high-ceilinged building. "I'm Abigail Greyson, this is my sister, Dottie, and her friend, Celia," she said, pointing to the shortest of them, a pretty young woman with doe-like features who stared, not saying a word.

Lida touched the edge of her hat, nodding to each of them in turn. Each of the women wore pressed, clean dresses and had their hair immaculately done. Their outfits weren't as nice as Mrs. Havish's, but still, Lida felt a tinge of self-consciousness standing in her hand-me-downs. "I'm here for the materials to deliver in Cedar Springs."

"Yes, this way." Lida followed Abigail to a side room while the other two shuffled between pews, rearranging several of the benches into a u-shape. "The women's club meets Tuesday nights. We prepare all day Monday for the event," Abigail explained. "Here we are."

In the room off the main chapel, two dozen stacks of reading materials had been sorted across a wooden floor that poked out beneath a vast, red and yellow patterned rug. Sunlight streamed in through several windows opposite the doorway, casting the pillars of books in grand shadows. The image made her breath catch, all these stories, all this information waiting in sacred silence to be shared.

Abigail directed her to the left-hand side of the room, then moved them clockwise around it as she spoke. "Here you'll find your magazines; *Woman's Own*, *Newsweek*, *National Geographic*. This stack is picture books. I'm afraid there's not many of them. My sister in Virginia says she's sending some next week, but you know how slow the post can be." She threw Lida a look, and when Lida didn't reply, she frowned slightly before continuing. "This here is your general fiction category. Your *Tom Sawyer*, your *David Copperfield*. And this here is from the ladies of the church, like myself." She beamed, her high cheeks growing pink with pride. "Copies of the Bible, King James version, of course, and pamphlets from different verses. Words of the disciples to help lift poor spirits. We thought that would be a nice thing to include."

Lida raised her brow, but upon realizing how serious she was, said, "Great, thank you."

Celia emerged with a piece of paper, handing it to Abigail. "Ah, yes, thank you, Celia." She turned back to Lida. "Here's the list Cynthia made for you. It tells you the families that signed up to receive materials and their addresses." Her light hazel eyes flew down the small print. Then she looked to Celia, who was flattening the skirt of her pastel-colored dress. "My, did you remember we have so many neighbors up in those hills? I can't imagine."

"Thank you," Lida said, taking the paper from her. The woman stared for a moment, then smiled curtly.

"Cynthia is so excited to make this happen, and we are just thrilled to be a part of it." Dottie beamed between her sister and Celia as she spoke. "Mr. Roosevelt is a saint. What an idea."

"What an idea," Lida echoed.

"Well, we'll let you get to choosin' what to bring. You're to come back every other Monday to pick up new materials to exchange with what you lend folks. Two pieces per household," she added, suddenly stern. "Don't let them claim lost items, either." She chuckled. "You know how people can be."

"Every two weeks. I understand."

The women exchanged looks, then stared a moment more, seeming to take in Lida's stature, her dark features. "Well, good luck." They disappeared to the back of the church. Their hushed voices floated toward her as she stared around at the room, but she ignored them. Looking down her list, a trill of excitement rose in her chest. This was the most freedom she'd ever had in a job. In the factories, she'd answered to angry men in offices who'd looked down upon their workers. There, she was as much a cog in the assembly line as the rusty belts endlessly carrying sheets of glass or woven fabric or whatever it was she was hired to prepare for somebody else.

Here, she got to choose what she did. She had the power to pick what people could read. She had a hand in something of worth. She understood the power of stories. Stories had carried her across the ocean on a giant liner packed tight with people clinging to hope in their one tattered suitcase on their way to America. Words of writers had lifted her out of dark places when her mother had died. She'd found solace in the prose. And she'd returned time and time again to familiar phrases when her father, as he inevitably did, took a turn down his own dark road, unable to find peace in anything but the bottom of a bottle.

A copy of *National Geographic* caught her eye. A bright hummingbird was frozen in the photo, its wings flitting so fast, not even the camera could capture its ferocity. It reminded her of this place, this part of the world. In one way, the still image reminded her of the way Cedar Springs seemed frozen in time. Pine City was modern in comparison, but the small mountain town, as far as she could tell, was behind in everything from fashion to equipment to advances like electricity. Still, Cedar Springs was grand in its own way, stunning in its colors and openness. So different from back east. She thought for a moment of her father, climbing down into the mine, his boisterous, eager personality stifled by the earth. The image on the cover shifted. The bold purple grew dull, the blazing greens falling to a pit of darkness. She shook her head to rid herself of the vision. She couldn't let herself think like that. She had to try to believe this would be different. Things already were. She only hoped it would last.

She waved to Abigail, Dottie, and Celia gawking behind her, no doubt curious about the tall, soft-spoken woman in the wide-brimmed hat. Let them wonder, Lida reminded herself. She had other things to worry about. She smiled at the books gathered in her arms. She had a job to do.

CHAPTER TEN

The second home Lida delivered to was the smallest one yet, and she feared for its ability to be a place capable of safe, healthy living. The ramshackle structure leaned to one side as if tired after years of sheltering those within. Astride Beth—who had shown hints of stubbornness away from Coffer's gloomy pen—she crossed a shallow creek, clear water running over smooth boulders as it cut down the mountainside. From there, she traversed uphill through fields of wild onion onto the lot of the Evanses' land.

A young girl of maybe four, with tight brown curls framing a cherubic face, sat in the dirt at the base of a worn stepladder below a hole-riddled porch. She sang something Lida didn't recognize as she swayed, drawing shapes and patterns into the dirt with a stick. The front door of the home looked ready to fall off. One window appeared covered in cobwebs, but as she drew closer, Lida realized the glass itself was cracked, splintered into a permanent pattern. Through layers of dirt on the glass, small spaces had been cleared, presumably to peer outside. A skinny line of smoke curled sadly out of a thin chimney. Lida smelled onions and some other wild herb.

When she drew Beth onto the dirt-laden drive, the young girl looked up. She'd arranged a few rocks into a formation that gave Lida the impression she intended them as a flower. Where the inspiration came from, Lida wasn't sure, as the land around the home was barren, pits of mud surrounding the home behind the girl and along the drive she rode now. She spotted a garden near the back, though it was small and nearly vacant of green.

"Who are you?" the girl asked, her voice high and curious. Her blue eyes blinked into the sunlight at Lida's back.

"I'm here to deliver some books." Lida slid off the horse, keeping the reins in her grip. "Do you know how to read?"

The girl shook her head.

"Well," Lida said, pulling one book and one magazine from the pannier, "I have a story here about a young boy, a little older than you, who lives in a wild jungle."

The girl's eyes grew wide.

"Do you like stories?"

She nodded vigorously and hurried to her feet, which were bare and as dirty as the rest of her legs that poked out from under the end of a faded red dress. Lida jumped when she ran to the house, hollering, "Momma, Momma. There's a lady bringing stories. Momma!"

She disappeared into the house. Lida glanced down at the copy of *The Jungle Book*. Behind that, she read the title of *Better Homes and Gardens*. The list prepared by Mrs. Havish hadn't named every resident within each home, so it was more challenging than Lida had thought to pick out materials. She figured this first round of deliveries would be a trial run, to gauge people's interests.

"You that book woman they said would be comin' round?"

Lida touched the end of her hat in greeting as a thin brunette woman stepped outside. A baby sat on her hip, reminding Lida of young Thomas. But this babe wore a dirty sleep dress, and Lida realized all three members of the Evans family had smudges of dirt on their hands and faces and shadows beneath their hungry eyes.

"Yes. I'm Lida. I'm the librarian here on behalf of the Pack Horse Library."

The woman seemed to watch her, still bouncing the baby on her hip. The same young girl appeared, poking her head out from behind the edge of her mother's pale blue dress.

"She's got a story for us, Momma."

"So you said, Evangeline."

Lida led Beth closer to a scraggly cottonwood tree and rested her reins atop a branch. "I've got two pieces here for you, Mrs. Evans." She extended the material as she walked toward the porch steps. "Now, if you look at these and don't care for them, let me know. I'll be here every other Monday. Likewise, if you want more of the same, tell me. I can't promise anything, since the library depends on donations, but I'll do my best."

Mrs. Evans took the book and magazine. She slowly read the title, "*The Jungle Book*." A small smile lifted her tired face. "I heard of this one."

Lida grinned. "It's quite good, if I may say so."

Mrs. Evans handed the book to Evangeline. She held it like a precious jewel, first out in front of her wide eyes, then brought it close to her chest, hugging it tight.

The reading materials in her patron's hands, Lida turned to go. She supposed her job here was done.

"My husband would like the magazine. He's down in Arizona, workin' an oil mine." Lida paused, turning back. The baby on Mrs. Evans's hip gurgled as she continued. "He went down there in February. Sends us letters when he can. Comin' back when he's got the means." Lida wondered at how difficult it must be to live out here with little ones to look after. "Just been me and my girls," she added, pressing her forehead to her baby's. "Of course, there's Mike, but now he's a workin' man, and we don't see him except for at dinner and on his day off."

Lida reached out as she listened. Mrs. Evans's baby took her finger, holding tight. "Mike, he's your son?"

"My boy, yes. He's workin' that mine now." Mrs. Evans glanced at Evangeline, who had plopped down onto the porch and opened to a page in the book. "Workin' to help out while his daddy's away."

"My father just started in the mine. Perhaps they've met."

"Perhaps," Mrs. Evans said, her tone faltering, implying that wasn't a word she used often. "He's takin' to going to the Old Lodge for lunch. Mike, I mean." She smiled. "I imagine he wants to feel like one of the boys." She swiped a fly from her face, then shooed it away when it tried to land on her baby's head. Her gaze cut to Lida's pants, then to the long coat she wore. "You new here?"

"Yes, ma'am."

"You been to the Lodge yet, Mrs...."

"Miss Jones. Lida is fine."

"You been down there yet, Lida?"

She flashed back to the warm Lodge, the hum of conversation. Then the memory was jarred as a blond vision with fiery blue eyes stared her down. "I have."

"Mrs. Thompson, she runs it, she's an angel. Serves those hungry boys every day. Makes the best fried chicken in Utah."

Lida smiled at the sentiment that seemed to run rampant through Cedar Springs. "It was quite good."

"Can we have chicken, Momma?" Evangeline asked, looking up from the book.

"Not today, honey."

After a moment, Lida said, "Well, I'll be back in two weeks." She knelt and tapped the pages of Evangeline's book. "Enjoy the jungle."

Evangeline's pout at the lack of chicken transformed into a smile. "I will!"

Lida said good-bye to Mrs. Evans as she led her girls back inside. Her next stop was three-quarters of a mile north, up a steep incline where the path dropped off near the edges of the mountain. She was careful to keep Beth to the inside, close to the wall of rock as they climbed higher. She breathed a sigh of relief when the road opened back up to a pasture where a young boy who looked like he couldn't be older than twelve stood near a log next to a pile of chopped wood. Ax in hand, he halted his swing and faced her, pulling himself up like a man of twenty as she approached. Five other children clung to the various pieces of their home beyond; some dangled from posts on the wide porch while others hid behind their big brother as he set aside his ax and greeted Lida, one arm extended.

"I'm Charlie. My daddy said you was comin'."

"Is your daddy Mr. Andrew Benter?"

"Yes, ma'am. He's at the mine."

"Mine, too."

Charlie's gaze had been hard, but it softened at this information. Lida pulled two books from her pannier behind the saddle. Beth snorted as one of the children walked up and tapped her front leg curiously. "Like I've told everybody, since this is my first delivery, I might have things you don't care for. I'll be back in two weeks, so if you want something specific, let me know next time."

The boy took both books. Three of his siblings stood on their tiptoes to try to see. All of them had dirty blond hair like Charlie, a mix of blue and hazel eyes vying curiously to know what he held. When his gaze stayed on the books, Lida said, "Have you read those?"

For the first time, he looked nervous as a small flush swam up his neck. "School closed down a long time ago. Haven't had much in the way of reading material lately."

She nodded. He read the first book's cover. "*The Advent…The Advent-chers of…*"

"That's right. *The Adventures of Huck…*"

"*Huckleberry Finn!*" he finished, looking up with bright eyes. He grinned, and Lida could see the pride in his young features. His siblings reached for the book. "My uncle read us some of this when he visited last spring. I never knew how it ended."

"Well, now you can find out." Lida glanced around at the clamoring bunch. One little girl had already lost interest and was offering a dandelion to Beth. "Maybe your mother can read some of it to you."

Charlie answered matter-of-factly, "Momma's gone." One of his siblings, with the same small nose and oval face, met her gaze. He nodded solemnly.

"Oh. Well, maybe your daddy, then, when he's home from work."

Charlie replied, "I can read to my brothers and sisters in the meantime."

"That's a very nice thing to do."

He lifted his chin. Lida glanced around at the pack of young children, alone here out on this land. She took in the pile of wood, the blisters on Charlie's hands, the well nestled near the line of trees at the edge of their property line. The towering pines nearby had been cleared in a fifty-yard space, the soil tilled in rows and hosting thin stalks of wheat. She glanced at the ax, the firewood, then at Charlie's younger brother as he ran off to shoo a lone chicken that had wandered nearby.

She faced Charlie. "Maybe I can come back soon and read some of Huck Finn's adventures, too. What do you say?"

He looked up from the book, a serious consideration between his brows. After a moment, he nodded.

"It's a deal." She stuck out her hand, and Charlie pulled back his shoulders again.

"Thank you kindly, Miss."

Lida wondered at this boy's resoluteness. He'd clearly taken the job of caretaker. She thought of the abandoned school, then of the children working in factories when she was younger. Out here, at least, they worked their own land. On the train, she'd imagined the west as a vast place of possibility. While it remained so, she realized no matter where she went, people's hardships merely took on different forms.

Nevertheless, the people of Cedar Springs, like Charlie Benter, seemed determined to make the best of what they had. And that was a concept Lida knew well.

CHAPTER ELEVEN

"Grandpa, wake up." Hazel nudged her grandfather's shoulder. He sat reclined, mouth partially open, in his rocking chair. He grunted then closed his mouth. Blinking slowly, he asked, "What's that? Huh?"

"It's nearly sundown. Your tea's ready." She handed him a china cup, all white save for a faint pink flower pattern that circled the rim. It had belonged to her great-grandmother and was one of four cups still intact after eighty-five years.

Silently, he took the tea after adjusting the knitted blanket that had fallen to one side of him. Hazel lit a gas lamp and placed it on a stand near the door before setting the table for dinner. When she only laid three places, he asked, "Where's your mother?"

"At the Lodge," she replied. "She wanted to make sure she was there to receive Mr. Davis with the week's supplies." Her grandfather snorted. Hazel shot him a look.

"And your brother?"

"Out back findin' more firewood." Hazel rummaged through the basket she'd packed from the Lodge: everything her mother had set aside throughout the day to bring home. Hazel had just spooned helpings of beans onto each plate when the faint sound of hooves sounded outside. "You hear that?" she asked, standing beside the table, beans dripping onto the plate.

Her grandfather gulped his tea, his brow furrowed. "We expectin' someone?"

She glanced through the back window, searching for Nicholas. "Not that I recall." Quickly, she set the food down and wiped her hands on a rag. When she stepped out onto the front porch, she spotted a horse and rider in the distance, coming up the ridge. In the fading sunlight, Hazel couldn't make out the rider, but she recognized the horse as one of Old Man Coffer's. Wondering at who it could be, she grabbed the broom next to the door and pretended to busy herself, pushing around a scattering of leaves. When the rider was thirty yards out at the edge of their property, Hazel straightened.

The woman from the Lodge sat atop the horse. Hazel remembered her hat, her coat, both more masculine than most women around here wore. Her pants were a hazelnut brown and tucked into nearly knee-high boots.

"What on Earth is she doin' here?" Hazel mumbled, one hand on top of the broom, the other on her hip.

Her grandfather called from inside. "Who is it?"

Hazel watched the woman a moment more, then replaced the broom. She poked her head through the doorway. "Ain't nobody, Grandpa. A tourist from the Lodge. Probably lost."

This seemed to satisfy him as he reached for his pipe. Hazel brushed a hand through her hair, then froze. Why did she do that? Nothing wrong with being presentable, she reasoned quickly before stepping back outside.

"Don't know when to leave well enough alone, do they?" she said under her breath behind a wide smile. Strolling across the porch, she waved.

The woman slowed the horse to a walk. Hazel could only see the top of her hat as the woman seemed fixated on her hands, clenching the reins. Her knuckles were nearly white in their efforts. *Tourists.*

She leaned against one of the wooden posts that framed the top of the five wide stone steps below the porch, then called, "Can I help you?"

Seemingly startled, the woman looked up. A pair of wide-set, deep brown eyes found Hazel. Strands of wavy, thick hair—as brown as molasses—framed a striking, heart-shaped face. Hazel shifted under her gaze, then forced hers away. She studied the woman's posture atop the horse. She looked calm enough, though her knees were flush against the horse's middle, and her back was rigid. Hazel wasn't surprised when the poor beast pulled back her lips, yanking the reins to one side.

Hazel nodded toward them. "You gotta nudge her forward, not push."

The woman gritted her teeth, her eyes on the gravel drive the horse kept starting and stopping on as she tried to steer them closer. Her voice was even and tight, like the grip she maintained on the rein. "It's been a while since I rode."

"I can see that."

The woman lifted her head, one brow raised.

Hazel crossed her arms. "Since when did Coffer start leasing his horses to tourists?"

The woman's mildly offended look withered to confusion. Hazel noticed the strong line of her jaw when she tilted her head. "I'm here on behalf of the Pack Horse Library."

"The Pack Horse...what?" Hazel uncrossed her arms, straightening. It had been amusing to watch this woman, clearly from out of town, try to ride a horse in a place she didn't seem to know much about, but now it was Hazel's turn to be in the dark. She tried to think if she'd ever heard of this library but didn't recall any such place.

"The Pack Horse Library," the woman repeated, bringing the horse to a stop just near the base of the porch steps. She exhaled, perhaps pleased she'd made it. "Is this the residence of Mrs. Clara Thompson?"

Hazel had been staring at the fullness of the woman's lips and cleared her throat. "You'll find her at the Old Lodge." She paused, waiting as the name settled into the woman's face, evidenced in the way her jaw clenched in recognition. Hazel was sure they were both picturing the bread spilling out across the Lodge floor.

"I see." She pulled a paper from inside her coat, unbuttoning the top part to do so. Hazel caught sight of a vest paired with a white blouse. "She signed up to receive materials from the Pack Horse Library. That's why I'm here."

There was a calm resoluteness to the woman's gaze. It held Hazel's steadily, and like the way she spoke now that she had come to a stop, was even and soothing. It reminded Hazel of a radio program she'd once heard. Not the dramatic kind where people hemmed and hawed, but the ones where someone read from a story over the invisible airwaves.

"Are you the book woman?"

Hazel jumped at Nicholas's question. He stood near the corner of the porch with a bundle of firewood in his arms, splinters in his hair and clinging to his jacket. He faced the woman atop the horse.

"Lord," Hazel said, strained laughter escaping her throat, "you can't sneak up on people like that."

The woman chuckled, then answered Nicholas. "I am."

He replied, "I'm Nicholas Thompson."

"Hi, Nicholas." She stuck out her hand, leaning down from her perch on the horse. Her brother set down the firewood, then shook it. "It's nice to meet you."

He pointed to her paper. "Clara Thompson is my mother. She's at the Lodge."

"So I've been told," she replied, cutting her gaze to Hazel. A wry smile lifted her cheeks. Was that a challenge in her eyes?

Nicholas looked between them. "That's my sister, Hazel."

"Hazel." The woman smiled as if she'd won whatever silent competition had been taking place between them in the last few seconds. Hazel recrossed her arms, all of the advantage she'd felt standing on the porch gone. "I'm Lida Jones."

Hazel tilted her head. "So not a tourist?"

"No." Lida dismounted, then sifted through a pannier draped behind the saddle. "I just moved here a week ago. Now I work delivering books to people in Cedar Springs."

"I see." Hazel played with the thin, white collar of her dress. Then, to Nicholas, she asked quietly, "Momma mention this to you?"

"Yes."

Would've been nice to know. "You deliverin' to everyone?"

"Just those who signed up. But anyone can partake if they want, those who might've missed sign-up or change their minds. I personally find it hard to resist a new book." Hazel caught the way she turned over a hardback in her hands, passing it carefully between them like it really was a treasured piece of gold and not a hundred pages stained with ink.

"Well, I am sorry my...our mother isn't here to greet you. You're welcome to head on over to the Lodge to catch her if you like."

"You don't want these?"

"No, I'm not saying that, I just mean..." What did she mean? She felt uneasy, standing here with this tall, striking woman staring at her with a bemused look in her eyes, half a grin on her face. "I just mean, I don't know if you need a signature or somethin' from the person who signed up. If you do, you'll have to go to the Lodge." Hazel could hear herself talking too fast. Her momma always said when she got nervous, she spoke like a jackrabbit in springtime. This woman's gaze prompted unnecessary words, pulling them from Hazel against her will to fill the space between them.

"There's no signature needed," Lida finally said, still smiling.

"I see."

"I'll take those," Nicholas said. Lida handed him two books. He read their titles. "*The Windy Hill* and *The Velveteen Rabbit*."

"What do you think?"

He held up the latter. "I've read this one already."

"Oh." Lida scrutinized Nicholas. "You like machines?"

"Yes. But I like birds more."

Lida dug through the pannier again, then through a satchel hanging from one side. She frowned. "I just gave away the last *National Geographic*. I'll be sure to set one aside for you next time. How does that sound?"

He nodded.

"What about you?"

Hazel had been watching Nicholas when she realized Lida was addressing her. "Me?"

"What do you like to read?"

"Oh, well, I like just about anything. I'm easy to please."

Lida raised her brow. Hazel felt a blush creep up the back of her neck. She hadn't intended that to come out the way it had. This is just silly, she thought, and scratched the base of her neck as it warmed.

"I'll make it a point to find something you may like next time I'm here." Lida held her gaze, and Hazel could see she was utterly amused by their exchange. She could only nod in response.

"Thank you," Nicholas was saying, placing the books atop the firewood, then carefully picking up the logs and heading up the porch steps.

"You're welcome," Lida called after him before mounting the horse.

Hazel, feeling lost in front of her own home, reached for the broom. She shoved the pile of leaves around before asking, "You'll be back, then?"

"In two weeks."

The words left Hazel's mouth before she could stop to think about what she was saying. "If you or your husband are ever hungry for some home cookin', head on over to the Old Lodge. We're open every day sunup to sundown, weather permittin'. The exception being Sunday, of course. The church that was built here originally burned down ten years ago, and we never rebuilt. Pastor moved on to Salt Lake." She shrugged. "Some folks make the trek to Pine City for worship. Them mountains are glorious enough for me."

"I'm not married."

Hazel bit her lip, but lifted her chin quickly and gave what she hoped was a surprised look. "Pardon me, that was a personal question."

Lida seemed unfazed. "I moved here with my father."

"Well, like I said, you're welcome to stop by." More words spilled out. *Lord, why am I blabbering?* "My momma, Clara Thompson, can fix y'all somethin' right up. We're known for our chicken."

"The best fried chicken in the state of Utah," Lida said, settling into the saddle.

Hazel bit her cheek to keep from smiling. "I see you've met some of the locals, then."

"They speak highly of your mother and her food."

The leaves kicked up in front of her broom, dancing skyward as if they were just as entertained by this conversation.

"Well," Lida said, and Hazel stopped sweeping to catch her touch the tip of her hat with two fingers. "It was nice to meet you, Hazel Thompson."

The chivalrous gesture was another left turn, and Hazel hesitated before saying, "Likewise, I'm sure."

Lida made a clicking noise and gently kicked the heel of her boot into the horse's side. They turned and headed back down the road. Hazel watched her a minute, then moved to go inside when the woman called, "Next time, I'll have to try the rolls."

The laughter surprised her. She waved as Lida Jones rode away. It took Hazel a minute to realize she was still smiling. She glanced around, feeling absolutely silly next to a pile of leaves and wisps of ragweed. The line of silent cedars stared at her, the wind whispering to them as if it could see the giddy whirl inside her chest. "Oh, hush," she said to the open alpine field, glaring at a nearby tree. Then Hazel set the broom aside, pulled her shoulders back, and walked inside.

CHAPTER TWELVE

Despite herself, Lida glanced over her shoulder as she left the Thompson property. When Hazel turned, too, Lida whipped around and flicked Beth's reins, urging her forward.

"Go on, girl. Let's get out of here."

Half a mile from the Seagers' home, Lida was still thinking about her meeting with Hazel Thompson. *Did she really invite me back to the Lodge? After the way she treated me last time?* Had Hazel forgotten how rude she was after Lida had spilled the rolls all over the floor? The memory flared in her mind like the sunlight glinting off the mountain as it began to set, and she saw the shock and frustration shining in Hazel's eyes. If looks could kill, she wasn't sure she'd still be here.

Beth brayed, and Lida surfaced from her thoughts enough to guide them down a right turn.

"You think she meant it?" she asked and was met with a twitch of Beth's ear. Lida had met plenty of people, like the women she'd worked with in factories back east, who'd invited her places. They used phrases like "stop by anytime" or "drop in, why don't you?" but often, their words rang hollow. Once, Lida had taken an invitation at face value from a girl she'd cut fabric with in Pittsburgh. She'd arrived at her home to find all ten members of the household eating dinner, packed tight in their one-room apartment, wondering at the strange woman in their doorway.

Men had invited her places, too, and while their words were

often genuine, they were usually laced with an underlying need she didn't want to fulfill.

Hazel, with her poise and fast talking, actually seemed sincere. Which only confused Lida further. The way Hazel had stared her down after their initial run-in was like a burning ray of light, hot and dizzying. It had left Lida reeling. How could she have implied wanting to see Lida again after a look like that?

"It was probably a pity invitation," she said. "She feels sorry I'm new in town and that I don't know anybody." Beth breathed loudly, bobbing her head. "Exactly. I *do* know people. I know Martha, William, and Little Thomas. Not to mention all the people I've met today." Another snort from Beth. Lida smiled. "And you, of course."

She continued to mull over her encounter with Hazel as she pulled up to the Seager property. Martha had shown her where to keep Beth; the old horse pen was starting to lean to one side, its back wall nearly eaten through by mites. Lida kept to the right of the building where a couple outdoor pens stood. Maybe she could help William fix up the barn. She didn't imagine Beth would much enjoy sleeping in the snow come winter. Permitting we're still here, Lida couldn't help but think. She glanced to the west, in the direction of the mine, and hoped her father was faring all right.

Removing the pannier and satchel, Lida moved to take off Beth's reins when the horse sniffed and nudged her coat.

"What is it?" Lida lifted her arm. "Oh." She laughed and pulled out an apple. "Even I forgot this was in here." Beth blinked at her. "First, let's get you situated." After the reins and saddle hung on the edge of a door, she led Beth into a pen. Pulling it closed, Lida leaned against the edge and took a bite of the fruit. Beth whinnied. "All right. You earned it."

She held the apple out, and Beth gobbled it in one go.

"I'm gonna have to find you more." Beth lifted one hoof, then stamped the ground in agreement. "I'll be back to say good night. I'll bring more apples, too."

A few hours later, Lida sat by a fire with a copy of *Swann's Way*. The day's activity had caught up with her, and she tiredly drew herself a bath outside with the nearby well water, boiling it to scrub away the dirt clinging to her after the ride through Cedar Springs. In the bath, she stretched like a cat, relishing the new ache in her limbs from a day's hard work.

Afterward, placing her half-eaten crust of bread on a plate next to her chair, she lit a candle resting in a metal tray. The sky had darkened, and she glanced out the window as the trees and mountains vanished behind a veil of black. It had grown cold outside, but inside, the fire and gas lamp created a warm, soft haze that beckoned her to unwind.

Voices outside pulled her attention. Moments later, her father opened the door. "Lida," he exclaimed like it had been a week, not twelve hours, that had passed since seeing her.

"Pa, are you all right?" Her book forgotten, she stood at the sight of her father in denim overalls and heavy black boots, all of it as dark as the streaks along his face and neck. The shirt Lida remembered as white was now charcoal. Bits of soot flew from his jacket as he removed it. "Where are your other clothes?" she asked.

He raised a potato sack she hadn't noticed. "Here. Foreman issued me uniform. And this." He removed the helmet, the headlamp still lit, and waved it proudly. "What do you think?"

"I think you need a bath."

"What did you expect?" He laughed, loud and animated. When Lida started for the back door, he held up a hand. "I'll fetch my own water. You sit."

"Are you sure? Pa, you've had a long day. Your first day in the mine."

"And what a great day it was." He held out his arms, and Lida stared at his tall figure. He looked like a raven preparing for flight. He kicked off his boots as Lida hurried to the kitchen and found half a loaf of bread. She checked the icebox and grabbed a cut of butter and a pear Martha must have left. She set all of it on the table. When her father returned with a giant bucket of water, he poured it into a large pot on the stove. Lida lit the gas for him. Meanwhile, he used the basin near the door to scrub his face and hands. The water darkened immediately.

She handed him a rag. "I suppose we had better boil all this, along with your shirt."

Spotting the food, he snatched up the pear and took a large bite. "Go, sit," he said again, shooing her away. "I will clean. Then I want to hear about your library horse." Lida grinned and threw up her hands.

She was in front of the fire on page forty-two when her father collapsed into the chair next to her in a clean pair of pants and a blue shirt, the buttons misaligned.

"Better?" she asked.

"I haven't felt like this in a while." He stretched his legs, his toes nearly reaching the fireplace edge. He raised his arms, giving an exaggerated groan. "It feels good, this work. Strong. I'm not as fast, yet, as some of the others. But I will get there."

Lida thought about reminding him not to compare himself to the younger men but decided against it.

"It's impressive," he continued. "The mine. How they can tunnel deep below, like clever badgers. These Americans are always relentless in their endeavors. All for black rock."

"That black rock powers half the country."

He waved a hand as if shooing a fly. "I know that. It's good work," he repeated. "I am glad for it."

"I'm glad for it, too." She held his gaze. "Congratulations, Pa, on your first day."

He grinned, his mustache lifting. "And many more to come."

The same evening, Hazel sat by the fire, jotting down a list of items they'd need to order in the next week for Mr. Davis to pick up. She bit the end of the pencil, squinting at the scrap of paper.

"Brussel sprouts or green beans?" she asked.

Nicholas lay on his stomach near the fire, a worn, red-patterned rug beneath him. Without looking up from his book, he said, "Brussel sprouts."

She jotted it down. The sound of their family's wagon came up the ridge, and a few minutes later, their mother hurried through the back door.

"Hi, Momma," Hazel said, scrawling sugar on the list, then looking up to find her mother shaking off her coat, her strong arms tugging at the sleeves.

"Hi, my darlin'. How was supper?"

"Fine, Momma. Beans were good today."

"I thought so, too." She moved past Hazel and Nicholas, placing a kiss on the top of each of their heads, and into the kitchen where she reached for the kettle.

"It's already boiled, Momma."

"You are a lifesaver, Hazel." She spooned loose chamomile leaves, bits of ginger root, and lemon peel into a silver tea egg and poured the hot water over it. Carefully, she carried the china cup to the living room and sat opposite where Hazel had the gas lamp lit low. Situated in the chair, she asked, "Grandpa?"

"In bed."

Her mother fidgeted, kicking off the low heels, then wiggled her toes in relief. "My dogs are barkin' today."

Hazel looked up from her grocery list. "Don't know why you still wear those for the night shift, Momma. Ain't nobody lookin' at your feet."

"Ain't proper to be in nothin' else." She opened the sugar jar Hazel had placed on the table, scooping three spoonfuls into her tea. "Besides, the only other pair I have is my boots."

"So wear those."

"I don't see you wearing boots, honey."

"Well," Hazel said, setting the list in her lap. "Maybe I'll start."

Her mother smiled and took a long drink. Hazel was running over her list when her mother asked, "What's that, Nicholas?"

He read for a moment more, then held up the book. "It's from the Pack Horse Library."

Hazel straightened. "Would've been nice to know they were comin' today."

Her mother frowned. "The Pack Horse Library? Shoot, I

reckoned they'd start in July at the earliest. When that lady from the city came around, one of them church ladies, askin' if we was interested in receiving books, she'd said they didn't have anyone to deliver materials yet." She took another sip, seemingly ignoring Hazel's perturbed look.

"Well, they found someone."

Nicholas said, "Her name's Lida."

"Miss Jones," Hazel countered, shooting her brother a look.

"Well, how was she?" her mother asked. She blinked slowly, and Hazel watched her frame settle into the old chair. Its arms creaked as her mother rested her elbows. "She from Pine City, this Miss Jones?"

"No. She's not from these parts." Hazel pictured Lida atop the horse, struggling to direct it.

"Where's she from, then?"

Hazel pulled herself away from the memory. "I…I didn't think to ask. She said her father just started in the mine."

"What's his name?" At Hazel's silence, her mother's eyes, which had been falling closed, flew open. "Surely I didn't raise my daughter to forget all pleasantries in conversation. You didn't ask after her daddy, neither?"

Hazel pressed back in her chair. "I was busy, Momma. I was… sweepin'." She grimaced, then dared a glance at her mother, who stared at her as if she'd grown an extra limb. "I invited them to the Lodge. Since her father's a miner, I reckon he'll be by anyway. Told 'em they're welcome any time."

Her mother set her tea aside. "Well, that's somethin'. Least you had a mind to do that. Not all your manners have flown the coop."

Hazel gave a half-hearted glare, then returned to her list.

A few minutes later, her mother was snoring softly in her chair. Hazel draped the knit blanket over her and sat as the fire dimmed. "Don't read all night now, Nicholas," she said. "Don't want you missin' the sun and being late for the Lodge."

"I won't."

She watched him for a while until her gaze drifted to the fire.

The light jumped, the yellow and red climbing over each other, vying for a spot among the charred logs. Eventually, Hazel closed her eyes, a wide-brimmed hat and striking brown eyes drifting in greeting at the edges of her dreaming mind.

CHAPTER THIRTEEN

H azel, honey, where's your brother?"
    Hazel swiveled as she passed into the Lodge's kitchen, a tray stacked with plates and cups balanced in her right hand. "I thought he was upstairs, checkin' the rooms for the renters this weekend. Straightening the sheets."

"I was just up there and couldn't find him." Her mother's brows knit as she pulled out half a dozen pieces of fried chicken from the cauldron. "He better not have run off again."

"I'm sure he's around here somewhere, Momma." The dirty dishes fell with a clamor into the wide sink. Hazel scurried to the oven to check the potatoes. "Ever since he got those books, he's been findin' corners to crawl into to read. He's probably out in the wagon or in the storage pantry. He likes it in there."

Her mother grumbled and swiftly filled four plates with identical pieces of chicken, large heaps of potatoes, a scoop of beans and a stream of gravy. "Lord, give me patience," she muttered before hurrying into the busy dining hall. On a Friday afternoon, it was buzzing with conversation, many of the miners eager for the coming weekend.

Moving from the pot of potatoes to the wide corner oven, Hazel donned oven mitts, then tugged a blueberry pie from the scorching bricks. She let it cool, then sliced it into equal pieces. When six of them were arranged in a circle on individual plates, she followed her mother into the raucous room.

Jerry's voice came from a table near the front. "That fella from the office come by, askin' if I'd heard any news of a union. I told him he ain't got nothin' to worry about," he was saying to a group of three, his face serious as he leaned forward. "'How do you know that?' office man asked. I told him, 'Because, it's my job, pal. I'm paid to *mine* my own business.'"

The table roared with laughter.

Hank shook his head. "Jerry, your wife laugh at those jokes?"

"She sure does. That's why she married me." He leaned back, a silly grin on his face.

Hazel dropped a plate of pie in front of each. "You boys just tell me when to get the hook, and we'll have him right out of here," she teased, giving Jerry a punch to the shoulder. She spotted Mike Evans across the room at a corner table, listening as men twice his size talked over empty plates. She crossed the room and lifted the dessert tray, showing off the two pieces left.

"Anyone fancy somethin' sweet?"

One of the men turned. "Only if you're offerin', honey."

She slapped his hand away. "No pie for you, then. Mike?" She didn't wait for him to reply before handing him a plate. He smiled, then dug into the golden crust. Meanwhile, the other men grumbled. She set the final piece between them. "Since there's only one gentleman at this table, the rest of you can fight for it like wolves." Then to Mike, she added, "Don't you let these rabblerousers make you think they know how to treat a person."

Above his mouthful of pie, Mike's eyes registered her humor. He fought a grin. "No, ma'am. My momma taught me manners."

"Well, I'm glad." She winked, then started back for the kitchen when she passed Jerry's table, the conversation catching her ear again.

"I still can't get over how tall he is," Hank said. "Like a giant. A huge Russian giant."

"How do you know he's Russian?" asked Steven.

Hank spoke through a mouthful of potatoes. "You heard him talk, didn't you?"

"No. Barely said a word whole time we was workin in the same shaft."

"Well, I heard him. Sounded Russian. Or you know"—Hank waved his fork—"over there."

Hazel ran to the kitchen and grabbed a pitcher of water, then returned to fill their cups, listening.

"The name is enough to tip ya off." Hank squinted, seemingly trying to recall. "Tarrow? Arrow?"

Jerry tossed a bite of chicken at him. "It ain't hard." He spoke slowly, drawing out the syllables. "Yah-row. Yaromir Jones."

Hazel interrupted, keeping her tone light. "Y'all talkin' about that new miner?"

They all nodded. Steven answered, "He's all right. Kinda... different."

"Just 'cause he don't share what he had for breakfast, lunch, and dinner for the last week don't mean he's missin' a screw."

Hank grumbled, wiping his hands across the front of his dirty overalls. "I know that. But Steven said it, he hardly said a word. Right nervous fella." More nods. "He nearly dropped the pickax on himself, then *did* drop it on poor Samuel."

"He seems fine. Kept his head down, worked all day. You boys could learn a thing or two from him," Jerry said, pointing his spoon at his colleagues. The men grunted and shoved each other's elbows. Hazel was still holding one of their cups, staring at the table when Jerry said, "You all right, Miss Hazel?"

"Hm? Oh, yes I'm fine." She'd conjured the image of Lida riding away on her horse. "This new miner, he was a Mr. Jones?"

"That's right."

"Well, I hope you boys showed him some Cedar Springs hospitality and invited him to lunch."

They all exchanged guilty glances. Jerry spoke quietly. "He had a lunch, Miss Hazel."

"Yeah, he stayed back with the ones who always do, like William Seager. Ate at the office," Steven added.

"Well, as I live and breathe. My boys didn't extend a hospitable hand?" Hazel was using them, but she hadn't been sure if her blurted, hasty invitation to Lida had been taken the right way. Since their conversation at her house, Hazel had found it difficult not to wonder if Lida might show up. She kept her eyes to the windows while she was at work, searching for the chestnut horse and the wide-brimmed hat.

Jerry cleared his throat. "We'll invite him 'round tonight."

"That's right," Hank said, pulling a toothpick from his pocket. "My cousin's comin' to town. He's bringing his fiddle. It'll be a grand ol' time."

"Well, I am glad to hear it," Hazel replied, excusing herself.

Maybe he would come, this Mr. Jones. If he did, maybe he'd bring Lida. Hazel forced herself to focus on her work, but as the afternoon ticked by, she was overcome with the need to run home and freshen up the second the lunch hour was over.

CHAPTER FOURTEEN

A week passed, and Saturday rolled over the mountainside, clear and warm. Lida woke with the sun. She took the morning slowly, greeting Martha, William, and Little Thomas when she dropped in for coffee.

"William tells me your father is doing well," Martha said, a skillet of eggs on the stove in front of her as she sliced an apple.

"That's kind of you to say," Lida said, standing behind the table with a cup of coffee in hand. She'd already dressed, but the Seagers were in nightshirts, and Little Thomas only wore a cloth diaper as he bounced in his father's lap.

William took a drink of coffee before offering a mashed bite of carrot to Thomas. "It's the truth, Miss Jones. He's a fine man. Quiet, but I never did see the use in talkin' much while we're down there. Always imagined the mountain preferred peace to the chattering of men."

When Martha offered her some of the eggs, Lida declined. "I was hoping to take Pa up the hill, go see Cedar Breaks. We haven't had a chance to explore yet." She hesitated before adding, "He's been awful tired each night."

William said, "It's tough work, Miss Jones. Hard on a man's body."

Martha hummed her agreement. "You slept like the dead that first month," she said to William. "I was afraid you wouldn't wake up in time for your shift."

They all smiled. Thomas gurgled, and William lifted him, patting him on the back. "Good thing we have a God-given alarm clock right here."

Lida laughed as Martha snapped her rag toward William, who grinned and dodged it. "Thank you for the coffee," Lida said.

"Here." Martha hurried to pour her another cup. "For your father. If you're gonna take him anywhere, he's gonna need that."

Lida lifted the cup in thanks.

"Y'all been over to the Lodge yet?" Martha asked. Lida was about to respond, but Martha had her eyes on Little Thomas, offering him more food and added, "Y'all outta head that way. It's nice on the weekends earlier in the day."

"What my wife is trying to say," William said, standing and lifting Thomas over his head, prompting a gleeful babble from the boy, "is it's more genteel this time of day. I reckon' the festivities from last night have finished, anyway."

Lida raised her brow. "That fun, huh?"

"As I am a devoted husband, I cannot say one way or another," William said.

Martha planted a kiss on his cheek, then gave his shoulder a swat. "Don't listen to him. But it may be good to show your father the Lodge. The miners all go there. William don't often, but the food is to die for. I go when I can get away. Clara Thompson, the proprietor, she's a saint incarnate. The nicest woman you ever met."

Lida smiled. "Well, we might just make it up there, then. Thanks again for the coffee." Walking outside, Lida figured it couldn't hurt to go by the Lodge again. She'd pushed the invitation from Hazel to the back of her mind, focusing on organizing her delivery materials and practicing her riding for the last week. A hearty breakfast in the cliffside Lodge did sound nice. It wouldn't hurt to help her father meet more people, either.

It shouldn't have surprised her, then, when she and her father walked into the Lodge an hour later and were greeted by none other than Hazel. She had on a primrose-colored dress under a white apron. Her short blond hair fell in frizzy waves over her face as she quickly wiped down a table, then swiftly lifted a tray piled with dishes. She didn't seem to notice them at first, only gave a mild, "Good morning, find your seats anywhere you like," as she scanned the chairs for scraps to toss into the fire.

Lida watched her a moment as her father hung up his hat and coat. Then she said, "Good morning."

Hazel's head jerked up, her eyes wide. "Oh." She took a couple of steps forward, then tripped on the leg of a chair. Lida moved to help balance the tray as it wavered. "Thank you kindly." Hazel situated the tray so that it rested between the inside of her wrist and her hip, then met Lida's gaze. "I wasn't expecting you."

"Should I have...telegrammed?" Lida asked, removing her hat.

Hazel stared at the wide brim a moment before responding. She blushed. "No, I mean, I would've..." She moved as if to fix her hair, then seemed to realize her hands were full. Blinking, she turned to Lida's father. "You must be Mr. Jones."

Her father had been staring up at the beams that met in a triangle to hold the high ceiling and breathing in the pungent cedar, then gawking at the pair of antlers atop the western wall near the stairs. He met Hazel's gaze and smiled. "Yaromir Jones."

Hazel nodded, and Lida didn't miss how she was careful in her pronunciation of his name when she repeated it. "Yaromir. My, what a unique name."

"It was my grandfather's."

"How wonderful. I'm named for my great-aunt, on my mother's side," Hazel replied before adjusting the tray still against her hip.

Lida broke the silence that followed. "So what's on the menu?"

Hazel brightened, seeming to regain her composure. "We got biscuits goin' this morning. Y'all like gravy?"

Lida nodded, and her father replied, "Does a mouse like cheese?"

Hazel indulged his comment with laughter, then hurried into the kitchen. Lida and her father found a seat in the left corner. Lida sat so she faced the fire and could partially see into the kitchen. Her father sat next to her.

"Fine place," he said. "The craftmanship is quite good." He patted the dark brown logs of the wall. "Solid."

Over his shoulder, Lida caught sight of Hazel in the kitchen. She was speaking to the same woman Lida had met before who bore a resemblance to Hazel. They wore similar outfits, even down to the shoes. Their foreheads were close as they spoke. The older woman placed her hands on her hips, and Hazel made a shooing motion. The older woman said something over her shoulder, then grabbed a carafe and two cups and strode toward their table.

"Good morning," her father said when the woman placed the two cups in front of them.

"Good morning. I'm Clara Thompson. Welcome to the Lodge."

"It is beautiful, this Lodge. It's yours?" her father asked.

"Yes, sir. My husband and I bought the land nearly twenty-five years ago. Built this here with the hardworkin' hands of the people of Cedar Springs. Wanted a place for the locals to congregate whenever they pleased."

Lida was impressed. Her father seemed to be, too, the way he glanced from Clara to the tall stone fireplace, then the nine large tables occupying the dining hall. He pointed to the stairs. "What is up there?"

"My office," Clara replied with a wink. "There's four rooms. One for myself to be here when we rent one of the other three. They're not very big ones, mind you, but enough for a single lodger in each. Folks passin' through who need a place to stay and can't afford a night in a hotel in Pine City can stay here."

"That's a good idea," Lida said.

"I thought so. You folks are new in town." It wasn't a question but the way people prompted for more information.

Her father took a sip of the steaming black coffee. "Yes. We moved here two weeks ago. I'm in the mine."

Clara held the carafe by the handle, her other hand on her waist much like Hazel had done. Lida caught a flicker of something in her eyes before she said, "Bless you. You keep that helmet they give you." She said this lightly, but Lida could sense something else behind her words.

"Won't leave home without it."

Clara smiled widely. "Good." She turned to Lida. "That makes you young Miss Jones, the Pack Horse librarian."

It amazed Lida how much town news Clara Thompson was able to gather in just a week's time. "Guilty."

"Well, my son, Nicholas, he's had his nose in that book you brought him for days." She waved a hand. "He's even off somewhere now, likely lost in the pages."

"I'm glad to hear he's enjoying it."

"Well, y'all drink up. I'll bring out the food here in a minute," Clara said, then returned to the kitchen.

Over the next half hour, more patrons trickled into the Lodge. Like Martha had predicted, though, it never got too busy. Lida wondered what the place must have been like the night before, filled with jubilant music and loud laughter to ring in the weekend. As she imagined the scene, sipping her coffee, she fought to keep her gaze from lingering on the kitchen and the pretty sight of Hazel, her strong hands kneading dough.

A short while later, they'd devoured their food. Her father picked up the last bite of his, using the bread as a sponge to absorb the final drops of gravy. Finishing it off, he patted his stomach, hardly protruding over the edge of his high-waisted trousers. "That is best gravy I've ever had."

Lida finished hers, too. "It really was delicious. We'll have to come back sometime for the chicken."

He agreed, accepting another refill of coffee from Clara as she hurried past. The restaurant was quiet now, the breakfast-goers finishing their meals. Her father took a sip, then said, "I'm going to find bathroom. I've never had so much coffee before noon."

Lida laughed. "I saw an outhouse in the back. Don't get lost."

He waved her off. Lida sipped her coffee, content. She pulled a copy of *The Silent Partner* from her pants pocket, the small, faded paperback cracked from dozens of readings. She flipped it open and was reading chapter seven when a voice interrupted.

"That one of your library books?" Hazel was running a rag over the next tabletop.

Lida decided not to comment on its already clean appearance. "No, this is one of mine. I'm afraid I packed more books than shirts when we moved here." She gave what she hoped was a charming smile. Of course, she only had three shirts, but that was beside the point.

"No wonder you took the job, then. We've got a bookworm in our midst."

"I've been called worse," Lida said, captivated by the sunlight streaming through a window that framed Hazel in a soft glow.

"Oh," she replied, her face falling, "I didn't mean that in any sorta way."

Lida blinked, refocusing. "I know."

Apparently deciding the table was now clean, Hazel glanced back at the kitchen, then took a seat in Lida's father's chair.

"Taking a break?" Lida asked, closing her book. She scooted back as a scent like cinnamon and berries wafted over her. She swallowed, her gaze drawn to Hazel's dimpled chin, her pink lips as she spoke.

"I've got some time before the lunch hour brings the folks who slept in." She reached over to tap a finger on the book. "This a good one?" Her fingers traced the printed letters.

Lida said, "It's one of my favorites."

"What's it about?"

"You ever heard of the Lowell factories?"

Hazel shook her head, then crossed her legs, her gaze focused on Lida.

"Well, back east, there's a lot of places—factories and mills, for instance—full of workers who aren't treated well. These places force people to work long hours for poor wages. Back when this book was written, even children weren't immune. And a lot of the work was dangerous. Still is, like those machines," Lida said, recalling the towering, screeching mountains of metal that loomed over the factory floor. "They don't care if you make a mistake. They don't care if your sleeve gets caught or your foot sticks. They'll take you right down and break you."

"Lord." Hazel's hand moved to the collar of her dress. Lida noticed the top button was undone. "You work in one of those places?"

"I did. Several, actually. We moved a lot," she explained at Hazel's curious gaze. "This book tells the story of some of the women there, in those mills. It talks about their lives, their hardships." Lida almost added that it also described a deep bond between two of the characters that Lida had always admired and secretly yearned for. She licked her lips, wondering if Hazel had ever longed for something similar.

"Maybe I'll have to borrow it one day," Hazel replied.

"Here." Lida slid it forward across the table. "I've read it a dozen times."

Hazel looked from the book to her, one hand coming to rest on top of it. "I can't take that."

"I insist." Lida rested her hand on top of Hazel's, pushing the book toward her.

Hazel held her gaze a moment, then pulled her hand and the book back. "That's mighty kind." She flipped through the pages. Lida appreciated the way Hazel's eyes lit up as they swept over the words. She was still watching Hazel as she said, "I miss reading. Haven't had much time for it, I'm afraid." She gestured behind her.

"You've always worked here?" Lida asked, pleased Hazel seemed open to continuing their conversation.

"Since I was sixteen. When my daddy passed, I took over a lot of his responsibilities, as much as I could, anyway. Woulda continued with school, but that closed down, so I started here full-time helpin' Momma."

Lida recalled the abandoned school building from her ride through town. "I'm sorry about your dad, and that's a shame about the school."

Hazel sighed. "I got through most of my learnin' years," she said, "but my brother, Nicholas, he was only a child when it closed. And the other young folk around here…" She trailed off, her eyes shining. "Well, it wasn't fair to them."

Lida wasn't sure what to do at the sight of Hazel's crestfallen face. She shifted in her seat and was about to reach out when Hazel gave an odd laugh.

"Look at me. Carryin' on." She pushed back her hair, swiping quickly at her eyes. "Well, at least we have the Pack Horse Library now." Something seemed to light itself in the back of her eyes when she tilted her head. "Say, where do you get the reading materials from? Somewhere in town?"

Lida was about to respond when a group of people came into the Lodge, loud and pulling everyone's gazes. One of them, a stocky man with a handsome, square face, noticed them. Rather, Lida noticed him notice Hazel.

"Hazel!" he called. "I thought I'd find you here."

Lida looked between them. Hazel's entire posture shifted. Lida hadn't even noticed they'd moved closer to one another, their chairs nearly side-by-side, when Hazel pushed herself back.

"Good morning," she said, her voice brusque.

The man said something to the others in his group before they sat near the fireplace. He made his way over and stood between Hazel and Lida.

Hazel's smile was tight when she said, "Paul, this is Miss Lida Jones. Lida, this is Mr. Paul Boley."

"How do you do?" she said, standing to shake his hand. She was pleased to find she was only an inch shorter than him.

He stepped back in surprise but took her hand. "It's a pleasure, Miss Jones."

Hazel, still seated, added, "Miss Jones just moved here."

"Really?" Paul said. He spoke loudly through a big smile. His cheeks and chin gleamed with aftershave, though they couldn't outshine the oil in his hair. "Where from?"

"Cincinnati most recently," she replied.

"Well, I'll be. I got a sister who married a fella from Columbus."

Her father returned, and Lida was glad to see him as he stood awkwardly behind his occupied chair. Paul looked at him with an expectant smile.

Lida said, "My father, Yaromir Jones."

Realizing his return, Hazel scurried to her feet. Paul and her father shook hands.

"Welcome to Cedar Springs, Mr. Jones. You any interest in cattle?"

"Not a lot," her father said. "They mostly stand in grass. Not very exciting."

Lida bit her cheek to hide her laughter as Paul nodded politely, a bewildered look on his face. She caught Hazel's amused grin.

"Well," Paul said, "you folks oughta come by my family's ranch some time. We're hosting the summer social this year. It's gonna be a swell time." He cut his gaze to Hazel, who had been reading the back cover of Lida's book.

"When is it?" Lida asked.

"July Fourth. It's sort of our way of celebrating Independence Day. Granted, I've missed the last few years, so the celebrations may have changed. I've been away on business a lot. My father and I get up to Salt Lake, dealing with the fellas in the industry."

Lida presumed he meant the cattle industry but didn't bother confirming as he added, "The cattle industry is hot, I mean hot. Made a pretty penny with all the hard work I've put in."

Her father muttered a congratulations, and she could tell he was feeling intimidated by Paul and his shiny hair and slick watch that poked out the cuff of his coat trimmed with fur. He glanced at it now, saying, "Only a month and a half till the social. I do hope to see y'all there."

Hazel had started to move past them to collect her rag when Paul added, "If I'm lucky, you'll find me with a pretty prize on my arm." He reached out and tickled Hazel's waist. She laughed, but it was high and sounded forced. Lida took a step forward but stopped. She wasn't sure why that small gesture bothered her so much. Maybe it was the ease with which Paul touched Hazel. Maybe it was the dark look in Hazel's eyes afterward. Maybe it had to do with the sharp odor dripping off Paul. Maybe it was all of those things.

Paul was grinning like a fool as her father sat. Hazel excused herself, tossing one more smile to Lida as she turned to go. A flare of jealousy sparked in Lida's chest when Paul bid them good-bye and followed Hazel into the kitchen.

CHAPTER FIFTEEN

Paul on her heels, Hazel slapped the rag into the sink, mumbling over her shoulder, "This ain't a good time."

"Looked like a good time between you and Miss Jones."

She turned, wanting to glare but decided not to give him the satisfaction. "The lunch hour's startin' soon. I need to—"

"Hazel, just hear me out."

She sighed, leaning against the counter. Over his broad shoulder, she caught sight of Lida. Her eyes were trained on Paul's back. Then they widened in surprise when Hazel grabbed Paul by the arm and said, "Not in here."

She shoved him through the back door, closing it behind her, out onto the dirt path lined with firewood and discarded flour bags. She glanced around, ensuring they were alone.

"I don't see why you're makin' such a fuss," Paul said.

"You put me on the spot in there. What'd you expect?"

He replied, "I expected you might take me up on my offer."

"You know what it means when people show up together at the summer social. People talk." She crossed her arms, her gaze darting to the Lodge.

Lines creased Paul's forehead as he looked at her like she'd said the wildest thing. Agitation grew in the corners of his downturned lips. Running a hand down the back of his hair, he said, "I've been mighty patient, Hazel. You know how often my momma asks after you? 'When you gonna bring the Thompson girl around?' It's like a damn anthem every time I'm home."

"I'm surprised your momma hasn't widened her rope. You get to Pine City, even Salt Lake. There's plenty of girls out there."

"They're not like you, Hazel." He stepped closer, the ends of his coat flicking up in the breeze. "They're swell, sure, but they don't want this life." He gestured to the towering pines, the snowcapped peaks. "You get it. You get what it's like to have pride in your hometown."

Hazel shifted. "Don't mean we gotta be joined at the hip, Paul."

"Why not?"

She looked skyward, wishing she could will herself into the hills and away from this conversation. "I've told you…I got my plate full. I got the Lodge, helpin' Momma, mindin' after Nicholas."

"We ain't gettin' any younger, ya know."

She scoffed. "I'm aware."

He shook his head, kicking around a pile of vegetable scraps near the soup cauldron. After a moment, he said, "I'll be fine for a few more years. It's easier for me, a man workin' hard, earnin' his keep. Out here, a man has some leeway before bein' expected to settle down." He paused, seeming to weigh his next words. "But, Hazel, we're both nearly twenty-six. You not bein' married…well, you said so yourself: people talk."

"People say a lot of things that don't mean nothin'," she fired back, hating the defensive tone she'd taken. More so, she hated the knowing look in his eyes after seeing her with Lida. It was like the look he'd had each time she'd rebuffed his proposals. Part of her feared he'd connected the dots. How much longer until he found the words they spelled out?

After a minute, Hazel said, "I've got to get back inside." Paul, who had been boring a hole into a nearby tree with his hard stare, side-stepped and cut her off. He leaned to one side, one arm across the door frame, blocking her. "Paul, let me pass."

"Just picture it, Hazel." He spoke low, his voice light, but a distant desperation slinking beneath each word. "You'd want for nothing with me. I could provide for you. I'd be happy to do it. We could live on the ranch. You wouldn't have to work another day." She'd turned her cheek but swung her gaze to meet his. "I like my work. I like my life." She tried to move past him, but he lowered his arm, hooking her waist.

"Hazel, come on."

"Don't, Paul."

He'd just put his other hand on her side when the kitchen door flew open. Her mother wore a smile, but there was fire in her eyes. "There you are, Hazel. I was lookin' everywhere."

Paul darted backward. He ran a hand down his face, seeming to collect himself. "Hi, Mrs. Thompson. Hazel and I were just catchin' up."

Hazel gave her mother a look, and she seemed to pick up on her silent message. "I reckon those friends of yours in there miss you, Mr. Boley."

"Yes, ma'am." He looked at Hazel once more, then disappeared inside.

Letting out a deep breath, Hazel smoothed her dress where Paul had held her. She felt her mother's gaze.

"Hazel…"

"I'm fine, Momma. You know Paul. He gets carried away."

"What was he on about?"

"The summer social." At her mother's raised brow, she added, "He's in town for it this year, apparently."

"Well, aren't we lucky."

Hazel laughed. "I don't know what to do about him, Momma."

Her mother chewed her lip, one hand on her hip. "The Boleys are a prominent family. Paul was a kind boy. Become a bit too big for his britches, mind you, but he's got a good heart."

Hazel nearly blurted out, "But he's a man, Momma," but turned away, one hand over her mouth. She closed her eyes, regaining her composure.

"Honey, you all right?" Her mother hurried down the steps and placed a hand on her shoulder.

"I'll be fine, Momma." Hazel didn't want to think about Paul. She didn't want to think about how many more times she'd have to dodge his requests. "Come on." Back inside, relief filled Hazel in the warm kitchen, surrounded by the familiar sounds of the lodgers.

"Stir that gravy now, honey." Her mother returned to the opposite countertop and swiftly chopped carrots into a pile, though Hazel felt her studying her.

"Yes, Momma." She lost herself in the familiar movements, the smell of the gravy spices as she shoved the interaction with Paul to the back of her mind. Only then did the pleasant memory of her chat with Lida return.

Hazel set the ladle aside. "I'm going to check on the Joneses' table."

"They're gone, honey. Left a few minutes ago."

"They've...what?" She turned. Sure enough, the table had been cleared. "Oh." She reached into her apron pocket, feeling for the paperback. She ran her fingers up the worn spine. It was like an anchor Hazel didn't know she'd needed as she'd felt adrift at the sight of Lida's vacant chair.

CHAPTER SIXTEEN

The weeks passed quickly, and Lida fell into a rhythm in their life in Cedar Springs. The mountains blossomed with summer; bright colors and lively sounds both unfamiliar and breathtaking drew her into daily explorations. With all the snowmelt nearly gone, it was like a wide ribbon of green had wrapped itself around the hillsides. Streams flowed with vigor, crisscrossing on her book route. Trees gleamed with ripe leaves, the pines towering pinnacles along the mountain's base. Sloping ridges and rockfaces were unveiled under the bright sun, greeting the world with their magnificent reds, browns, and yellows.

Lida would wander near the Seagers' property, sometimes with William, other times with Martha, Little Thomas wrapped in a swaddle on her back. They pointed out the different flora and fauna, and Lida drank it all in. She'd appreciated their willingness to show her around this untamed world, so different from the one she'd known. It seemed incredible that this was the same country she'd lived in for two decades. How could each half look and feel so different?

She was glad, too, to lose herself in the scenery after the encounter with Hazel at the Lodge. Lida had done her best not to let her mind wander after seeing the way Paul interacted with her or the way Hazel had pulled him outside to be alone. She'd seen Hazel react to him and knew they weren't compatible. Still, the image of her hand on Paul's arm made Lida squirm. It also lit a spark of uncertainty in her new, tenuous relationship with Hazel. There was a connection between them, Lida knew. At night, lying in bed, she'd stare into the night sky imagining the feel of Hazel's hand beneath hers. Hazel's fingers would trace the letters on a book cover. She pictured Hazel thumbing through the pages. When her dreams lingered, Lida reminded herself it might not be worth pursuing. Every city she'd lived in for the last ten years had had a time stamp. Though there was an undercurrent of difference here. Things had seemed to be going well in this town for her and her father. Maybe, she hoped, they would stay awhile.

Exploration also meant more time spent riding, much to Beth's delight. Both she and Lida were much more comfortable with each other, and Lida more confident. Once they knew the delivery route without a map, Lida leaned into Beth's intuition as the mare picked up quickly on which slopes were most troublesome or where the tastiest grass waited.

This Monday, they were making a delivery to the Evanses, who had become one of Lida's favorite stops.

Little Evangeline ran outside to greet her. Much like every other time, she recounted the events of the book Lida had left them, then eagerly accepted the new ones.

"She's gotten so she'll only fall asleep with a story," Mrs. Evans told Lida, smiling at her daughter plopping onto the porch and staring at the cover of *The Tale of Peter Rabbit*.

Lida handed Evangeline a lemon candy. There had been a bowl full of them at the church when she'd exchanged materials yesterday. Celia and Dottie had greeted her but were busy talking endlessly about the upcoming social and hardly said a word to her.

As Evangeline took the candy and relocated inside, Lida asked, "How's Mike?" She hadn't seen him save for one day when they'd crossed paths while she was hiking with William.

"Oh, he's workin'. You know." Mrs. Evans peeked inside, pushing the front door open more. An old wicker bassinet sat next to a table, and baby Katherine slept soundly. "I can tell he's proud of his work. Proud to be contributing. I just wish…" She paused, her words seeming to catch in her throat. "I just worry about him being down there all day. He comes home exhausted. Sometimes he can't hardly see, there's so much of that rock in his eyes."

Lida understood. Some nights, it took two baths for her father to scrape the soot from his tired limbs. "Any word from your husband?"

Wiping her eyes with the hem of her apron, Mrs. Evans said, "No, nothin' recently."

"Hopefully soon."

"Yes, hopefully."

After the Evans's, she continued through town, dropping off a *Better Homes and Gardens* magazine to the Benters. It contained a number of simple recipes. Young Charlie had mentioned wanting to make something for the summer social, but he'd lost his mother's cookbook.

"Thank you, thank you," he'd said, his brow covered in sweat under the midday sun. Two of his siblings were in the garden behind him plucking sad-looking tomatoes.

As she rode on, glancing back at the children, Lida thought about her conversation with Hazel in the Lodge. She imagined the Benter children in a school, learning to write and read instead of seeing after tasks from sunup to sundown on the harsh, wild land.

When Lida came to another stream on her way to the Thompson house, she dismounted, deciding she had time to spare. It was a warm day, made warmer by the sun that seemed like it was sitting on her shoulder.

"Let's just cool off a minute, what do you say?" she said, leading Beth to the water. Lida knelt and scooped some into her hand. She relished the cool drink as it quenched her dry throat. "Certainly didn't have this in Cincinnati."

All around her, the stalwart mountains, the tall grass, the fir trees were like something out of a postcard. She found it difficult to believe this was where she lived. Each ride across Cedar Springs offered new discoveries, especially as summer opened her arms. Wildlife seemed to be everywhere. Squirrels and deer ran abundant. William had trapped a couple rabbits, and they'd enjoyed several pots of stew. The variety of birds was enough to leave her dizzy, their gentle trills a welcome change compared to the sharp whistles of trains and trollies. Their songs followed her each day, and she welcomed them.

Of course, there were hazards as the seasons changed. Two streams met near the bend before the road at Old Man Coffer's property, forming part of a river that swelled with snowmelt. "Gotta be careful. That water ain't messin' if she sweeps you up," Martha had said. "Best let the fish do the swimmin'." Lida wasn't much of a swimmer anyway and was content to sit by the water and watch the clear blue race by.

She'd also been cautioned to be wary of bears, but Lida was more concerned about wildcats. The week before, she'd been leaving the Benter property when not a mile away, Beth had stopped in her tracks on the thin rocky slope.

"Go on, girl," Lida had urged, but Beth wouldn't budge. A moment later, Lida discovered why.

A mountain lion stood high on a ridge fifty yards away. It blended with the rockface, and only when it opened its mouth in a lazy yawn did Lida see it. She had tried to back up, to coax Beth into moving, but she wouldn't. Eventually, the lion disappeared into the mountainside. Only then did Beth whinny in relief, her strong body quivering as Lida ushered them onward.

Fortunately, there hadn't been any more such encounters.

Lida rolled up her sleeves after taking another drink from the stream. It was so warm, she'd opted to leave her coat at home. Her vest provided an extra layer when the breeze picked up, but she was tempted to remove it. She took off her hat, instead, splashing the rim with water before doing the same to her face and neck. Then she replaced it, grateful for a shield from the bright rays.

Mounting, Lida took a deep breath as a flutter started in her stomach. Even her body knew where she was heading next: the Thompson house. After three deliveries, Lida had come to learn the times Hazel was likely to be home and had seen her each of the last times she'd been by.

"I'm halfway through *The Silent Partner*," Hazel had told her two weeks ago. "I can't put it down. Momma had to save the chicken the other day. I plumb forgot it was fryin'."

"I don't mean to distract you from your work," Lida had told her, though she secretly swelled at Hazel liking the book.

"Nonsense." Hazel's gaze had gone from the book in her hand to Lida. "Besides, some distractions are welcome."

Comments like this confirmed Lida's belief in their connection and helped her forget about shiny Paul and the way he'd looked at Hazel. Still, Lida began to wish their conversations weren't always on a timer. Each visit, Hazel stayed on her porch, and Lida remained atop Beth. Lida felt like there was a glass inside her that filled itself up each time she talked to Hazel. But as their visits ended, the glass tipped, spilling out the joy their time together brought as Lida rode away.

"Maybe today, I'll make it onto the porch," she said, and Beth brayed at her optimism. Lida gave her a pat on the neck as they pulled up the front drive of the Thompson house.

It seemed quiet. Frowning, Lida pulled out her pocket watch. Three o'clock. After the lunch hour. Lida directed Beth to the base of the porch steps. She called, "Hello. Pack Horse Library."

Silence.

"Hello?"

More silence. She was about to call again when an odd sound came from inside, like somebody hammering a steady beat against the floorboards, followed by the front door opening. An elderly man on crutches with the same blue eyes as Hazel squinted at her.

"What's that?" he asked, a pipe sticking out the corner of his mouth. His shoulders were hunched as he situated himself in the door frame. Lida's eyes were on his right pant leg, which was clipped at the knee and sewn closed, when she realized she was staring.

"Hello. I'm with the Pack Horse Library. Is Mrs. Thompson home?" She hesitated before adding, "Or her daughter, Miss Hazel Thompson?"

He sucked on the end of his pipe, then rested his right crutch against the wall and leaned to the left to scrutinize her. "They ain't back yet."

Lida reached behind her into the pannier. "I've got new materials for them. But I need the old ones to exchange."

He blew a cloud of tobacco smoke, then was about to say something when a spattering of coughs erupted from his mouth.

"Are you all right?" she asked, dismounting as he staggered, nearly losing his balance. He was more agile than she expected, though, and leaned heavily on the single crutch, hobbling forward to the porch railing.

After more wheezes, he replaced the pipe and said, "Damn lungs ain't what they were."

Lida, books under one arm, stood on the steps, still afraid he might topple as he insisted on holding the pipe and not the railing. This close, she could see the black stains around his fingernails, the sinewy muscles in his arms, and hear the wheeze in his chest.

"Did you work in the mine, sir?"

"Mr. Criley," he said through the side of his mouth.

Lida had seen that name. She'd seen it on the sign at the front of town. There was even a Criley road just outside of Pine City. "Mr. Criley."

"I did. Worked that mine for twenty-three years."

"My father works there now."

Mr. Criley studied his pipe. "My son-in-law worked, too. My daughter works the Lodge."

"Mrs. Thompson. Yes, we've met."

He took another draw from his pipe, eyeing her pants, her hat. "I'll fetch your books."

He limped to the doorway, still only using one crutch, then reappeared with the books. "What'd you say your name was?"

"Lida Jones, sir."

"Lida. I heard of you. Hazel mentioned you and"—he motioned to Beth—"this library stuff."

Trying not to smile at the fact Hazel had talked about her, she thanked him and handed him the new materials, a *National*

Geographic magazine for Nicholas and a tattered copy of *The House of Seven Gables* for Hazel. She'd remembered how passionately Hazel spoke of *The Scarlet Letter* and imagined she'd like another one by Hawthorne. Mr. Criley gave a half-hearted wave and went inside.

Lida led Beth to the barn stall once they returned to the Seagers'. The disappointment at not seeing Hazel surprised her. She wondered where Hazel was. Surely the Lodge was busy. The few times she'd seen Hazel there, the work seemed endless, and her enthusiasm to please the customers equally so. It was probably work, Lida assured herself, that kept Hazel from home.

Disheartened, Lida lost herself in the pages of a book after dinner. She was engulfed in the story and hardly heard the door when her father came home.

"Hi, Pa," she said without looking up. When he didn't respond, she found him wearing a sullen look as he hung up his coat. "Pa, what is it?"

He set his helmet outside and his metal lunchbox by the door. She wasn't sure he'd heard her and was about to ask again when he said, "Nothing, Lida."

"Pa. It's not nothing." They'd been side by side in life, on this fraught journey west for nearly a decade. She knew when something wasn't right. She stood, a spike of panic in her chest. "Is it work? Did something happen?"

He bent to wash his face and hands, drying them on a stained rag. "Lida, not now, please."

"Pa." She moved to face him. "What happened?"

Finally, he turned, his gaze lowered. "I was late coming back from lunch." He shrugged, waving a casual hand. She glanced at the metal lunchbox, then grabbed it. Setting it on the table, she opened it to find the bread, cheese, and apple she'd packed him that morning.

"Pa."

"I went to Lodge. You should be happy. I make friends."

"Was William there?"

"No. I went with others. After, we got distracted and were late."

He kept staring over her shoulder or at the fire, anywhere but at her. Not caring that his shirt was filthy with soot, she reached out, grabbing his shoulders, making him look at her.

She stepped back at the shine in his glazed eyes. "You've been drinking."

"I had…three." He held up four fingers. "Maybe more."

"How? When?"

"We stopped at Jackson Ansom's property. He had some mountain whiskey. Have you ever had mountain whiskey? It is so good." At her incredulous look, he added, "We had time, Lida. We had time." He shrugged again. "Until we didn't."

Lida blinked. She could see the guilt creeping up her father's neck, swirls of red penetrating the black.

He said softly, "Foreman gave us warning."

"You're lucky that's all he did."

He brought his tall figure up, looming over her. "Do not speak to me as if I'm child." The sternness of his tone took her aback.

She swallowed but was too shocked to be intimidated. "Don't you know how dangerous it could have been? To be working in such a state?"

"We didn't work. Foreman dismissed us."

Lida frowned. "Then where have you been?"

"Walking."

Lida scoffed. "Walking." Her body was tight with frustration. Her fists clenched at her side. Agitated, she slammed the lunchbox shut. Her father flinched. They both held each other's gazes. Finally, she sighed, her voice softening. "You have to be careful, Pa. You know how quickly things can change." *How quickly you can be fired*, she almost added. *How quickly we have to pack our bags and leave.*

"I know what I'm doing, Lida. I know I made mistake." He gave her a smile. "You worry too much."

"I've had reason to."

His smile fell, and his gaze turned hard. "I do not mind our talks, Lida. I am glad for them most days. But this…it's like you don't care."

Her jaw nearly fell to the floor. "Like I don't care? Pa, what are you—"

"Do you even remember what week it is?"

She was spinning in her anger, and it took a moment to focus on the calendar behind him on the wall. Finally, she found today's date, then slid her gaze to the twenty-fifth of June.

"Pa," she said, her voice barely a whisper.

"Eight years. Eight years without her. Can I not mourn?"

"We've mourned her, Pa. We need to honor Momma now."

"Then let me honor in my own way."

"Not like this," she countered sharply.

He was crying, tears making rivets in his stained cheeks. "I want to make her proud. But I can't seem to find the right way."

"Pa—"

He coughed to hide his cries. It broke Lida to see her father like this. It broke her a little each time it happened. The first time had been a month after her mother's funeral, when he'd gone out at lunch and didn't come home until dinner the next day. He could hardly stand when he'd staggered through the door. Each time since then was another crack in Lida's armor, the armor she wore for her father. The armor he'd forced her into as he coped in the only way he seemed to know how. The armor she had to wear as the inevitable pitying looks and nattering gossip trailed her father from his work into their home. The armor she wore to prepare herself for another train, another town, another life.

"Come on." She tugged him to a chair by the fire, then filled a bucket and found a rag. Silently, she removed his socks and rolled up his pant legs. He was sobbing now, openly, and into his wide hands. She brought his feet into the water, then let him weep, let him miss her mother. Then Lida washed the soot and dirt from his tired body, wishing it were as easy to wash away his sorrow as it was to erase the mountain's mark upon his skin.

CHAPTER SEVENTEEN

Tuesday morning, Hazel dressed quickly, choosing a denim-blue dress with a soft floral pattern stitched along the hem and collar. She snatched up Lida's book from her bed, then hurried into the main room.

"Morning, Grandpa." She kissed the top of his head and pulled up the knit blanket that had fallen to one side. Morning sunlight streamed in once she opened the curtains, though clouds gathered in the distance. "Might rain come nightfall," she said over her shoulder.

He grumbled in his rocking chair. "What're you still doin' here?" he asked, groggy with sleep.

She tossed the book into a satchel and poured a glass of milk from the small icebox. Handing it to him, she said, "Was workin' late yesterday helpin' Momma get ready for the social." They'd pickled ten jars of beets and organized the preserves for more pies they would bake today. At the kitchen table, Hazel sliced a piece of bread. "You were already asleep when I came home last night," she teased before exchanging his empty glass for the bread.

He took a hungry bite, speaking through the crumbs. "Tell your momma she works too dang hard for that event."

"Grandpa, the summer social is Cedar Springs' biggest night. You started it," she reminded him with a pointed look as she found her shoes by the back door.

"Worst mistake I made," he said, but she could see the glimmer of fond memories in his eyes. "Nothin' but a bunch of hooligans gettin' into trouble. Used to be a patriotic ceremony. Used to have respect."

She gasped, adding a fainting motion for effect. "Grandpa, you don't really believe there are hooligans in Cedar Springs, do you?"

He grunted. "That night there are."

She laughed. "Here I was thinkin' it was a glorious tradition bringin' the townsfolk together. Didn't you propose to Grandma at the social back in seventy-five?"

Another grunt.

"I thought so." She grabbed her satchel and said, "Nicholas will be here at ten o'clock. Don't forget to send him back by noon. He's so lost in his books lately, he's liable to forget what day it is."

She was halfway out the door when her grandpa called, "That lady came by yesterday. The one with them books."

Hazel paused, one hand on the door. "Miss Jones?" She glanced at the calendar hanging on an old nail. "Lord, I beat Nicholas to it. Plumb forgot." She glanced outside, scanning the open fields as if doing so might make Lida reappear.

"I gave her back those books." He pointed to the base of his side table. "She left these."

Hazel hurried over. Crouching, she found a *National Geographic*, then smiled at the Nathaniel Hawthorne. "Thanks, Grandpa." She gave him another kiss, then ran out the door.

❖

"This makes seven, Momma." Hazel pulled the blackberry pie from the oven. She placed it at the end of the counter in front of Nicholas, where he sat hunched over the magazine, glued to an article on thrushes.

"Perfect, honey," her mother said, swiping her forearm across her brow. Both of them looked harried after a busy day. They hadn't even had too many customers to serve, but all of the baking, cooking, and organizing for the social in one week's time had them on their feet nonstop.

"I reckon that stew out there's just about done," Arthur said as he lumbered through the back door, the oversized cauldron simmering behind him over a low fire.

"Thank you, Arthur," her mother said. Hazel grinned at the look they shared. Arthur had been by the last few days, claiming to have forgotten to deliver some of his usual items. Both she and her mother ignored the fact that he'd always had an impeccable memory. From the way he fidgeted with the band on his suspenders, Hazel had an inkling he was workin' himself up to something. So she'd invited him to stay and help after his delivery that morning. She was pleased at the lightness in her mother's step when he was around.

"You've been mighty helpful," her mother said to him, taking a moment to lean against the counter. "Not sure if we coulda done all this without you."

Arthur grinned. "I'm sure you'd be just fine."

Hazel pursed her lips and hid her face, turning to wash her hands. She waved good-bye to Jerry and Hank, the last patrons to leave after the dinner hour. The sun was still up, but beginning its descent in the late June sky. As she'd predicted, more storm clouds were rolling in, but they only hovered, ominous and gray over the hills.

After Hazel cleared the table, she caught Arthur's pensive look as he stood beside her mother, the two of them chopping carrots in compatible silence.

"Mr. Davis, mind helpin' me with the firewood?" He followed her outside. Checking that her mother was still busy, she said quietly, "Mr. Davis, somethin' on your mind?"

He looked bashfully around, and Hazel couldn't help finding his uncertainty endearing. "Well, Miss Hazel, I was considerin' asking your mother if she'd accompany me to the summer social." Hazel smiled at the brightness in his gaze as he threw a look inside. "She's a mighty good woman, your mother."

"Yes, she is." Hazel placed her hands on her hips. "And if I may, Mr. Davis, you're a mighty good man."

He dipped his chin. "Thank you. Well, what do you say, Miss Hazel?"

"I say there's only one way to find out." She winked, then gently pushed him back inside. "Nicholas," she called, "come on." Her mother looked up, mid-chop. "Where you off to?" "Errand to run. We'll see you at home." "We gotta close up, honey. The front porch needs seein' to. The fire needs puttin' out. We gotta check on the rooms upstairs and—" "If I may," Arthur said, "Clara, I'd be happy to stay and help." Her mother blushed at Arthur's use of her first name. Hazel registered the knowing look in her mother's eyes. Then she tugged Nicholas from his stool.

"We'll see you two later," she called, then caught Arthur's gaze. He gave a grateful nod before she left them alone, a feeling of possibility filling her chest.

"The fruit-hunter thrush enjoys berries and nuts in its native Borneo," said Nicholas.

"Is that so?" Hazel replied. She and Nicholas sat under a wide weeping mulberry tree. The sun was setting, gray clouds settled over a layer of deep pink slowly giving way to red beyond the mountains. They'd have to get back to Grandpa soon but had time to spare. She leaned back, soaking in the cool evening air, hoping her mother would say yes to Arthur Davis. Since her father died, her mother had thrown herself into the Lodge. Hazel had been happy to help, eager to take up her father's mantle as the co-proprietor, but that had left little room in either of their lives for anything else. Her mother was at the Lodge six days a week, sometimes before dawn and well after dark.

"What do you think of Mr. Davis, Nicholas?" she asked.

He lay on his back a few feet away, the magazine close to his face in the fading light. Their wagon sat on the road twenty yards behind them, and she wondered how long it would take him to remember they had a lamp he could use to read by. "He's nice."

"I agree."

"He's alone."

"Yes," Hazel said, "he came up here by himself from Georgia."

They sat in the peaceful quiet of the coming night until a sudden bray sounded nearby. Nicholas frowned, turning over on his stomach. "What was that?"

"Sounded like a horse."

They listened. Hazel leaned, peering into the trees. A woman's voice came from somewhere close, followed by another series of brays. "Stay here." She hurried to her feet. Around the trunk of a pine, she spotted Lida and her horse, who had her hooves planted firmly, refusing to move. Lida had dismounted, revealing a disheveled braid after removing her hat. She pulled in vain on Beth's reins.

Hazel waited a moment, then moved forward saying, "Havin' trouble?"

Lida straightened, a small flush flying to her cheeks. She looked behind Hazel, then around. "Where did you come from?"

Hazel hitched a thumb over her shoulder. "One of my spots." She smiled. "Taking in the sunset with Nicholas."

Lida nodded, then grimaced as she gestured to Beth. "I don't know what happened. We were on our way home when she just stopped. We'd never been this way. I wanted to become more familiar with alternate routes, just in case, but I'm coming to regret that decision." Beth snorted, shaking her head.

Hazel crossed her arms. "Well, she certainly is speaking her mind."

"I wish I could read it. I don't understand why she's stopped. My bags are empty, so they're not weighing her down."

"Hmm." Hazel walked closer. Lida stepped back, replacing her hat. "Have you tried letting her go? Just to see if she'll move without you holdin' her?"

"I'm afraid she'll run off."

"She done that before?"

"No, but…" Lida trailed off, and Beth snorted again, seeming to nod along with Hazel's suggestion. "I guess it's worth a try."

Hazel took the reins from Lida. She placed them over the pommel of Beth's saddle, then gave her neck a pat. "What is it, sweetie? What do you want?"

Quickly, Beth whinnied and trotted back up the ridge ten yards, then stretched her neck into the high branches of a tree. Hazel and Lida exchanged glances, then hurried after her.

"I should have known," Lida said, shaking her head. Beth was tugging a ripe peach from its limb, her large teeth nibbling on the flesh. "She never could resist something sweet."

Hazel laughed. "She's got a good nose on her. I didn't even know these were here."

"I have to be careful with what I keep in my pockets," Lida said, both of them watching Beth munch happily. "She sniffs out apples like a keen-nosed wolf."

"I believe it." In the fading light, Hazel took in Lida's figure. Her dark gaze studied Beth, and Hazel was tempted to reach out and play with the ends of Lida's long braid. She wanted to run her fingers through Lida's thick, dark hair. The vest she wore over a long-sleeve white shirt fitted over her chest. That combined with her snug riding pants revealed a figure Hazel found absolutely intoxicating, the kind she wanted to trace every inch of with her hands.

Feeling self-conscious at these sudden thoughts, she took a step back. "Well, I am glad we solved the mystery. Hopefully, she won't give you any more trouble now." She started to walk away.

Lida called, "May I join you?" Turning, Hazel met her gaze. "To see the sunset. Beth's going to need to digest a minute anyway."

Hazel raised one eyebrow at the flimsy excuse, but she didn't care. "Of course. This way." She led Lida toward the bluff where Nicholas lay, nose back in his book. "Look who's here."

Nicholas, on his stomach, looked up. He smiled. "Hi, Lida." Hazel cleared her throat. "I mean, Miss Jones."

Lida laughed, securing Beth to a low branch near Sasha, who whinnied at the mare in greeting. "Lida is fine, Nicholas."

Hazel felt Lida's gaze on her as they took a seat next to Nicholas atop the soft grass. Shadows grew thick along the rock-littered cliffside, the sky dimming and the darkness stretching its waking arms around them. Nicholas fetched the lamp from their wagon. He placed it between the three of them, his feet to the drop-off and mountains beyond. Hazel stretched out again, cutting her gaze to Lida, who had one arm resting over the knee propped close to her chest.

"It's beautiful here," Lida said after a moment.

"No sunsets in Cincinnati?"

"Not like this."

Hazel tried to keep her gaze focused on the hills, but having Lida so close made that difficult. Though the silence was comfortable, Hazel's mind hummed with questions. "How's your father?" she eventually asked.

Lida was quiet for a moment. "He's doing okay. The past week has been hard."

"They workin' him too much?" Hazel straightened. "He ain't hardly been there a month. I'd tell that foreman what for if he's abusing his power. They always do, but that don't make it right. Your father's gotta make sure he makes it known he won't take it if they're workin' him too hard," she repeated, feeling fired up, then embarrassed by the soft smile on Lida's face.

"It's not work."

"Oh."

"Well, it is, but also…" She seemed to search Hazel's eyes, and Hazel wondered at the swirls of dark brown. "My mother passed away eight years ago yesterday."

Hazel wanted to reach out, but she sensed a quiet acceptance in Lida. "I'm so sorry."

"It's hard to believe it's been that long. I still remember that day. I was home, helping tend to her, feeding her ice chips. We were living in New York, in a crowded apartment building as old as the city itself." Lida moved to sit cross-legged, picking at a blade of grass, running it between her fingers as she spoke. "We knew at that point, my father and I. We knew she was leaving us. She'd been sick a long time. I can still smell the bedsheets, sticky with her sweat. I can hear her rattled breathing." She gave a sad laugh. "Even the doctor with his long beard and small glasses. I can see him, proclaiming the time of her death with his silver pocket watch." She turned to Hazel, who soaked in the shape of Lida's face lit in the soft glow of the lamp. "I can see all of that, but I can hardly remember what she was like before. Each day that goes by, it's harder to picture my mother…the way she was."

A dull, aching sensation crawled into Hazel's chest. She hadn't felt it in a while, but it was always there. She nodded, understanding the cruel tricks time played on memories.

"The day my daddy died was one of the worst of my life." She hadn't spoken to anyone about her father's passing in a long time and was surprised by the ease with which the words escaped her now. "That was the only time I've seen my momma cry. When they came by…those miner boys with their dirty faces and dirtier hats gripped in their shaking hands, bringing my daddy's helmet home…God, it was awful. Like a train came bulldozing through our lives, wreckin' everything." She was watching Nicholas, who didn't seem to hear her. This was one of those times she was extra grateful for the way he focused so hard on something, the rest of the world simply didn't exist.

She jumped, surprised when Lida's cool hand rested on hers. Hazel swallowed and used the dark to trace her gaze over Lida's fingers, up her arm, and to the eyes staring back at her with a look of…what was that? Gratitude? Understanding? It made Hazel's skin warm, her chest feel like it was brimming with something she couldn't quite name.

Hazel continued. "People showed up after he was gone. The people my daddy and momma spent years lookin' after, spent years building a community with, they showed up. Looked after Nicholas and Grandpa so I could help Momma."

Lida said, "It's a good town. Full of good people."

"The best." She took a breath, pulling her hand back to wrap her arms around herself as cold fell over them once the sun dipped behind the mountain. "Which is another reason why I can't stand to see folks leavin' for greener pastures. There's plenty of green right here." She sighed. "I'm not blind, mind you. I know the opportunities aren't exactly fallin' from trees like they once did. But if people leave the first chance they get, what chance does Cedar

Springs have? And sendin' our boys into those hills? It ain't the way to do it." She glanced over at Nicholas reading. "I wish that school hadn't closed."

Even in the near-complete darkness, as a slim crescent moon rose to the east and stars littered the night sky, she could see Lida was thinking. She could see it in the way her eyes stared just past Hazel. She could see it in the way she had shredded the blade of grass into tiny pieces. Hazel knew she was thinking of something kind to say, something to ease her mind. It was a nice gesture but wouldn't fix the feeling of helplessness as the future of Cedar Springs seemed to teeter on the cliff's edge.

"Well," Hazel said after a time, "we'd better get back. Come on, Nicholas."

He rose, tucking the magazine into his pocket and walking to the wagon, the lamp swinging at his side. Lida stood, offering her hand.

"They teach everyone chivalry back east?" she asked, taking it.

Lida grinned. "Sometimes."

They were at the wagon, their horses whinnying restlessly, eager to get home. Nicholas was already in the seat, adjusting Sasha's reins. Hazel was about to join him when Lida reached out, pressing lightly on her arm.

"What if," Lida started, and Hazel turned. "What if I could get more materials? More books. More...supplies. Enough to provide for a school."

Hazel blinked. "Well, I...I don't know. How?"

"The Havishes. They're the ones who hired me. They're the organizers of this sect of the Pack Horse Library. I could talk to them. See if there's a way to bring in more than the library deliveries."

Hazel's chest felt ready to burst. "You would do that?"

Lida smiled. "I'd be happy to."

"Well, that would be wonderful."

Nodding, Lida leaned forward, then stepped back, biting her bottom lip as if swallowing her words. Hazel wished she hadn't. Then she touched the brim of her hat.

"You'll make it back okay?" Hazel asked. "It's mighty dark."

Lida mounted. "I'll find the way." She said good-bye to Nicholas, who waved as Hazel climbed to sit next to him.

As Lida disappeared into the dark fold of trees, he said, "I like her."

Hazel leaned into him. "Me too, Nicholas. Me too."

CHAPTER EIGHTEEN

Once her father left for work with William, Lida readied Beth, then rode down the mountain into Pine City. Each time she visited, the bustle of the city had become increasingly jarring. Sights and sounds that had once been as familiar as her own face now seemed too loud, too much compared to the peaceful hillsides of Cedar Springs. Still, she did appreciate the city and its commodities, as she stopped into the butcher's and picked up a pound of steak to surprise the Seagers with. Her pay from the Pack Horse Library, while not grand, was still a pleasant addition to her father's income. She tucked the delicacy into her saddlebag.

It was nearly eleven by the time she made it to the Havishes'. She'd asked after their address when she'd exchanged materials at the church. Dottie had given her directions, hardly looking up from the red, white, and blue quilt she was working on which, Lida learned, was to be auctioned at the social. Apparently, some of the folks of Pine City climbed up the mountain once a year to mingle with their neighbors.

Securing Beth to the black iron gate, Lida took in the two-story Victorian house. It sat at the top of a keyhole road off the main street, the paved concrete lined with lampposts marking each home's front drive. Like the Havish's, each lawn was framed by front gates standing guard over trimmed green lawns and rosebushes. Sunshine brightened the blue sky on another early warm summer day.

On the wide, ornate front porch, Lida removed her hat and

WILDFLOWER WORDS

knocked. Moments later, an old woman with dark brown hair and dark eyes opened the door. For a moment, Lida thought she'd fallen back in time and was staring at one of her neighbors from the old country. But there was no recognition in the woman's gaze, and Lida knew it wasn't her. Still, she recognized the features of a countrywoman in her thin frame, which barely filled the confines of her black and white maid's outfit.

"Good morning," Lida said. "Is Mrs. Havish home?"

"Who's calling?" Her accent was thicker than Lida's father's.

"Miss Jones. Lida Jones."

The woman gave a curt nod, then closed the door. After several minutes, it was opened wide by Mrs. Havish.

"Miss Jones! What a surprise. Come in, come in." The maid took Lida's hat and coat. Mrs. Havish, wearing low heels and a matching red dress as fashionable as the last one Lida had seen her in, motioned for her to follow. "Whatever brings you this way, Miss Jones?" she asked, returning to a wing-back leather chair in a parlor room off the main entry. Lida blinked at the chandelier hanging overhead, its dozen or so electric bulbs waiting for the sun to go down in order to dazzle the room. Meanwhile, sunlight from the window grazed the patterned wallpaper and a plethora of fringed lampshades that encircled the room. Mrs. Havish picked up a newspaper from a tea tray. "Is everything going all right? We left your pay at the church."

"Yes, I got it, thank you. Everything is going well," she said.

Mrs. Havish motioned for her to sit, and she did, careful as she rested her boots upon an intricately patterned rug. "Tea?" she asked, leaning forward to pour another cup.

"No, thank you. I don't want to keep you." She glanced around. "Is Mr. Havish home?"

"Oh no, dear. He's away on business. I imagine he'll be back just before the July Fourth festivities."

Lida was unsure how to broach the topic of requesting more materials. Mrs. Havish seemed to sense her trepidation as she put down the newspaper. "I'd be happy to help with whatever brought you here, my dear." She gave a wry smile. "My husband may be the one who signs the paperwork, but he has to get the inspiration for his deals from somewhere."

"Well, it's about the materials for the library."

"Everything's been coming in on time, so far. As regular as a clock," she said, winking.

"Yes." Lida smiled. "As you may recall, the school in Cedar Springs closed some years ago."

Sitting back, Mrs. Havish said, "Yes. I imagine it's difficult to keep a teacher up there. We have a hard enough time of it in Pine City."

"Would it be possible to inquire about more materials? Materials to help revitalize the school?"

"Have they a new teacher? Is Cedar Springs planning to reopen the school?"

Lida fidgeted with the frayed end of her sleeve. "Well, no. But if they had the materials, that would be a start."

A small smile lifted Mrs. Havish's cherry-red lips. "Remind me," she said, "you've been there nearly three months now, is that right?"

"Yes."

"It must be some town to make such an impression on you. To want to make such a request."

"It's a good place, full of kind, hardworking people." She pictured Hazel in her dress. When she glanced at Mrs. Havish, she looked utterly tickled.

"So I see." She took a sip of tea and sat back again, crossing her arms. "I would very much like to help you, Miss Jones."

"Really?" Lida worked to keep her voice steady, but excitement expanded in her chest.

"Absolutely. I admire a woman who isn't afraid to ask for things. Just like you did on your father's behalf the first time Walter and I met you. The West needs more women like you." Lida felt herself blush at the compliment. "Besides, you've been an exemplary member of the Pack Horse Library initiative. Well," she added with a grin, "you've been its only member so far, but you've proven yourself greatly. I'll telephone Walter tonight and tell him he must request more materials for the good people of Cedar Springs."

Lida sprang from her chair, Mrs. Havish giving a startled laugh as she hurried forward. "Thank you, Mrs. Havish." Lida stuck out her hand.

"Please," she said, standing and shaking it. "Call me Cynthia. I'll let you know as soon as I hear something. Hopefully, we can have things ready in a month or so."

Lida thanked her again then found her hat and coat before hurrying out the door, feeling like she might float all the way back to Cedar Springs.

❖

"Hey, you're Yaro's kid," a man with a scraggly beard and straw-yellow hair hollered at the base of the Lodge steps as Lida dismounted. She eyed his sloppy grin, the wobble in his step. "Tell him we missed him at lunch today. Hope he comes by the Boley Ranch Thursday." He guffawed, the men on either side of him cackling before they wandered away, not waiting for her to respond.

She took their comment to believe her father had stayed near the mine with William for lunch, a good sign he wasn't getting carried away by other offers. Lida climbed the Lodge steps and could hear the packed dining hall before she saw it. Sure enough, every table was full of miners in dirty coveralls in the thick of the lunch hour.

Lida removed her hat, scanning the room. When Mrs. Clara Thompson blew through, a pitcher of water in one hand, Lida stopped her. "Is Hazel here?"

"Why, Miss Jones," Clara said, filling six cups for the men at a table by the door, one hand on her hip. "How's your father?"

"He's well, thank you."

Lida caught the way Clara seemed to study her as she searched over the heads of everyone in the room. There was something in Clara's gaze when she said, "You'll find her in the kitchen. We've got our hands full with the social only two days away."

Lida took that to mean she shouldn't stay long. "Yes, ma'am." Then she wove through the tables, scooting between chairs. In the kitchen doorway, she found Hazel with Nicholas and a tall man with broad shoulders who saw her first.

"Can I help you?" he asked.

"I was hoping to speak with Hazel."

The smile Hazel wore at seeing Lida made her heart seem to skip. "Lida, hi, everythin' okay? It's not Monday, is it?" She tossed Nicholas a look. He shook his head and returned to stirring what looked like a creamy pie filling. "No, can't be Monday. Social's on Thursday. Right around the corner. You know, every year, we think we'll be ahead of schedule, on top of the menu, the planning." She blew a strand of hair out of her face as she rigorously rolled a piecrust out. Nicholas stole a bite of dough. "But seems like we always run right up to the day, workin' till the very minute it starts." She took a breath, giving Lida a tired smile.

Lida nodded, taking in the frenetic kitchen that seemed to sing with activity. Every stovetop was lit, cast-iron skillets sizzling; the wide brick oven encased the already warm room in heat, filling it with a dizzying mixture of tantalizing scents. When Clara scooted past, a pile of dishes on a tray, Lida's enthusiasm from visiting Mrs. Havish dimmed. Overwhelmed and out of place at the sight of Hazel and her family throwing all their effort into the upcoming social, Lida hesitated. She realized, also, she wanted to be alone with Hazel to tell her the news.

"Well, I was just passing by." Tearing her gaze from Hazel, she realized Clara was eyeing her as she scrubbed a dish. Dipping her chin, she turned to go.

"You'll be there, won't you?"

Lida turned. She noticed the man chopping onions give Clara a look, which Hazel didn't seem to notice as she added, "At the social, I mean. You'll be there?"

She hesitated. "I…well, I hadn't decided, to be honest. The Seagers may go. I'm not sure if my father will be up for it."

"Whole town'll be there," Clara said, not looking up from the bubble-laden sink. Was that a challenge in her voice or an invitation?

"In that case"—she looked back at Hazel—"I'll do my best." Hazel's posture seemed to relax as she laid the dough over a pie. "Perfect." Then, seeming to realize her mother stood nearby, added, "We'll see you there." Lida bit her cheek to keep herself from grinning. She donned her hat and tipped the brim to Clara.

Outside, she ran a hand down Beth's neck, who whinnied and twitched one ear as she seemed to sense the eagerness in Lida's movements. "Well, girl, looks like I better find something to wear."

SAM LEDEL

CHAPTER NINETEEN

Hazel hopped down from the wagon. "Nicholas, you grab the pies. Momma, you need me to get the chicken?"

Arthur helped her mother down from the back of the packed wagon. He looked handsome in beige trousers and a matching hat. A pressed denim shirt sat under brown suspenders. He even wore a jacket, like many of the other men accompanying ladies onto the grounds of the Boley Ranch.

"No, honey, you take these tablecloths here and see they get laid out on those tables." Her mother—in her best lavender-checked dress—searched the vast property from just outside the front fence where they'd parked their wagon alongside dozens of others. The consistent bray of mules and horses filled the air. "If you can find the tables," she added. "Lord, I knew we shoulda gotten here earlier." She handed a large pot to Arthur, then licked her thumb and cleaned a smudge on Nicholas's cheek. "If someone hadn't decided to chase after a crow, we might've been on time."

Nicholas frowned, trying to dodge their mother's hand.

Hazel grabbed the red and white tablecloths, then gave Arthur a pleading look. Nicholas had a look of his own that warned he might run off again.

"Clara," Arthur said, "why don't we go find Mrs. Boley so we know where she'd like all this set up?"

More people hurried by as her mother straightened Nicholas's tie. Children ran in between women in fresh dresses, the smell of clean linens nearly as thick as the scent of hair oil every man seemed to have in their combed locks.

Hazel spotted Jerry and gave him a wave as he strolled onto the ranch arm-in-arm with his young wife.

"All right," her mother finally said. Nicholas dipped away to escape her grasp and stood next to Hazel. "Keep an eye on your brother," she said before they started for the expansive front lawn.

By the next hour, nearly three hundred people milled about the ranch, shouting greetings and cries of "Happy Fourth!" To the right of the front entrance, several games of horseshoes had begun. Lanes were made for potato sack races, and children practiced for wheelbarrow competitions. To the left of the front gate sat the first rows of long picnic tables, each large enough to hold twenty guests.

The opening ceremonies would start soon. Mrs. Boley, per tradition, would give a welcome speech from her front porch. Hank Cavill's wife would sing "The Star-Spangled Banner," then the food would be served, and the social would be underway. Hazel could feel the buzz of anticipation as all of Cedar Springs and some of Pine City poured onto the ranch, eager for a day of fun.

Weaving through people, she took in the grounds. The house looked like an elaborate cake draped in banners and holiday trimmings. Blankets lay strewn like patches where people sat with little ones. Older men and women sat stoically in chairs near the outskirts, looking on with bright eyes but dour expressions. Nearly everyone wore a fine dress or sharp jacket over shined boots. Hazel briefly wondered what Lida would wear if she did come.

"I do hope to see you on the dance floor, Hazel."

She spun around to find Paul. He wore what looked like a new hat, his jacket crisp over his starched white shirt and black trousers. His black shoes shined as much as his hair. She slowed her work to lay out a tablecloth, not wanting to give him the impression she had time to talk. Nicholas, meanwhile, had given up and sat on a bench nearby, his arms crossed as he watched a sparrow pick at the ground.

"Is that what that is?" Hazel gestured to the fifty yards of green by a gazebo strung with lights. She noticed a folding table hosting a gleaming mahogany radio.

"I thought it would be fun to hop on the dance-a-thon bandwagon." At her furrowed brow he added, "It's the newest craze, Hazel. Went to one when I was up in Salt Lake. It was a real doozy. Folks dancin' till they can't no more. Why, I saw a pair sleepin' on each other's shoulders, still swayin' after six hours."

"That is somethin'." She made a note to stay as far away from there as possible. Dancing for hours with Paul was the last thing she wanted to do. She was glad when her mother called from the other end of the tables, motioning for her. "If you'll excuse me," she said. Paul's face fell, but he didn't protest as she grabbed Nicholas and hurried away.

Her brother was untucking his shirt as he said, "I want to go home."

"We just got here."

"I want to be with Grandpa. It's too loud here."

Hazel sighed. Sometimes crowds were too much for Nicholas. Two years ago, at the Christmas dance at the Lodge, he'd been sitting in the kitchen when somebody started playing a trumpet. He'd clamped his hands over his ears, screamed, and run out the back straight into the falling snow. She and Momma had to pull him back inside so he wouldn't freeze, then took him home.

She gave him a nudge with her elbow. "You sure you don't wanna go climbin' up that tree again?" she teased, hoping to make him smile.

It seemed to work, but only for a moment before he kicked a rock, both hands planted firmly in his pockets. She wished she'd brought him a book, something to keep him busy. He didn't fall into sour moods often, but when he did, getting him to do anything was like pulling teeth.

He sat glumly on a large boulder as she helped Momma get the food ready. Many women had brought their own desserts while her mother supplied the chicken and sides. Though her mother couldn't resist baking a few of her own pies. Hazel wasn't sure how there were any chickens left in this part of Utah after they'd spent days plucking and cleaning endlessly. The large cauldron, supplied by Mrs. Boley, was already bubbling with oil and fat, ready to fry.

"I should've borrowed your perfume, Momma," Hazel said as they skewered the first birds and lowered them into the liquid. They stood at the head of an assembly line: a long table hosting clay dishes covered in towels to keep flies from the food. "I couldn't scrub hard enough to get the smell of chicken outta my hair."

"Oh, hush, honey. Ain't nobody payin' no mind," she said, her hands working deftly to pull one bird from the oil and replacing it with another.

Hazel brushed strands away from her face but still wished she wouldn't be stuck here behind the uncooked meat. When, if, Lida arrived, she wanted to be at her best. How awful, she thought, to smell like unseasoned chicken. She had searched for Lida since arriving but had seen no sign of her or her father.

An hour later, after the ceremonies, they'd served nearly half of the social-goers lunch. Hazel had moved from the chicken to dish out sides to people in line. Spooning another scoop of creamed corn, she took the plate offered to her and was about to ask how much to serve when she looked up to find Lida.

Hazel dropped the large spoon, quickly recovering it. It would take her much longer, though, to recover from the sight of Lida standing on the other side of the table. She wore her signature wide-brimmed hat over her typical braid, except this time, it fell gently over her left shoulder. The vest she usually wore was gone. Instead, over the fitted white shirt—the sleeves rolled to her elbows—Lida wore a dashing pair of suspenders. Hazel traced the way they hugged her breasts, then jerked her gaze back up.

"Hi," Lida said.

"Hi, yourself." Hazel swallowed, glad the man in line behind Lida seemed too preoccupied with deciding between coleslaw and potato salad to notice her near disaster with the corn. The fitted trousers Lida wore made it difficult for Hazel to remember a proper greeting. She reached for Lida's plate again, scooping corn, then beans, onto it. Finally, she managed to say, "You made it."

"It took me some time to find something to wear." She glanced down. "Turns out William's old suspenders fit me pretty well."

I'll say. She noticed the top button of Lida's shirt was open at the collar, exposing the hollow of her neck.

"I think you better save some beans for the next person."

Hazel looked down to find she'd scooped three heaping helpings onto Lida's plate. Blush warmed her cheeks. "Lord, I'm so sorry."

Lida laughed, took her plate, and continued slowly down the line.

"Is your father here?" Hazel asked, careful to serve the next guest only one spoonful of vegetables.

"Over there," Lida said, pointing four tables away. Hazel spotted Mr. Jones's tall figure as he spoke to William Seager and his wife, their son cooing happily in his mother's arms.

"Well, tell them they must try the blackberry pie later."

Lida smiled. "I will."

Hazel caught the way Lida's gaze lingered on her dress before she made her way back to her table.

Later, Hazel switched out the now empty vegetable dishes for the desserts. Her calves ached from standing so long, but she did enjoy getting to catch up with folks she hadn't seen in a while as they had come through the social for a good meal.

"I thought I was gonna have to go back and scrounge for scraps when the collards were low." Her mother swiped at her brow, throwing a dish towel over one shoulder.

"Baloney, Momma. We had plenty."

The picnic tables, which had been packed tight as everyone ate, began to thin as people finished their meals. Children ran off to the southeastern corner, eager to begin the potato sack races. Hazel found Lida at her table, still eating and talking with the Seagers and her father.

"I'll be right back, Momma," she said, checking to make sure Nicholas was still eating in his seat behind them. The growing number of birds swooping in to pick up leftovers seemed to entertain him.

Her mother carefully arranged the pies along the table. "Make it quick, honey. These won't slice themselves."

Hazel made her way to Lida's table. She decided it'd be rude to just sit, so she pulled up near Mr. Jones and Mr. Seager, asking, "How's everything?"

"Just fine, Miss Thompson," Martha said, offering Thomas a spoonful of mashed potatoes. "Y'all outdid yourselves."

"That's mighty kind," she replied, trying not to focus on Lida, who she could feel watching her.

"This lemonade is delicious," Mr. Jones said.

"I'm more of a Coca-Cola fan, myself." William raised his glass bottle. "I wait every year for the Boleys and their shipment of this stuff." He took a large gulp, then made an exaggerated *ah* sound.

Laughing, Hazel slid her gaze to Lida. "Everything all right for you?"

"Wonderful."

Little Thomas gave a cry. William finished the last of his Coca-Cola, then stood. "I reckon he's wantin' another tour of the grounds. First time on such a grand ranch for our little man."

Martha stood, too, brushing crumbs from her lap. "I'll join you," she said, and they disappeared into the crowd.

Yaromir smacked his lips. "I see the pies," he said, rubbing his stomach.

Hazel glanced over at the dessert table. Her mother seemed to be giving Arthur directions on how to slice. "I'd grab some while you can, Mr. Jones."

"You don't have to tell me twice," he said before hurrying away.

Watching him go, Hazel glanced at the now empty seat across from Lida, then took it.

"Busy day," Lida said, taking a drink from her lemonade.

"The busiest. Busiest week is more like it." Hazel glanced around. Everyone was there, every member of Cedar Springs, together. The sights and sounds filled her up, leaving her giddy at the sense of pride and community that overwhelmed her.

"I can't believe you do this every year."

Hazel laughed. "Neither can I. But I kind of love it." Lida's inquisitive brow prompted her to explain. "I know it's a lot. It's a lot of work every year, and every year I always wonder if we'll pull it off. Seems like we're workin' day and night nonstop, but then"— she gestured around—"it's all worth it when it comes together."

Lida had a look in her eye that made Hazel fidget in her seat. "You're like Elizabeth Bennet."

Not expecting this, she replied, "From *Pride and Prejudice?*"

"She always seemed to thrive at the social events in her world. When I pictured her exchanging banter with Darcy, I imagined the same spark I see in your eyes at being around all of this."

Hazel could only listen. Nobody had ever likened her to a literary character before.

Lida searched her face. "Perhaps a bit of Mrs. Dalloway, too."

"I'm afraid I don't know that one."

"*Mrs. Dalloway* by Virginia Woolf."

Hazel shook her head, smoothing the lap of her dress, embarrassed at not recognizing the name.

"It's an interesting story. The entire thing spans one day. Mrs. Dalloway is said to be the perfect hostess, gracious to all of her guests, attune to everyone's needs."

Hazel reached up, playing with the end of her hair, shy with Lida's comparisons. "Well, technically, the Boleys are hosting. Momma and me, we just provide the food."

Lida took another sip. Hazel was drawn to the shine of her lips from the drink. "You're selling yourself short."

Hazel attempted to regain her composure. She crossed her legs, meeting Lida's gaze. "If I didn't know any better, I'd say you were trying to figure me out, Miss Jones."

Propping one elbow on the table, Lida leaned forward. "Maybe I am."

Hazel's stomach flip-flopped. She worked to keep an even face. "What else have you figured out, then?"

Lida smiled, then seemed to try to contain it as she said, "I can tell how much you care about every person here. I can tell how much you enjoy seeing them happy. I can see you're proud of what you've put into this."

It was Hazel's turn to lean forward. She sensed Lida holding back her next words. "But..."

Lida licked her lips. "But...I sense it's been a long time since you enjoyed yourself at the Cedar Springs social."

The words didn't seem intended as rude, but Hazel grew defensive as she scoffed. "I'm not sure what you mean. I'm here every year."

"Making sure everyone else is happy."

"Are you implying I'm not?"

"No." Lida stretched out her hand, resting it in front of Hazel in a conceding gesture. "I didn't mean that. I just meant"—she nodded to the games getting underway—"when was the last time you let yourself have fun?"

Hazel felt warm as Lida's bright gaze held hers. She studied Lida's hand as she mulled over her words. She was right, and Hazel wasn't sure what to make of that. How could this woman she'd met only a few months ago seem to know her so well?

Unable to withstand the intoxicating challenge in Lida's eyes, Hazel stood. "I need to get back."

Lida's shoulders seemed to fall. She leaned to one side, looking past Hazel. "It seems like things are under control."

"Momma needs my help. And Nicholas needs seein' after." Hazel was starting to feel like a fish out of water, which only drove her crazy since she was standing in the middle of her own town.

Reaching into her pocket, Lida said, "I found this article when I was exchanging materials the other day. Thought Nicholas might like it." She unfolded the newspaper clipping, handing it to Hazel.

"Thank you." The fine print labeled different parts of a factory machine below a grainy picture. "I really should get back now."

"Or you and I could sign up for the next game of horseshoes."

Hazel hesitated, unable to hide a smile. "I'd like to, but..." She looked back at the dessert table. A long line had formed as people waited for a serving. Momma waved, shooting her a "What's taking you so long?" look.

"I understand," Lida said, returning to her food.

Later, when Hazel had sliced and served what must have been her thousandth piece of pie, she looked through the crowds. The Seagers were back. Lida's father sat behind an empty plate, bouncing Thomas on his knee.

She wasn't sure what it was, but something had happened during her conversation with Lida. It was like a seed had been planted as soon as Hazel had sat, and each word, each uncanny observation from Lida pulled the sapling from its roots. Vines had grown, thin but hardy, and stretched across the lawn from Hazel, searching for the one who had inspired it to begin. Searching for Lida.

She glanced at the empty pie trays, then did a quick count on how many people were left to serve. After handing a healthy slice of blueberry pie to Charlie Benter, she side-stepped to Arthur. He'd been diligently collecting empty pie tins.

"Mr. Davis," she said, "do you reckon you can cover for me with the rest of these?"

"Yes, I reckon we're nearly done, anyway." He cut his gaze to her. "Where you goin'?"

She took a breath, wiping her hands clean. "Just don't wanna miss my chance at the fun is all."

He smiled. "I can't argue with that."

"If Momma asks, I'll be back to help clean up when Mrs. Boley brings out the beer before the fireworks." He nodded, and she squeezed his arm in thanks. "Oh, here." She dug into her dress pocket for the article. "This outta keep Nicholas busy."

"I'll see he gets it."

Hazel slipped quietly away. The afternoon sun dipped lower, the sky a beautiful shade of deepening blue with streaks of pink. The mountains looked on as the festivities continued.

Tapping Lida's shoulder, she tried to keep the anticipation from her voice as she asked, "So, you still up for that game?"

CHAPTER TWENTY

L ida cheered alongside Hazel and two dozen spectators as ten wide-eyed potato sack racers hurried to the finish line.

"Go, Charlie!" she shouted as he pulled ahead of his siblings and Mike Evans. With a final, emphatic hop, he dove forward over the finish line to a roar of cheers. Mr. Benter, flushed from a day of hearty food, scooped up his eldest son, raising him high to soak up the adulation. Laughing, Lida said, "That was great."

"Better than when we beat Hank and Jerry in horseshoes?" Hazel asked, still clapping as more children ran by for high fives.

"That was pretty fun," she said. "Seems like my father is doing well, too." He stood next to William in the horseshoe area. Her father spoke animatedly as William tossed the iron shoe at a stake forty feet away. The beer in his hand was half-empty, but Lida refrained from walking over to check on him. It was only one beer. She didn't want to be a nag. Besides, she'd been having fun and didn't want to leave Hazel.

"Horseshoe skills must run in the family," Hazel was saying, tossing Lida a smile before she waved to more people.

Lida chuckled. "I think it was beginner's luck." The sun was setting on the ranch lawns. She'd seen Paul skulking about, but since a makeshift game of baseball had started at the back edge of the property, he'd been busy. Tracing her gaze along the mountain edges, something caught her eye. "What is that?"

Hazel followed her finger to the flagpole planted next to the eastern wall of the Boley Ranch house. "Oh, that's this year's pole sitter."

Lida blinked. "What?"

"You've never seen pole sitting?" Hazel laughed. "Not as entertaining as potato sack racin', but it's a tradition."

"What happens, exactly?"

"It's pretty much how it sounds." Hazel shielded her eyes from the setting sun that cast long shadows over the rolling grass. "Looks like Stephen Akers is tryin' to break his own record. Sat up there for seventeen hours last year."

Gaping, Lida said, "He just sat there? Willingly?"

"Sure did. Think you could do it?"

Lida shook her head. "I'd need a lot of books."

A surge of music struck up on the far end of the grounds. Hazel grinned, then grabbed Lida's hand. "Let's go see what's happening."

Lida let Hazel lead her around to the back side of the house. The home certainly was the nicest one in Cedar Springs by far, with a wide, wraparound porch and intricately planted front garden. She eyed the shining, black-iron weather vane, the sharp gleam reminding her of Paul.

The dance floor came into view. Hazel slowed, releasing Lida's hand. She was peering into a large red barn. A Chevy of some kind sat in the cavernous space amidst bales of hay and other farming tools. Behind it, animal pens stretched into the shadowy depths. The dull bleat of sheep came from even farther beyond the hillside.

Lida found the source of music. It flowed from an expensive-looking radio, though several men had found instruments of their own and struck up a twangy tune to accompany the invisible orchestra flying in over the airwaves.

Men and women dipped one another, stamping their feet and loosely swinging side to side as the musicians yipped and hollered their encouragement. She glanced at Hazel, who seemed to be scanning the social-goers. What would she say if Lida asked her to dance? The idea was frivolous. Lida could dance; she just preferred not to most of the time. Despite that, she found she wanted to if it was Hazel she was dancing with.

"Oh no." Hazel's voice pulled Lida from her thoughts. "Paul."

"What?"

"Quick. Back here."

Lida tried to find him through the shadows and twilight that crept over the mountainside but couldn't before she was pulled into the barn. Hazel gently pushed her a few feet within the open doorway, then peeked around the corner. After a minute, she leaned back against the barn wall, exhaling.

"Is he gone?" Lida asked.

"His mother summoned him to the house. Thank goodness."

"Thank goodness," Lida echoed. Her eyes drifted to Hazel's lips, then down to her neck when she brushed back her short blond waves. A thin sheen of perspiration dotted her skin. Lida wondered if it might taste as sweet as she smelled. Realizing she was staring, Lida cleared her throat. "I hate to think how many times you've hidden somewhere to avoid him."

Hazel rolled her eyes. "Too many, I'm afraid."

The music carried on outside, but it was muffled by the barn wall, creating the sense of being completely encased, separate from the rest of the world. The sensation made Lida feel bold, and she nearly reached out, the urge to run a finger down Hazel's neck, to feel the smoothness of her hair, overrunning every other thought. Then she remembered. "I wanted to tell you," she said, "that I spoke with the Havishes about materials."

Hazel pushed herself off the wall. "You did?"

"Well, I spoke with Mrs. Havish. I asked if she could request more items, like school texts and things like that." Hazel's hopeful gaze searched hers. Lida felt light as she said, "She told me she has to speak with her husband, but she'd be happy to help us." She clamped her mouth shut. *Us.* "I mean, happy to help any way she can," she stammered, her throat going dry.

Surprise and joy sat in the corners of Hazel's upturned lips and wide eyes. Then Lida nearly fell back as Hazel jumped forward, throwing her arms around Lida's neck in a fierce hug. "Thank you," she said over Lida's shoulder.

"You're welcome," she replied, impressed she was able to speak at the feeling of Hazel flush against her. She slowly brought her hands to rest on the small of Hazel's back. As she did, though, Hazel leaned back wearing a wide smile beneath shining eyes.

"Thank you so much," she said again, then leaned forward, kissing Lida.

The softness of Hazel's lips was what she noticed first, followed by the burst of cinnamon and sweet berries that encircled her. A quick heat stirred below Lida's stomach. She reached up, framing Hazel's face, wanting to pull her closer when Hazel stepped abruptly back.

Lida opened her eyes. Hazel seemed like she'd seen a ghost, one hand over her mouth as she stared in disbelief.

"Hazel, are you all right?"

She nodded, but her hand stayed where it was, her gaze wide and startled.

"Are you sure?" Lida wasn't sure what to do as they stood frozen in the darkening barn. She furrowed her brow and almost stepped forward but decided against it, giving Hazel space.

Finally, her hand fell. "I've never…" Her voice broke, and she started again. "I've never done that before." Hazel seemed to hesitate before asking, "Have you?"

Lida swallowed. "Only once," she said after a moment. She flashed back to a kiss she shared with a woman from the fabric mill. Their encounter had been brief but confirmed Lida's suspicions of her own inclinations. It paled in comparison to Hazel's kiss moments ago, and Lida yearned for more.

Hazel seemed to absorb this information as she nodded slowly. Lida relished the way Hazel's gaze went up her legs, lingered on her waist, then held her own. She stepped closer.

Lida didn't try to hide her smile when Hazel reached up, hesitating only a moment before cupping her face. Her heart beat wildly, and she bit her lip to keep a patient mind as she stared into Hazel's bright eyes. Finally, she said, "I don't want you to feel like you have to do anything here."

"I know I don't have to," Hazel said, her voice low, "I want to." Lida pushed forward and fell into another kiss. The first one had taken her by surprise. This time, she pulled Hazel against her. She could feel Hazel tilt her chin up, as if she strived to be as close as possible as her arms wrapped around Lida's shoulders. Lida ran her hands up Hazel's back, feeling her supple body beneath the fabric of her dress.

When her hat bumped Hazel's forehead, she reached up, but Hazel beat her to it. They parted, breaking their kiss, their breathing coming fast. She caught the pleasure in Hazel's eyes as she tossed the hat aside, then pulled Lida back into a kiss.

Jubilant shouts sounded outside, cutting through the continuing music. Lida stepped backward, and Hazel helped lead her farther inside the barn. It was darker, but only briefly before a piercing whistle scraped across the sky, followed by a sharp boom that bellowed overhead.

Mid-kiss, Lida pulled back, searching the high ceiling.

"Fireworks," Hazel said, her forefinger against Lida's chin, her gaze eyeing the button on Lida's shirt.

Lida's heart pounded at the look in Hazel's eyes. She kissed her again, then gave a surprised gasp when Hazel turned her gently, pushing her against the wall.

Streaks of color and sound raced across the mountainside, lighting the night in fierce reds and glowing whites. Inside the barn, Lida held on to Hazel, losing herself in the truest and most unexpected woman she'd ever met.

CHAPTER TWENTY-ONE

A week after the social, it happened again. Hazel ran right smack into Arthur and sent half the sugar bag flying across the Lodge kitchen.

"You all right, Miss Hazel?"

She hardly heard the question. Hazel stared at the sweet crystals that floated briefly across the warm air. It dazzled her, the carefree vision glistening before her eyes, and something struck her, quick, like the pluck of a banjo string. She realized this vision was what she'd been feeling since her kiss with Lida.

Merely recalling the hot, passionate moment they'd shared in the welcoming dark sent flutters to Hazel's stomach. Remembering the lights and music that exploded in celebration as she had kissed Lida sent a warmth spinning in her chest. It spread through her as she recalled tracing her lips down Lida's neck and how her hands had seemed to ache with need. Each replay of these moments left her dizzy in a whirl of crystal sweetness.

Unfortunately, it also made her prone to accidents.

"Lord, honey, what's next, the preserves smashed to pieces?" Her mother grabbed a rag mop to clean up.

"I'm sorry, Momma," she said, like she had after each burnt pie or overcooked chicken since the Fourth.

"I don't reckon those boys haul themselves up here for lunch just to be served blackened meat and sugar-coated collards," her mother huffed before handing her the mop to finish.

Nicholas laughed from his stool as he rolled out a pie crust. Hazel grumbled, "Yes, Momma." She sighed. She was trying to keep herself on the ground, but how could she after that night? A week had passed, and Hazel could still feel Lida's body against hers, could smell her skin. She could hear her own heart thundering as the fireworks bowed overhead in a grand finale, and they had, sadly, forced themselves to stop and rejoin the social.

One night at home a few days later, she was recalling the feel of Lida's hips under her hands when her grandpa's voice interrupted her reverie. "I wonder where her head's at."

Her mother replied, "Been like this since the Fourth."

"That so?" Her grandpa grunted. "I know what's gotten into her, then."

Hazel half listened but continued to sort the coins from this week's register without looking up.

"Well," her mother said, "spit it out."

"I reckon our Hazel had herself a time at that social. And I'd put money on it being with one Mr. Paul Boley."

Losing count, Hazel shot him a look.

"See?" he said, wagging his pipe her direction. "*That* is the look of a woman who's smitten."

Her mother, Hazel happily noticed, didn't look completely convinced. Nicholas, in his usual spot by the fire, asked, "What's smitten?"

"It means Hazel has finally given up her foolish ways and done the right thing," he said. Hazel stared as he added in a proud tone, "She's given in to the proposals of that fine young man."

Incredulous, Hazel scoffed.

"Hazel doesn't like Paul."

All gazes swung to Nicholas.

Their grandpa laughed. "So says you."

Shaking her head, Hazel said, "He's not wrong, Grandpa."

He crossed his arms, clamping his teeth over his pipe. "Malarkey."

"You're the one talkin' malarkey." She glanced over to find her mother watching her. "Momma, tell him how ridiculous he's bein'."

She stared at Hazel a moment, her small blue eyes seeming to search for a sign, a symptom to explain her behavior. "You have been mighty clumsy lately, honey. Not thinkin' straight. Distracted."

To Hazel, the stuffy room now felt hot. "I'm tired is all," she said, averting her gaze. "The social was a lot of work."

Her mother grunted and returned to her grocery list. Her grandpa puffed on his pipe. Feeling the need to fill the silence, Hazel added, "Besides, Paul would be the last man I'd pick." Putting on a lighter air, she said, "I have all the men I need in my life." She nudged Nicholas with her foot, making him smile.

Her grandpa gave a defeated harumph.

The next day, Hazel was careful to keep her conversation with Lida short when she made her delivery.

"Is everything okay?" Lida asked, putting away the magazines Hazel returned. "You seem...tense."

From the edge of the porch, Hazel glanced inside, then hurried down the steps. She stood close to Beth, who whinnied in greeting as she patted her neck. In a low voice, she said, "Can you meet me near the Breaks?"

Lida smiled. "I'd like to, but I can't today." She motioned to the pannier with books still to deliver.

"How about later this week?"

"How's early Thursday? Before I see Mr. Coffer?"

"Perfect." Hazel started to reach for Lida but stopped herself. A sense of risk grew into a pressure at the back of her neck. Hazel could only imagine what her grandpa would say if he decided to get up out of his chair and caught them being too affectionate through the window. "I'll see you then."

Tipping the brim of her hat, Lida guided Beth toward the drive. "Oh." She pointed over her shoulder to the book in Hazel's hands. "Chapter twenty is my favorite. Page ninety-seven." Then she tossed Hazel a grin and was gone.

That night, alone in her room, Hazel flipped to page ninety-seven. A slip of torn paper fell out. In the dim lamplight, Hazel read Lida's cursive script:

I can't stop thinking about the fireworks.

Folding it, Hazel clutched the paper over her heart, eager to sleep knowing what dreams would come.

❖

Lida lay next to Hazel in a tranquil alpine meadow. Dragonflies swooped overhead, searching for puddles from last week's storm. Smatterings of larkspur and primrose littered the grass surrounded by tall spruce trees. Hazel had brought a knitted blanket when she'd met Lida here at dawn.

"Told Grandpa I was gettin' an early start at the Lodge," she had said as Lida admired her soft pink blouse tucked into a long skirt.

She'd used a similar excuse, rising early under claims of heading into town to see the Havishes. Her father had raised a curious brow over his eggs, but that was all.

Now, the sun was just over the eastern ridge. They had both taken their horses a half mile north of the Lodge, overlooking parts of Cedar Breaks National Monument. Lida enjoyed Hazel's insight on the landscape about this spot, which according to her, tourists didn't know about. She explained how the rock below gained its colors, how wind had swept over the ridges and dips for eons to create the scenery people traveled miles to get a glimpse at.

This morning, Lida was delighted to switch roles, sharing her specialty: stories. She closed the book, resting it atop her stomach.

"I liked that one," Hazel said next to her.

Lida smiled, gazing at the long limbs of the towering pine overhead that met the stretch of blue growing more cerulean by the minute.

"You'd be a fine narrator," Hazel mused, rolling onto her side. She rested her head in her right palm. "Folks would love listenin' to you read."

She turned her head. "You think so?"

"Absolutely." Hazel moved the book so she could rest her hand on Lida. Then she traced the buttons of Lida's blue linen shirt.

A hum escaped Lida's throat. She collected herself before

replying, "That wouldn't be allowed at my readings, Miss Thompson." She gave half a grin. "Too distracting."

"Is that so?" Now tracing her collar, Hazel found her neck. The feel of Hazel's fingers grazing her skin was elating. Lida wanted to pull her close. She wanted to take Hazel's hand, lower it, be as close as possible to this woman she couldn't get enough of.

A swallow sang from deep in the trees. The sound pulled Lida back into the meadow.

"Hazel." She grabbed her hand, using all of her willpower to simply kiss Hazel's knuckles. "What are we doing?"

A small frown creased Hazel's fair forehead. "I thought we were enjoying each other's company." A lilt of uncertainty made her voice catch. "Aren't we?"

"We are," Lida assured her. She hadn't meant to ask that aloud, but it was out now. It had been in the back of her mind since their kiss. It lingered in the shadowy corners as she tried to subdue it with the way Hazel's dress clung to her small chest and the curve of her hips. The question didn't stem from uncertainty. She absolutely wanted Hazel. Rather, it came from her inability to express those desires. Physical longing overpowered her each time Hazel was near. Sometimes she feared it was palpable, and somebody would see them. Somebody would see the line drawing them together. "I'm just…not used to this," she finally said. It was as close to the truth as she could get with Hazel near and the sun rising to the east, their time alone coming to an end.

"It's new for me, too." Hazel searched her face. "Honestly, I've no idea what I'm doin'." She gave a nervous laugh, rolling onto her side. Lida watched her scan the tufts of white forming overhead. "I always knew I wouldn't go for men. I just never reckoned I'd meet anyone." She faced Lida. "It's like one of your books. Like somethin' somebody wrote."

"Like a fairy tale?" Lida asked, tugging at the sleeve of Hazel's dress.

"They write fairy tales about Utah cooks?"

"They ought to."

Hazel was smiling. "Utah cooks and enigmatic women who show up outta the blue."

"Technically, I came in on a train."

Hazel swatted her arm.

Laughing, Lida leaned in, unable to resist kissing her. A pinecone fell, nearly hitting Lida in the shoulder and breaking their kiss.

"What the devil?" Hazel, still cupping Lida's face, looked up. Lida followed suit, peering into the thick green needles. Then Hazel huffed, hurrying to her feet. "I don't believe it."

"What?" Lida pushed herself up, still trying to find what Hazel glared at as she brushed off her skirt and took a defiant stance.

"Nicholas Thompson," Hazel called, "get yourself down here this minute."

Scrambling to her feet, Lida's skin pricked. *Nicholas is here?* How long had he been up there? Her throat went dry as another question formed: what had he seen?

Moments later, Nicholas swung down from a low branch, landing near his sister with surprising ease. Lida wasn't sure what to do. She glanced over at the horses, who chewed on a patch of grass, oblivious to her dilemma. Ultimately, she decided to mimic Hazel, pulling herself up in an authoritative stance.

"What in heaven's name were you doin' up there?" Hazel seemed to do her best to loom over her taller brother, but Lida could see he was utterly unafraid.

He plucked a dandelion before responding. "Bird watching."

Hazel threw Lida a look that seemed to say "Should I believe that?" Lida honestly wasn't sure. She'd known from the moment she met Nicholas that his mind was different. That didn't mean he didn't understand things. Often, he seemed to understand better than most. Lida's palms sweated at the notion.

Hazel must have been at a loss for any other words as she repeated, "Bird watching?"

Nicholas nodded. Glancing at Lida, he waved.

"Hi, Nicholas." She looked to Hazel, but she seemed disoriented by her brother's presence. She stared at his wrinkled shirt, his unruly hair, like an explanation might be found in his disheveled appearance. Lida asked, "What did you think of the article on thrushes?"

"It was good." He blinked several times, looking past her shoulder.

"I'll have to find you another one."

The air in the meadow grew thick. Warm wind blew as the sun rose higher. Part of Lida wanted to bolt, grab Beth, and run full speed down the mountain. But a look of determination graced Hazel's face, making her wait.

"Nicholas," Hazel said, "did you see us?"

The bold question ran Lida's throat dry. She held her breath. When Nicholas didn't answer, Hazel spoke more slowly. "Lida and me. Did you see us?"

He looked between them, then at the blanket, then back again. "Yes."

Lida inhaled, catching Hazel's gaze. Frantic, she stepped forward. "Nicholas, let me explain."

But Hazel moved forward, too, one hand up. "Let's both explain," she said, and the look in her eyes told Lida that she had a plan. "You remember that day you asked me about Paul and his cologne?"

Confused, Lida tilted her head, running an anxious hand along her belt. *What does Paul have to do with this?*

"Remember how we talked later about how people like different things about different people? No one really knows why, that's just the way it is?"

Nicholas said, "The way Paul likes you, but you don't like him."

Lida hid a smile.

"Yes," Hazel said. "And how Momma and Mr. Arthur like each other, but Momma's too stubborn to admit it."

A small smile lifted Nicholas's lips. He looked toward Lida. "She's the one you like."

Lida wasn't sure if he was asking her a question. Heat crept up the back of her neck.

"Yes." Hazel pulled their gazes. "She's the one I like."

This seemed to satisfy Nicholas as he blew the dandelion seeds into the wind and started for the horses. Lida and Hazel exchanged looks. Was that it? Did Nicholas understand what so many people seemed unable to grasp?

Hazel must have been wondering that, too, as she called after him. "All right, Nicholas?" The lump in Lida's throat felt like a rock. They'd been seen. Nicholas wouldn't say anything, she told herself. *Would he?*

He patted Beth, his expression completely serious when he said, "Lida smells better, anyway."

They both broke into laughter. While some of the tension remained in Lida's chest, much of it lifted from the meadow at his remark. Grateful for Nicholas, she bent to help Hazel collect their things.

"Be careful," she said to Hazel, "more conversations like that and I may have to stick around for a while."

Hazel held the blanket when Lida handed it to her, keeping her hands in place. "I hope so."

The sentiment lingered, and Lida realized how much she meant what she'd said. She realized how much she liked it here. Cedar Springs was a spellbinding change Lida hadn't expected to love so much.

Love. She slid her gaze to Hazel. Was that what she was feeling beneath the quick beating of her heart?

Maybe, Lida thought, helping Hazel onto her horse. Maybe.

CHAPTER TWENTY-TWO

To Lida, August rushed by like the frigid creek waters racing down the mountainside. The thick of summer brought an influx of tourists to Cedar Springs, making the population swell like the warm winds.

The Pack Horse Library routes kept her busy, and the flock of easterners to the west meant the Lodge seemed to never close, always whirring with activity.

"It's bedlam but great for business," Hazel told her one Monday afternoon when she made a delivery. Behind a coy smile she added, "I'm sorry I haven't been able to get away."

Sincerity sat in Hazel's eyes, but so did the endless to-do lists as her mother hollered for her to come inside. Lida didn't want to infringe upon her work, but she was finding it difficult to keep her distance. They'd been careful around Hazel's family when Lida made deliveries or stopped by the Lodge, but the more time between their meetings, the more Lida longed to be alone with her.

It was a double-edged knife, then, that they both were so occupied. Lida enjoyed her stops to her library patrons. Evangeline had become a diligent study and could sound out one-syllable words now. She'd run out of her house as Lida approached, waving her small hand to show Lida where she'd written the first letters of her name in the dirt.

Charlie Benter, too, sprouted like the garden that looked fuller on his family's land. He constantly requested scrapbooks and magazines to learn more about cooking, which seemed to impress his haggard, hardworking father the few times Lida encountered him.

The entire mountainside vibrated with positivity as summer gave way to cooler nights and shorter days. The first week of September, Little Thomas took his first steps in the front yard. Lida and her father had been chatting with the Seagers on their porch one night when Thomas stepped forward, his bare feet on the creaky planks, then again, then one more time before tumbling into William's proud arms.

When it came time to pay Mr. Coffer again to extend Beth's lease, Lida was tempted to leave the money under one of the old lanterns that perennially sat on the porch. She didn't want anything, like a visit to the grouchy Coffer, to bring her down now that she had found a blissful rhythm in Cedar Springs.

Dismounting, she eyed his dark home and crouched on the front step to carefully lift the lantern. A strangled shout came from inside. Lida straightened, listening. She knocked.

"Mr. Coffer?" To her surprise, a string of Spanish curses followed. Several women in the New York factories spoke it, and Lida recognized the flowing language. Even its blasphemies were lovely. She gently pushed open the door. "Hello?"

He stood near his old stove, waving his right hand, seeming to search for something. His face was etched with pain.

"Are you all right?" She closed the door as he found an empty water basin and plunged what Lida realized was his burnt right hand into the water.

"Damn bacon grease jumped outta the skillet and bit me."

She eyed the ancient-looking skillet where a single strip of bacon now sizzled indifferently. Mr. Coffer's hands trembled; his eyes closed as he let the water ease his burn.

After a minute, they both seemed to realize she was inside his home. She stepped back at his startled gaze. Then she said the only thing she could think of. "I didn't know you spoke Spanish."

His gaze narrowed. "Heard that, did ya?"

Lida glanced around the dark room. She found a crooked frame on the far wall, a copper coin with the figurehead of a woman engraved on it behind the cracked glass.

He followed her gaze. "My father's. He sailed from Spain, landed in the Americas and migrated to California."

Lida raised her eyebrow. "Your family immigrated here?"

Fervently, he shook his head.

"But—"

"I was born in America."

Lida raised one hand in defense. "But your father came here from Spain." At his silence, she added, "Like how my father and I came here from Russia."

"That's different."

"How?"

Mr. Coffer pulled his hand out of the water, wrapping it in a dirty rag. "Different times."

"But our families had the same idea," she said slowly, tilting her head. "Coffer isn't Spanish."

"My father changed it. Cordova sounded too…"

"Different?"

His jaw clenched. "I see what you're trying to do, Miss Jones. And I ain't gonna have it."

"Mr. Coffer—"

"You can set the money on the table and be on your way." His gaze was on the floor, his haggard frame swaying from the last five minutes. "Go on, then. I appreciate your concern, but I can handle myself."

She placed sixty cents on the table. When she was on the porch, he stood in the open doorway.

"And don't tell no one what you heard, you hear?"

"It's not a bad thing, to speak your family's language."

For a moment, his hard gaze softened. Were those tears? "Ain't no place for it here," he finally said. "Ain't no place for different."

"With respect, Mr. Coffer, I think you're wrong." His gaze

widened but she continued, recalling the dozens of languages that swam through the streets of New York. The sounds shifted into Hazel's voice, bright and welcoming. "America is the ideal place for different. We shouldn't have to hide it."

His grizzly jaw tightened, but he only turned and slammed the door behind him. Lida's interaction with Coffer lingered in her mind when she went into town to collect her pay later that week. Dottie found her as she sifted through children's books.

"Good morning," Lida said, trying to decide between *Winnie the Pooh* and *Raggedy Ann* for the Evans.

Dottie held out a telegram, giving her vest and dirty boots a once-over. "Message from Mr. Havish."

Lida set the books aside, eagerly taking the note. "Thank you."

When Dottie hurried back to her post with Celia at the catalog desk, Lida unfolded the telegram.

Cynthia told me of your query. Not able to fulfill due to union strikes. Shipments soon to be delayed. Limit library exchanges to one per household.

Lida reread the note. A queasy feeling squirmed in her stomach. No extra materials would come. No schoolbooks. No chance at revitalizing this community the way Hazel had dreamed would be possible.

Outside, a crisp breeze licked at the ends of her coat. She pulled up her collar, shoving the telegram into her pocket. She considered riding over to the Havishes'. Surely they would understand the need of her request. They would understand a town like Cedar Springs stood on the precipice of falling away, yielding to larger places like Pine City and Salt Lake without an investment in education, in its young people's future.

After completing her deliveries the next day, Lida was still in a fitful mood over the unfortunate news. She almost rode over to the Lodge, knowing she needed to tell Hazel. She balked, though, when she pictured Hazel's reaction and imagined the disappointment in her eyes.

Deciding she needed time to work out how to tell Hazel, Lida headed for home. Upon reaching the Seagers' drive, Lida was struck with the discordant cries of Little Thomas. He sat in Martha's lap in a chair outside the front door.

"What's going on?" Lida asked, pulling Beth up to the porch. Thomas was red in the face, his eyes pinched tight as he continued to holler.

Martha spoke in between his screams. "He's got a fever, so we're getting some air before going back inside." She paused, a sympathetic look on her tired face. "Noise out back ain't helpin' him sleep."

Lida dismounted. William hurried outside with a bottle of milk he handed to Martha. His arms and face were still smudged after what looked like a half-hearted attempt to clean the mine off. The look he gave Lida turned her feet to lead.

"William?"

He took Beth's reins. "I convinced them to come here so he'd be at home." He winced at his son's continued wails. "Not sure I made the right decision but figured your father's safer here than on the other side of the mountain." He paused, speaking lower. "Don't think he'd have made it back, considering the state he's in."

Lida swallowed, guilt trickling down her spine as she took the pannier and her satchel before William led Beth to the stable.

Standing outside her front door, Lida waited, pressing her ear to listen. Harsh drunken laughter bounced around inside like a bee in springtime. The clinking of glass was followed by slurred speech.

Steeling herself, she opened the door. The scent of corn whiskey hit her like a wall.

"Lida!" Her father stood next to the fireplace, his arms out wide as he greeted her, nearly spilling the short glass of liquor in his hand. The rug between him and two scraggly men held a plate full of bread and cheese, their week's worth.

One of the men, his eyes shining like her father's but his nose much redder, gave her a snaggle-toothed grin from a chair. "The long-lost daughter returns," he said, prompting more laughter. Lida recognized him from that day at the Lodge. She stared back, then at the other man, who poured more drink into their glasses from a clay jug. "Come join us."

Lida was surprised when the tightness in her chest didn't ignite the whisky swimming across the room, sending them all up in an angry blaze. She was certain her father could feel her fury as it clenched in her fists. The evening sun cast an orange glow over his face as he took a long drink.

"Pa," she said through a tight jaw, "we better let these gentlemen get home. We've got supper to make."

He smacked his lips, swiping at the droplets in his mustache. "Nonsense, Lida. We have plenty to share."

They didn't, and she knew he knew that, too. At least, he had when he left for work that morning.

She didn't say anything but gave each of the men a tight smile. The snaggle-toothed one finished his drink, then threw up a hand. "I reckon we best be goin, Yaro."

"No," he said, teetering. "Stay."

"Naw," he replied, standing and stealing the rest of the bread. "We best get movin'." His companion stood, and they grabbed their hats and coats, careful to skirt around Lida. He called to her father, "Good luck." He tipped his hat. "As they say, 'Hell hath no fury.'"

She clenched her jaw, willing herself not to shove these men outside. "Good night."

The fire crackled as if in anticipation now that Lida and her father were alone. Shadows grew along the walls and floorboards as dusk poured over the mountain. Lida lit the lamps, her movements slow as she tried to calm her frustration. "How was work?" she eventually asked, hands on her hips.

Her father kept his eyes on his glass. "We were released early." She grunted. He gave her a pointed look. "It's true. Foreman's wife went into labor. Shut down at noon."

She glanced at her pocket watch. Irritation flared in her gut. "Since noon, Pa?"

He passed the glass to his other hand. "We are letting off steam, Lida. It's not easy, this work."

She scrutinized the new hunch in his shoulders from bending, striking all day against the rock with a pickax. The bags under his eyes drooped over smudged cheeks. He ran a dirty hand through his hair, then repeated, "It's not easy."

"I know it's not." She sighed. Things had never been particularly easy for most of her life. But at least when her mother was alive, they had been happy in their togetherness. Even if the city was filthy, its air strangling, its work demeaning, the three of them had one another for comfort. The last eight years had seen her mother's vacancy bring her and her father closer, but the space between them morphed into a different beast over time. Its face changed each place they wandered, but it always followed, stowed away beneath their feet on each train fleeing father west. "Why didn't you come home with William?"

"I didn't want to bother him. Besides, he has Martha and young Thomas." His glassy gaze seemed to peer through the wall, searching for the Seagers.

"Pa, they wouldn't think that of you."

"They're a family. I didn't want to intrude."

The words held an undercurrent she couldn't pinpoint, but it made her skin itch. "So you found two local lushes instead?"

His eyes widened at her punitive words. "You should not judge those men, Lida."

"You shouldn't let them push you into this." She gestured to the clay jug. At his incredulous look, she moved closer and picked it up by the handle. When she made for the back door, ready to empty it, her father leapt forward.

"Don't." He stood between her and the door, swaying slightly.

"Pa, move."

"Lida, I need it."

The confession rocked her. It wrapped around her like the aroma of stale whiskey on her father's breath. "No, Pa, you don't."

His dark eyes spilled tears. "I do."

She shook her head. "You just...you're tired. You're working too hard." Dizzy and suddenly small, Lida kept the jug behind her, like she was keeping it from a needy child.

He looked from it to her. "Lida. I am tired. But not tired from mine." His swallow was audible.

"What do you mean?"

He motioned for her to sit. She hesitated but took a seat, keeping the jug beside her chair. Her father slowly sat across from her. "I don't know if I can explain."

"Try."

He took a shaky breath. "It's like...the sadness hasn't left. Since your mother...it's been here." He rapped his knuckles over his heart. "It's festered like a wound, settling deep."

Lida's head began to ache as she fought tears.

"But now," he said, bringing his fingers to his temple, "it's here. And it never leaves."

Lida had seen people succumb to sadness. A neighbor in New York had lost her husband in a factory accident. Afterward, she'd never left her room. Lida and her parents had watched her wither away, wrapped in unshakable shrouds of grief.

But her father was strong. He wasn't like that woman. He had continued on, finding work each time things went sour. He was still willing to move, always in search of brighter prospects. She'd always made sure he could, even when it was difficult. They'd both survived without their mother, even if it was hard.

Memories of hasty packing, of rushing to stations, searching the destinations, and flinging their hopes onto the next place made Lida shudder.

"With them," her father said, pulling her from her thoughts, "those men, I'm not alone."

"Pa, you're not alone. You have me."

He shook his head as it fell between his legs, his elbows on his knees.

"Yes, you do."

He startled her when he choked out a sob. "No. Lida, you are not here. You are gone."

"What are you—"

"You have the library. You have your routes, which seem to keep you later each week. When you are here, you are in a book.

Always in a book." He sobbed harder. "You are not here. You don't feel it like I do."

Lida stared as he wept into his hands, his breathing staggered. She combed her mind to replay the last few months. She thought he had been doing well. Aside from that one incident, he'd been going to work every day. She grimaced, knowing he probably wouldn't make it tomorrow. But this was a minor hiccup. Things were going well, she told herself again. She pictured Hazel. Had she been caught up in their new romance? Had she been neglecting things at home, not paying close enough attention?

"I miss her," her father said, still crying. "I miss her, and I don't want to be alone."

Lida pulled her chair closer. "I'm here, Pa." She found his hands, clutching them between her own. "You're not alone. I'm here."

CHAPTER TWENTY-THREE

When Lida didn't make her delivery on Monday, Hazel spent the afternoon in a gray cloud.

"What's burnt your biscuit?" her mother asked in passing, a tray of dirty dishes on her shoulder. The full dining room rang with conversation behind her.

"Nothin', Momma." Hazel scrubbed clumps of gravy off plates. She felt her mother's eyes on her.

"You lookin' forward to a new book that bad?"

Hazel glanced across the room, then buried her gaze in the suds, hoping to keep the fact that she missed Lida hidden beneath the bubbles. "I might've been. Nicholas is hankerin' for a new article," she added for good measure.

When Saturday rolled around and she still hadn't heard from Lida, Hazel began to worry. It was a slow day at the Lodge, so after the lunch hour, she said, "Think I'll go check in on the Joneses. You ain't seen Mr. Jones lately, have you, Momma?"

Her mother puckered her lips in thought as she added a twist of lemon to the tea. "Come to think of it, I haven't."

On her way outside, Hazel ran into Jerry. Buttoning her coat against the mid-September wind, she asked, "Mr. Jones been at work?"

"No, ma'am," he said, tethering his horse. "Been out a full week now."

Hazel hopped into their wagon, and Sasha led them down the hillside. A strange feeling had taken residence in her stomach. It tightened her grip on the reins and coaxed Sasha into a trot until they hurried onto the Seager property.

Deciding not to disturb Martha, who sounded like she was dealing with a disgruntled Little Thomas, Hazel led Sasha around the back. A small log cabin, shabby in nearly every way save for the clean windows and a porch that looked swept, came into view. A line of smoke curled out the chimney.

Hazel tethered her horse to one of the porch posts. She smoothed the skirt of her paisley blue dress, adjusted her coat collar, and ran a hand through her hair. Then she knocked.

"Hazel." Lida's wide eyes flew from her to the road beyond, then back. "What are you doing here?"

Mildly offended, she put on a smile to cover her uncertainty. "Hi to you, too."

"I'm sorry." Lida seemed to gather herself as Hazel tried to look over her shoulder. The house was dim. The smell of chicken broth wafted out. Noticing her prying gaze, Lida stepped onto the porch, closing the door behind her. "I wasn't expecting you."

Hazel could see that. Lida wore what looked like an old pair of trousers, a tear in one of the knees. Her white linen button-down was wrinkled and her dark hair twisted in an unkempt braid. She looked tired, and Hazel's anxiety grew with each furtive glance Lida threw over her shoulder.

"You missed this week's delivery," she finally said.

Lida didn't say anything.

"And I haven't seen you around." A muffled groan came from inside. "Heard your daddy's missed work lately. He doin' okay?"

Lida brushed hair from her forehead. She seemed to be looking anywhere but at Hazel. "He's sick."

"I'm sorry to hear that." Hazel shuffled sideways, trying to meet Lida's gaze. "I make a mean broth. Happy to get one ready for him. I can bring it by tonight."

"I've made some already."

Hazel searched Lida's face as she shoved one hand into her

pocket. "Well," she said, trying to understand why Lida was keeping her distance, "the offer stands if you change your mind."

"Thanks."

Hazel reached out, unable to stand Lida's sad gaze boring into the grass beyond. She gently cupped her elbow. "Are you okay?" Tears welled in Lida's eyes, and she leaned her head back, smiling. "I'm fine."

"You don't seem fine." Hazel stepped closer, but Lida waved her arm, keeping her back.

"You didn't need to come here."

Taken aback by Lida's sharp tone, Hazel said, "I know I didn't need to." She took a breath. "I was worried about you."

"Well, I'm fine." She sniffled. "Don't you have a whole town to look after?"

Hazel's mouth fell open. This wasn't the Lida she knew. Hazel could see the pain fixed in her face, in the crease between her brows. She crossed her arms and gave her a pointed look. "Lida, what's going on?"

She rubbed her hands together, taking a shaky breath. "Nothing. I told you, I'm—"

"Fine." Hazel finished sharply. "Yeah, somethin' don't feel true about that."

Lida's shoulders fell as she sighed. The sight of her like this made Hazel's chest ache. What was going on that she couldn't even talk about? Why was she trying to send her away?

Using a different approach, Hazel softened her voice. "Will he be okay?" she asked, gesturing to the house.

Lida wiped her eyes, shrugging. "I don't know." Her voice broke. "I'm not sure if this is the best place…for him."

It felt like the porch had given out beneath Hazel's feet. "What?"

Lida was crying. "We may have to go if…if he doesn't get better." Then she met Hazel's gaze. The fear and grief swimming in them left Hazel dizzy. "The mine may not be good for him."

Each word clawed its way to Hazel, each syllable intended to mar her vision and judgment. She swiped at her eyes, stinging with tears. It took a moment to find her words. "What are you saying?"

"I don't know."

"You saying you're gonna leave?"

She gave a sad shrug.

Hazel was certain she'd been kicked by some invisible force. It hit her low and deep in the gut. She fought to keep herself from doubling over. "You can't." She hardly recognized her own voice as she reached out, making Lida face her. "You can't just…leave." *Not now that I've found you. Not now that I've found who I want.*

Then Lida was kissing her, hard and fast. Hazel tasted tears as she cupped her face, trying to ease the agony radiating from the beautiful woman in front of her.

A soft cry escaped Lida's lips, and she pulled back. Hastily, she pushed something into Hazel's hand. Through her confused tears, she could see a crumpled telegram note. Before she could finish reading it, Lida muttered, "I'm sorry," and shut the door behind her, leaving Hazel alone and feeling like the very world had gone dark.

Lida slid down the door into a crouch. She listened for the sound of retreating steps, then hooves. Certain Hazel was gone, she wept silently, one arm over her mouth to stifle her cries.

When she managed to collect herself, she crossed the room to check on her father. He lay on his side, facing the wall in the rickety cot shoved into the corner. She pulled the blanket over his shoulders.

"You are crying." His voice was weak.

She swiped her nose on her sleeve. "I'm all right. You rest. Come Monday, you're going back to work."

He nodded into the pillow.

She'd poured out the remaining corn whiskey and did the same to her father's vodka. He had only stared solemnly from the window as she dashed it into the mud.

October came, and the first true snowfall blanketed Cedar Springs. By the second week, her father had returned to himself, though Lida was careful to monitor his demeanor like a hawk. When the sadness threatened to keep him in bed, seeming to lock his limbs in place, she was there, encouraging him to continue.

She was grateful for the return of their routine, including her library deliveries. After parting from the Evanses with a pencil drawing of a mountain from Evangeline in her pocket, Lida found herself leading Beth to the Lodge. She'd avoided Hazel for nearly a month, too embarrassed to even chance an encounter. She'd been leaving the Thompson books on their porch, then would find Nicholas for the returns when she knew Hazel wouldn't be home. A feeling she'd been trying to shove aside, the feeling of missing Hazel, forced itself to the forefront of her mind. It compelled her to the Lodge on Friday evening, and she let it.

Lida secured Beth alongside the other horses. Inside, the dining hall overflowed with lively conversation. She spotted Jerry and Steven Akers at a table near the fire. After hanging her hat and coat, she asked to join them.

"Sure thing, Miss Jones," Jerry said, taking a swig of his beer. "Real good to see Yaromir back."

She gave them a smile. "He's glad to be back, too."

Clara swept through, pouring a glass of water. "Miss Jones, good evenin'."

"Hi, Mrs. Thompson." She peered past her, hoping to catch a glimpse of Hazel.

"We got chicken with potatoes and okra today. Would you like butter with the roll?"

"Hmm? Oh." She refocused, sliding her water glass closer. "Yes, please."

Jerry and Steven chatted away over their meals. Lida listened, sipping her water. When Hazel emerged from the kitchen with her food, she straightened. Her mind raced with a dozen things to say. Hazel set the plate in front of her with a loud clatter, the noise dissolving Lida's resolve.

"Afraid we're outta butter," Hazel said. Then she turned on a dime and was gone.

Lida felt her cheeks grow hot. She swallowed, staring at the steaming plate, a single roll dropped unceremoniously into the gravy.

Jerry leaned forward. "She been like that for weeks. Nearly set the place on fire last Tuesday. Whole hall smelled like charred bird."

Lida bit her cheek, poking at the potatoes with her spoon.

"My money's on whoever she met at the social went and messed things up."

A piece of okra caught in her throat. Lida coughed, and Jerry patted her back before handing her water.

He said to Steven, "Ain't nothin but gossip."

"Ain't just gossip. I saw it." Still coughing, Lida listened intently and took another drink. "I was sittin' up on that pole. I was watchin' them folks on the dance floor. Including Mister Two-Left-Feet over here." He grinned, nudging Jerry. "That's when I saw Miss Hazel slip into the barn with someone."

Sweat trickled down Lida's neck. She adjusted the cuff of her shirtsleeve.

"Had to be Paul Boley," Jerry said matter-of-factly.

"Might've been." Steven leaned back, his thumbs moving up and down his suspenders. "Didn't get a good look at the fella. But whoever he was, he had Hazel in a giddy whirl right after."

Lida chewed through a smile, relieved they didn't know who had been in the barn with Hazel that day.

"Done stepped in it, though, whoever he is. Now she's angrier than a hornet's nest."

Lida dared a look toward the kitchen. Hazel mashed a pot of potatoes like they were trying to fight her. She grimaced. Of course Hazel was upset. She had a right to be after the way Lida had handled things.

"Well," she said, cutting into the chicken. "I do hope they do the right thing." An irksome guilt burrowed in her chest. Lida had only wanted to make Hazel happy; she loathed the fact that she'd been the cause of her distress.

Jerry and Steven nodded and Lida chewed on a plan to get back into Hazel's good graces.

CHAPTER TWENTY-FOUR

Nicholas, stir that gravy, will you?" Hazel hurried behind him in the busy kitchen. He tossed another sweet almond into his mouth.

Their mother swatted his hand. "Those are for the patrons."

"Why are they in here?" he asked, picking up the gravy ladle.

"Because," their mother huffed, "I don't have eight arms, that's why."

Arthur swooped between them, scooping up the almond bowl. "I'll see to it, Clara."

"Thank you, Arthur. Mind checkin' on the turkey out back once you're done?"

"Happy to."

"Don't forget your coat this time," she called after him. Then to Hazel, "I swear, just 'cause he's built like a mountain don't mean he can't catch cold."

Hazel grinned at her mother's attentive gaze trailing after Arthur. She glanced at the wall clock. "Nearly six thirty. Only an hour before folks start comin' for dinner."

"Another Thanksgiving," her mother said, shaking her head. "Can't hardly believe it."

Hazel smiled, scooping up the cutlery Nicholas had organized on the counter. "I'll set the tables, Momma."

Thanksgiving at the Lodge was a smaller occasion compared to the summer social. Only the regulars ventured out for Clara's traditional turkey dinner. Christmas was a bigger to-do, when folks were tired of bein' shut in from the snow and ready for some merriment.

"Check on your grandpa while you're doin' so," her mother called.

In the dining hall, Hazel skidded to a halt at the sight of her grandpa in conversation with Paul.

"Look who dropped in," he said before banging on his chest in a futile effort to quiet his coughs. He reached for his pipe on the table. Her grandpa was tucked under a blanket in a chair on the other side of the fire, his crutches resting in the corner. Paul struck a match and lit it for him as his coughs sputtered to an end.

"Evenin', Hazel," he said genially.

"Hi, there."

"Mr. Boley was tellin' me about a cattle company out in Colorado. They're lookin to make a deal with the Boleys." He hacked again, wiping his mouth with a handkerchief. "Ain't that somethin?"

"Sure is," Hazel said, proceeding to set the tables. They were draped in burnt-orange tablecloths for the holiday, a maple leaf centerpiece atop each one. She was arranging the knives on the second table when Paul came up beside her.

"That's actually why I came by." He removed his hat, the gesture sending notes of musky cologne toward her. "I know I've asked a lot of questions, Hazel. But I reckon I got maybe one or two more in me before I'm liable to give up."

She tossed him a smile, wondering if that could be true.

"Well, see, I was wonderin' what you'd say to Thanksgiving in the city."

Hazel paused. Her silence seemed to encourage him.

"See, I'm takin' Mother up to Salt Lake here in half an hour before I go on to Denver. Gonna treat her to a real fine time. Won't be no trouble to buy another ticket." He glanced at her grandpa, who nodded encouragingly. "Well, Hazel, what do you say?"

She blinked, stepping back to create space between her and the shining aura that always seemed to encapsulate Paul. She shot her grandpa a look for his incessant need to make him a part of her life. One hand on her hip, she leaned against a chair. Paul's blue gaze was bright, his cheeks pink from the cold. She had to give him credit; he was persistent. Too persistent for too long, but still…even for all his insistence, her family was right: he was a good man. He would treat her right. He would take care of her. He'd give her the life he thought she wanted.

But he wasn't who she wanted. Her mind conjured Lida as she stared at the shine of the silverware. She wished Lida were the one asking her to spend the holiday together. Hazel was still annoyed, confused by Lida's behavior the last time they spoke. But, she admitted, she hadn't been the most gracious either when she'd seen her at the Lodge.

"Paul," she finally said, "I—"

The door opened, sending cold air across the room. The fire danced as Lida hurried to close it. She kicked snow from her boots. Melted snowflakes dotted her hat and wool coat. Hazel hadn't realized she'd stopped talking until her grandpa gave a muttered greeting and adjusted the blanket over his legs.

"Mr. Criley," Lida said, tapping the brim of her hat.

"Ms. Jones."

She started to undo her scarf. "I was hoping to find—" She spotted Hazel. "Oh." Lida glanced at Paul, then back at her. "Hi."

"Hi."

The word snapped the tension that had formed between the three of them. Hazel bit her lip, averting her gaze and tinkering with the silverware. When she looked at Paul, a look she hadn't seen before crossed his face. It drew slowly over him, his irises turning a forlorn shade of blue. The disappointment shifted quickly, though, a dark anger taking its place.

"Are you joking?" he asked, his gaze holding hers and his tone frighteningly even.

Deep panic gripped Hazel's legs, rooting her to the floor. She worked to keep her voice calm. "Paul."

"What're you on about?" her grandpa called from the corner.

Paul's jaw clenched, sending Hazel's panic shooting through

her body like a hot poker. Still facing her, he called over his shoulder, "Mr. Criley, I reckon I know why your granddaughter won't take my offer."

Her grandpa huffed. "What do you mean?"

Hazel wanted to shout, but her throat felt constricted. Across from her, Paul's eyes burned, and in them, she saw what she'd always feared: he knew.

"You ever ask her who she was with in that barn on July Fourth?" His eyes flickered to Lida. "If you did, you'd know. You'd know the reason she keeps rejecting me. Me," he repeated, jabbing a finger into his own chest.

The room grew quiet, the few diners watching wide-eyed and slack-jawed.

"Tell them," Paul said, stepping closer. "Tell them, Hazel."

"Paul, you need to go."

"Tell them or I will."

From the corner of her eye, Hazel saw Lida step forward, one fist clenched at her side. She swallowed, sensing the attention of everyone in the room on her and Paul. *God, this couldn't be happening.*

Paul was in her face now. She saw tears in his eyes, but his voice came out in a snarl. "Tell them about—"

Footsteps hurried from behind her, and her mother stood between them. The fire that had filled her eyes last time Paul had been there seeped into her voice, coming out thick and laced with urgent warning. "I reckon you best not finish that thought, Mr. Boley."

He fell back, but regained his composure. "Clara, with respect—"

"It's always been Mrs. Thompson to you, Paul Boley."

Finally, Hazel's voice returned. Softly, she said, "Momma."

But her mother held up a hand, still staring at Paul. "Now, I ain't got no idea what's passing through this room, but you need to back off." When he didn't move, she stepped forward, lowering her voice to a whisper. "I don't know what you think you know, but you take another step to Hazel, you will wish you'd already taken whatever fancy train it is you're leavin' on tonight." She stepped back. Louder, she added, "Hear me?" Her gaze swept over the diners. "Anyone who thinks this is the way to speak to Hazel, or anybody, isn't welcome at the Lodge. No rest from the cold, no food in your belly, nothin'. Understood?"

Mutters of "Yes, ma'am," drifted uneasily through the room. Still seething, Paul shoved his hands into his pockets and stormed toward the door. When Hazel started after him, both her mother and Lida reached out.

"It's all right," she told them, appreciative of their concerned looks. "I just need one minute."

Her mother squeezed her hand, and Lida nodded. She ran outside after Paul, who was already at his car. "Wait, Paul."

"We're done, Hazel." He yanked the door open. "I'm done."

"You won't..." She took a breath to steady herself, glancing back at the Lodge. "You won't say anything, will you?"

He shook his head, his gaze boring into his steering wheel like he couldn't bring himself to look at her. "It's your life. Your choice."

He got into the car, starting it. Clouds of smoke billowed out from the exhaust. She stepped back when he rolled down the window. Finally meeting her gaze, his voice was the sincerest she'd heard it in a long time when he asked, "What kind of life can she give you?"

Hazel knew he wouldn't understand. Not many people could. What she and Lida had was theirs and, she realized she didn't need to explain herself to anyone. "Like you said, Paul, it's my life. My choice."

She let the words hang between them. Finally, he gave a small nod and rolled up the window before driving away.

"What in tarnation was all that about?" her grandpa asked when she returned. Her mother was back in the kitchen, her movements tight as she chopped potatoes. Most of the diners had gone. Steven Akers shot her a look from behind his piece of chicken, but she ignored it.

"Nothin, Grandpa. Paul just had to learn how to take no for an answer, that's all."

Her grandpa muttered but turned to Lida, who was warming her hands near the fire. "Were you lookin' for Nicholas?" her grandpa asked. Hazel quickly set the other tables, exhaling to gather herself after the commotion with Paul, using the corner of her eye to admire the wine-red scarf that complemented Lida's complexion. She wore her high boots and riding pants, and Hazel tried not to stare at how they clung to her hips. The sight of her quelled the unease from the altercation moments before.

Lida replied, "Oh, no, actually." Hazel hadn't noticed the book in her gloved hand. Lida pulled it closer. "I was hoping...I was hoping to speak with Hazel a moment."

Hazel's heart sped up, and she smoothed the already even tablecloth to gather her thoughts. "We're mighty busy," she said, adjusting the already perfect centerpiece. "It bein' Thanksgiving and all." She pulled back her shoulders and placed her hands on her hips, giving off as much a sense of apathy as possible. She reminded herself she and Lida were on uneasy terms, though after what just transpired and the concerned look in Lida's gaze, Hazel began to feel a little silly.

"Hogwash," her grandpa chimed in behind a cloud of tobacco smoke. "Your momma will be fine for five minutes."

Hazel pursed her lips. Lida smiled as she hung up her hat and scarf but kept her coat on. After shooting her grandpa a look, Hazel motioned for her to follow. They sat at a table near the stairs.

"Are you all right?" Lida asked, nodding to the doorway where Paul had stormed out.

"I'm fine," she said, overwhelmed at the look in Lida's eyes. The drum of Lida's fingers against the book in her lap gave Hazel the confidence to say, "I hear your father's doin' better."

"Yes." Lida chewed her lip. She seemed to contemplate her words. "Hazel..." She pulled her chair closer, throwing a glance across the room. Hazel temporarily lost herself in the way her name sounded when Lida said it. "I need to apologize."

Right, Hazel thought. She was mad. She leaned back in her seat, crossing her arms and legs.

"I was rude that day you visited. You were reaching out in kindness, and I should have returned the courtesy."

Hazel fidgeted. "I suppose you had a lot on your plate, your daddy bein' sick and all." Lida licked her lips. When she glanced again at Hazel's grandpa, Hazel uncrossed her arms and leaned forward. "What is it?"

Lida stared at the table. Her voice was a whisper when she said, "I want to tell you things."

Hazel's heart nearly burst at the longing in Lida's voice. She reached out, resting her hand next to Lida's. "You can."

She gave a small nod, then seemed to steel herself. "My father has battled certain demons since my mother died. Sometimes, he can overcome them on his own, but sometimes, he can't."

Hazel searched Lida's eyes, sifting through the dark pools for understanding. "He was in the throes of a battle when I showed up."

Lida nodded.

Making sure her grandpa wasn't paying attention, Hazel rested her hand on Lida's. "I reckon it's tough, trying to keep pryin' eyes from a man's struggle. And there I was, pushing myself into your trouble like I belonged."

Lida, who had looked ready to cry, smiled. "That's the thing. I wanted you there. I just…" A "v" formed between her brows. "I felt shame. Shame at what was on the other side of my door. Shame at this secret that drives us across this country."

Hazel studied Lida, pieces of her story resurfacing. New York. Pittsburgh. Columbus. Cincinnati. "That's why y'all have moved so much," she said, her voice low.

"It's why he has trouble staying in one place, at one job."

Hazel swallowed, recalling Lida's pained warning. *We may have to leave.*

"But he's better now?" she asked, almost afraid of the answer.

"Now." Lida held her gaze. "But it may return. It will," she corrected, pain thick in her voice.

Hazel wished she'd thought to speak somewhere more private. She wanted to pull Lida close, hold her until the pain went away.

"Hey," she said, taking Lida's hands. "It's all right." She understood Lida's wariness. If her father couldn't keep the mining job, there wasn't anything for him here. He'd have to find something else, somewhere else. The thought of Lida leaving poured into Hazel's grip as she clung to her hands. Lida stared at their fingers and smiled. "Where is your father now?"

"At home. Well, with the Seagers. They made a small dinner for today." She gently set the book on the table.

Hazel tilted her head. "I thought the deliveries were done till spring."

"This is one of mine."

"Oh."

Lida nudged it forward. Turning it over, Hazel read the cover. "*A Room with a View*."

"It was my mother's. She's lined the margins with notes. There's one quote in particular I'm fond of."

She picked it up, and the pages fell open. Tucked between two of them, the white petals of a sego lily stared up at her. Delicately, she moved the pressed wildflower to find a line circled in ink. She followed along as Lida said, "'Let yourself go. Pull out from the depths those thoughts that you do not understand, and spread them out in the sunlight and know the meaning of them.'"

Hazel reread the words twice. She had heard of women growing faint from an act of love, a romantic gesture so grand it made people swoon. She wondered if this wasn't one of those moments as her head spun, and she found a welcoming fixture in Lida's gaze. "It's beautiful."

"It's yours. Take it as a token of gratitude for speaking to me after the way I acted."

Hazel carefully replaced the wildflower. When Lida stood, she sprang to her feet. "Where are you going?"

"Back home."

"Wait," Hazel said, one finger up as she clutched the gift in her other hand. She called to the kitchen, "Momma, we have room for one more, don't we?"

Her mother stepped into the doorway, her brow glistening as

she stirred a bowl of batter at her hip. She was still red in the face after speaking to Paul, but her eyes softened at the sight of them. "Why, Miss Jones. How are you?" Hazel tucked the book behind her when her mother eyed it curiously. "I reckon we got room. Extra chairs are upstairs."

Hazel grinned and happily took Lida's coat.

CHAPTER TWENTY-FIVE

In front of the fire, Lida wrapped her arms around herself. She closed her eyes and fell into the warm recollection of Thanksgiving Day at the Lodge. The memories shielded her from the wind forcing its way through their cabin walls and the unease in her mind for her father's condition. Hazel's bright laugh filled her mind, chasing away a new uncertainty. It was the uncertainty of her future. The holiday spent with the Thompsons had shifted something in her chest, moving the ready suitcase and pulling her gaze from the next destination, fixing it instead on this town. On Hazel.

Paul's shadow was gone, revealing a path Lida didn't even know was possible to walk. Was it, really? What if he started talking? What were the odds, truly, that she could have a future with Hazel? Inhaling deeply, Lida shook her head and forced herself to dwell in the good memories she'd formed since coming to Cedar Springs.

When she caught a glimpse of Sasha pulling the Thompson wagon to the Seagers' drive, she quickly checked on her father. Grateful to find him still asleep after a fitful night, Lida left her book at the kitchen table and hurried to the door.

She was surprised to find not Hazel but Clara hopping down from the high seat. Her stout frame landed with a sturdy thud into the packed snow in front of the porch. The icy white crunched beneath her high boots.

"Good morning," Lida called, raising a hand to the sun tearing through the sheet of gray overhead. Harsh wind cut across her face.

Clara had wrapped a scarf around her head, adding a layer above brown earmuffs. Lida closed the door behind her, throwing her own scarf around her neck and pulling her coat tight.

"Morning," Clara replied. She lifted a small pot from the back of the wagon. "Heard this house may benefit from a hearty meal."

Lida shoved her hands in her pockets. The mine had closed for the season last week. Unfortunately, the new free time had created opportunities for her father to stumble. News of her father's struggle had become public when William had found him in Pine City on Sunday. Her father had gone into town, so he told Lida, to buy material to make new mittens. He'd lingered, and after hours at the Canyon Café, William—who had been across the street purchasing nails to repair the barn—had spotted him weepy and disoriented in an alley.

Lida knew the people of Pine City would talk, and the talk carried right up the mountain.

"Thank you," Lida said. When Clara stood expectantly at the base of the steps, tufts of blond hair whipping around her oval face, she added, "Please, come in."

Quickly, Lida lit their second gas lamp and threw another log on the fire. She opened one of the curtains and was about to throw open the second when Clara said, "He's still sleepin'. Don't bother."

Lida followed her gaze to her father's passed-out figure on the corner cot. His tall frame hardly fit; one foot dangled off the end.

Clara set the pot on the stovetop. Lida grimaced at their sparse shelves as Clara squinted at a sad-looking pair of turnips and a basket of potatoes on the table.

"It's kind of you to bring that by." Lida wasn't sure why she felt nervous in front of Clara. Maybe it was because she didn't seem as talkative as she normally was, spewing spitfire strings of words across the Lodge dining room. Maybe it had to do with the way Clara rested one hand on her hip and seemed to wait for Lida to speak. "How's the Lodge?" she finally asked.

"Quiet. Always is this time of year. Ain't many folks feeling adventurous come December." She smiled, and Lida's shoulders relaxed.

"I didn't realize the roads would stay closed so long." She gestured to the window, the grim sky threatening more snow. Four inches had fallen overnight after two the night before.

"Ain't able to clear it like they can in other parts. Folks here are used to it, though, and everyone does their part to make sure we can move around safely. Come Christmas, we clear a decent stretch so folks can visit one another." She stepped to the other side of the kitchen, glancing out the back window. "Oughta get William to tarp that firewood." She gestured to their wood-burning stove. "Be sure to clean that out. And check the windows. Glass likes to crack when it's this cold."

Lida nodded. She wanted to ask after Hazel. With the weather turning the way it was, the library route, like the mine, was suspended until Spring. Her father's persistent need for tending-to made venturing to the Lodge more and more difficult.

"Hazel sends her regards," Clara said, snapping Lida back to attention. A blush warmed her face, but she hoped it would be mistaken for the cold. "Nicholas, too. That magazine you lent him on birds…" Clara clucked her tongue. "Lord, that child slept with that thing under his pillow for weeks straight. Can recite every fact from it now."

Laughing, Lida said, "It took a while to get that one back."

Clara smiled. "Even my daddy, you met him, he's stubborn as a mule and can't hardly read more than a page without gettin' a headache, but he likes them books, too."

She pictured the Thompson clan all sitting around a fire, exchanging words and facts from the Pack Horse materials. She imagined Hazel, curled in a chair, her lips shining as she read. "I'm glad," she managed to say.

Clara tossed another look toward Lida's father, who had begun to snore. "I best be goin', then." She adjusted her scarf but paused at the door. "You know what I find does a man good when he's feelin' lonely?"

Lida swallowed at Clara's ability to see through her father's pain.

"Some time with the community. Bein' around other folks. I reckon it may do him good."

Lida's eyes stung with tears. She couldn't find her voice and was glad when Clara added, "Did Hazel mention we do Christmas at the Lodge? Well." She pulled herself up, thumbs hitched in her brown coat. "I do hope to see you and your father come by on December twenty-fifth. We do dinner at three o'clock."

For a moment, Lida could only blink at Clara. Here was this woman—the fiery, tough proprietor of the Lodge with a million things to do at any moment—in Lida's home, bringing her stew and inviting her to spend Christmas with her people.

Could they be Lida's people, too?

"Thank you, Mrs. Thompson. We'd be honored."

She gave a resolute nod. "Very well, Miss Jones. Don't forget the stew, now."

"I won't. And please, call me Lida."

With a soft smile, Clara took her leave. Lida watched her wagon retreat back down the hill as snow started to fall. Then she ran to the calendar. She circled the twenty-fifth, then stepped back. Warmth trickled down her shoulders as if winter wasn't wrapping its chilled fingers around the land. Instead, Lida was light-headed at the new promise of the holiday.

Later, she ran a cool rag over her father's forehead. Flashes of harsh winters in crowded apartments sprang forward in her mind. Harsh smells, jarring city sounds, the undercurrent of desperation in every hungry face she ever spent a holiday with coursed through her. Slowly, all of that faded as Clara's invitation came back to her. After another glance at the calendar, she focused on her father. She would help him heal. He would be better by then, and together they would join Clara, Nicholas, Hazel, and the people of Cedar Springs for their first Christmas at the Lodge.

CHAPTER TWENTY-SIX

"Quit pullin' at the lace, honey. You'll tug the threads right out."
Hazel frowned at her reflection in the narrow mirror resting against the wall inside the door. She was upstairs in one of the spare lodger rooms, dressing with her mother for the night. Her grandpa and Nicholas were next door, doing the same. They'd all been there since seven that morning, fussing about downstairs to get ready for Christmas dinner.

Admittedly, she was glad for the extra time because she hadn't once in her life worried so much over what she was wearing. She wanted Lida to look at her, to really see her. The very thought sent a flutter through her stomach. For a moment, the flash of other holidays, other moments with Lida, filled her mind. It was their future, but what would it look like? She didn't think Paul would be back and could only hope he'd keep his mouth shut. Even if he did, what if Lida grew tired of her? She was used to the fast pace of the city. What if she wasn't looking for a small-town life?

"Momma, you sure this looks all right?" She tilted her head, tucking hair behind her ear. Her fingers bumped a pair of small pearl earrings. They'd been her grandmother's, and Hazel only wore them on rare occasions. They went well with her dress, which had white buttons below the neck and down her back. The deep red of the material had reminded her of Lida's scarf. The more she stared and huffed, though, the more she feared she looked like a sweaty tomato.

Her mother stood behind her. "Darlin', quit fussin'." She grabbed Hazel by the shoulders. "You look beautiful."

Hazel twisted, gazing at the velvet material that cut into a "v" between her shoulder blades. The long sleeves were cuffed with white lace. She'd tied a black sash around her waist in the hope of creating the semblance of a figure. After fiddling with it, she glanced up to find her mother's eyes shining. "Momma?"

"You really are quite the young woman."

Taken aback, Hazel found her mother's hand still on her shoulder. "Well, I have you to thank."

Her mother laughed. "Hush now. Come on, guests'll be here any minute. Best go make sure your brother has his shoes on and Grandpa remembered his tie."

Downstairs, Arthur was dressing the tree with the final strings of red ribbon.

"Oh, Arthur, it's lovely," her mother said. Hazel had to agree. The entire room looked as if she'd walked into a holiday card. It reminded her of an advertisement she'd seen in a magazine for a fancy lady's home somewhere far away. Candles sat on every table in metal trays lined with holly leaves. Hank and Jerry had helped her mother find and chop a strong fir tree. It loomed in the corner next to the kitchen. The scent of its thick green needles mingled with warm spices from mulled wine and dozens of baked goods. A hint of cooked meat wafted beneath it all as the fire blazed, and lights cast a warm halo along the walls.

Her grandpa made his way downstairs, Nicholas helping him. After recovering his breath, hunched over his crutches, he said, "I'm liable to choke on all this holly." At the base of the stairs, he wobbled, lifting a hand to wave aside a bundle of green hanging from a string above his head.

"That's mistletoe, Grandpa."

He grumbled, and they helped him to his corner seat. Shortly after, guests began to arrive. Hazel was in the kitchen, tightening the lid on a jar of honey when she heard Mr. Jones's voice and hurried to greet him.

"Mr. Jones, welcome," she said, taking his hat and coat.

"We could not celebrate Christmas where we came from," he announced, peering at the tall tree, the tables set for six and gleaming with fine china.

"That was a long time ago, Pa." Lida stood behind him, giving her father a look.

"I know," he replied. "This is..." He raised a hand as if to measure the tree. "A taller Christmas tree than even New York." He chuckled. "I didn't think was possible."

"We try our best," Hazel replied. She bit her lip at the sight of the wine-red scarf Lida hung alongside her hat and coat. She and her father both wore pressed white shirts. While Mr. Jones wore a jacket he kept on, Lida sported a vest above a pair of dark brown trousers. She kicked snow from her boots near the door. Hazel realized she was still wearing her apron. She tugged it off and ran a hand down her hair to smooth it as Mr. Jones wandered away to gawk at the tree.

"Can I offer you somethin' to drink?" she asked Lida, who, to Hazel's delight, was staring at the off-shoulder cut of her neckline.

"I'll have what he's having." She pointed to William, who sat with Martha and Little Thomas nearby. A steaming mug rested on the table.

She nodded. Hesitating, she glanced at Lida then asked, "And for you, Mr. Jones?"

Lida's father scanned the frothy beer glasses on the table between Jerry and Mr. Benter before saying, "Have any spiced cider?"

She smiled, feeling hope and seeing a glimmer of it in Lida's eyes. "Comin' right up."

The meal, unsurprisingly, was a hit. They'd dined on pork roast, sweet potatoes, beets, and cabbage salad. For dessert, plates of sugar cookies and cherry cobbler were passed around. Hazel took Nicholas's empty pudding glass but not before he licked the last of it from the spoon.

"That was incredible," Lida's father said at their table when Hazel returned from the kitchen. She sat next to Lida, who she'd caught eyeing the black sash throughout the evening. Each glance ran her throat dry, and she felt a familiar longing building within her. Outside, night had fallen, but inside, the Lodge was bright.

Hank opened his violin case while Mr. Benter pulled out a harmonica. They dragged chairs near the fire and to a faint chorus of applause, started a song.

Over the soft music, Hazel said, "I am glad you enjoyed it, Mr. Jones." Hazel's mother yawned after a sip of her wine, the plum color staining her mouth. "Can I get anyone more food?" Hazel asked. She was met with satisfied refusals, so she leaned back, herself content after such a meal. Noticing Lida scan the crowded dining room, she asked, "Somethin' on your mind?"

Lida stared at the fire, then at the Evanses sitting at the next table, then at Hazel. "You do this every year?"

Hazel smiled at the same question she'd asked on the Fourth as her mother answered. "Sure do. Ever since we hammered in the last nail in these here walls."

A look passed between Lida and her father. Hazel longed to believe it was a look of hope. Hope that they may be around for another night like this next year.

"Looks like Akers found his banjo," Arthur said across the table, munching on candied almonds.

Her mother fanned her flushed neck. "Lord help us. The dancin's startin'."

As if on cue, half the room stood. As Lida and her father sat, seemingly bewildered, Hazel helped Jerry and the boys make more room near the fire. Hank sang an old folk tune, and couples jumped and stamped along.

Mr. Jones stood, offering his hand to Lida. She glanced at Hazel.

"I'm dyin' to see this," she said.

Lida grinned and took to the floor.

A few moments later, Arthur said, "I always wondered what a flamingo would look like if it tried to dance."

Hazel smacked Arthur's arm at the same time as her mother.

"Arthur Davis, I don't see you out there," Hazel teased, though she had to admit, Mr. Jones did resemble an awkward, gangly bird trying to take flight. Lida, though, moved gracefully and tried to lead her father across the floor.

"You're right, Miss Hazel. We oughta fix that." To her mother, he said, "May I have the honor?"

Her mother took another sip of wine, then caught Hazel's eye. She nodded encouragement, but her mother didn't budge. "You know I got two left feet," she protested.

Hazel waved away the comment. "Nonsense."

"You have one left foot," Nicholas added.

"Exactly," Arthur said, taking her mother's hand and twirling her onto the floor.

Her mother's smile spread, her high-pitched laughter scattering between the other dancers. It broke joyously into the corners of the Lodge, bouncing back in gleeful yips from the musicians. Hazel's gaze drifted to Lida, who'd exchanged partners and danced with William while Yaromir gave a frightened-looking Mrs. Evans a twirl. Lida's dark braid spun out behind her, pulling Hazel's focus. She'd never noticed how strong her arms looked. Her face caught the glow from the lamps, and Hazel admired the heart-like curve of her jaw when Lida laughed at William's exaggerated bow.

"All right, we can't miss out on all the fun," she said, tugging Nicholas behind her.

He sighed but seemed pleased to join the steady beat that had possessed the room. Everyone stomped and clapped in tune to the music, now a faster, wilder song that seemed to push against the walls, seeking the wide mountain range beyond. The sound filled the room, packed it tight with music and laughter.

When Hank called for a partner change, her brother found Mrs. Benter, and Hazel caught her mother's hand, giving her a twirl. Another song prompted another change. She caught Lida's gaze, who smiled and winked over Nicholas's shoulder. Hazel spun her mother back to Arthur, then found herself looking up at Mr. Jones.

"You follow, Miss Thompson. I try not to squash feet." She held on to his lanky frame and was so dizzy by the time the next partner change rang out, she nearly fell into Lida.

"I've got you."

Hazel breathed a laugh. "Is it just me, or is the door on the wrong side o' the room?"

Lida braced her, taking one of Hazel's hands. "Just you, I'm afraid." When Lida's hand came to rest on her waist, Hazel's world shot into focus. She gripped Lida's shoulder if for any other reason than to keep herself from falling into the gorgeous dark browns of Lida's eyes. "Ready?"

Hazel could only nod as Lida led her around the floor. She shocked Hazel with the ease with which she wove them in and out of everyone else. A decent dancer herself, Hazel thrilled at the effortlessness of their movements together.

This close, Hazel's senses seemed to pick up on details she hadn't noticed before. The scent of rose petals that lingered near Lida's neck. The surrounding light accentuated subtle shades of hickory brown in her thick braid. Hazel was struck, as she was in July, with the urge to dive into that braid and run her fingers through the lush strands.

The partner change called, and Hazel was certain the disheartened look in Lida's eyes matched her own. The sudden space between them was vast, like the canyon outside, and Hazel stumbled off the floor, unable to bear it.

"You all right, Hazel?"

One hand on the table, she fell into the chair next to her grandpa. "Just a little light-headed." She found Lida, who was keeping up with Charlie Benter's enthusiastic steps. When she turned, her grandpa wore a strange look. She took a deep breath. "What is it?"

He puffed on his pipe, then lifted his chin toward Mr. Jones. "Can't decide what I make of him."

"Mr. Jones? He's mighty nice." She grimaced as his hearty claps nearly elbowed Martha in the face. "Not a graceful man but a kind one."

"Man's got demons."

She spun around, wide-eyed at his candidness. "Grandpa, ain't no way to speak about a person. And on Christmas, too."

He grunted.

"Besides," she said after a minute, "we all got somethin'."

He caught her eye. "Folks love comin' west, thinkin' it'll cure what ails 'em where they came from. Think the big sky will take 'em in, heal what hurts, what drove 'em out here."

Hazel studied Mr. Jones. "What's so wrong with that?"

"Ain't nothin' wrong. But even this big ol' sky has limits." He rubbed his knee, his gnarled knuckles finding the sewn cuff of his pant leg. "And that man don't know where to even look for help."

A quick reply came but fell on Hazel's lips. The one downside to a small town, though she loathed to admit it, was how fast gossip spread.

"Well," Hazel said as the music dipped before building into a final, twangy beat. "Maybe Cedar Springs is just what he needs." Lida's laughter called, spinning Hazel back onto the dance floor before the blissful sound burrowed into her heart. Under her breath, she added, "Maybe it's just what *they* need."

CHAPTER TWENTY-SEVEN

L ida said good-bye to the Thompsons, draping her scarf around her neck and buttoning her coat. She felt content in a way she hadn't in some time after hours of dancing, wine, and good food. "Glad y'all could be here," Mrs. Thompson said proudly, though she teetered slightly into Arthur, who shook their hands.

"Looks like someone may need a ride home," Hazel teased, giving Arthur a look.

Lida laughed, pulling the Lodge door open. The Seagers were preparing the wagon. Her father tipped his hat and walked outside.

Arthur led a chatty Clara to the kitchen. Watching them, Lida said, "Your momma is quite the banjo player."

Hazel laughed. "First time I ever heard it." She shook her head. "She works so hard all year. It's nice when she can have a night like this." She flicked a rag toward the back. "Arthur's a good man. He'll see she gets home all right."

Lida noticed Mr. Criley eye her as he stood to gather his crutches with Nicholas's help. Outside, voices grew distant as the revelers journeyed home. "Well, thank you for a delightful time." She put on her hat right before she was surprised by Hazel, who leapt forward to hug her. Smiling, Lida closed her eyes, ready to sink into Hazel's arms. Then she remembered the others and cleared her throat.

"Merry Christmas," Hazel said, a sweet smile greeting Lida as she stepped back.

Her father called, but Lida didn't move. She didn't want to. She wanted to be here with Hazel. Gesturing to the tables, she said, "I could help, if you need it."

For a second, it looked like Hazel was going to agree, but she shook her head. "I got it. It's my Christmas gift to Momma. I always tidy up afterward." They held each other's gazes. "I reckon your clan is eager to get home."

Reluctantly, Lida pulled up the collar of her coat, bracing for the cold. Then she hurried outside and onto the wagon. Once they were home—Little Thomas asleep in his bundle of blankets—Lida walked toward the front porch with her father.

"This isn't like the snow back east," she said, sweeping her gaze across the thick layers glistening under a bright half-moon. "Everything is so quiet here." The surrounding trees stood stalwart, silent above the mountain town. Chilled, she dove her hands into her coat pockets. Her right hand collided with something hard and cold.

"I'll start fire," her father said, but Lida was focused on the small mason jar she held between her thumb and forefinger. Thick golden honey shined inside the glass. A red ribbon was tied around the lid and wove through a hole attaching a note.

Holding it to the moonlight, she read, "Something sweet for my book woman."

"Lida?"

She was still standing on the porch. Her father had lit a lamp and started a small fire. He stared at her in the doorway, his bushy brows low.

"I have to go," she said.

"Go where?"

"The Lodge. I…" She shoved the gift into her pocket. "I forgot something."

He studied her as if ticking off a mental list of everything she'd gone there with.

"I'll take Beth." Then she ran inside and hugged him. "Merry Christmas, Pa. I'll be back."

A smile crept from under his mustache. "Merry Christmas."

She hesitated. "You'll be okay?"

He replied with a wave. "I'm fine."

She watched him a moment, then raced out into the night, back to the Lodge.

❖

Hazel scrubbed more cranberry cocktail from a glass, humming to herself. She let the monotonous movements strum up the memory of dancing with Lida, their bodies in perfect sync with one another. The sound of the Lodge door opening made her look up. "Who's there?"

Moments later, Lida appeared in the doorway.

"Lida." She set the dishes aside and quickly dried her hands. "Is everything all right?"

"Everything's fine."

Hazel took off her apron, slowly moving to stand at the end of the counter. She leaned against it, acutely aware of the fact that she and Lida were the only two in the Lodge. "Did you forget something?"

Lida gave half a smile as she tossed her hat onto Nicholas's stool. "I did." She pulled out the jar of honey Hazel had slipped into her coat earlier between dinner and dessert.

"I see you found it."

"I love it." Lida stepped closer, replacing the jar in her pocket. "Thank you."

Swallowing, Hazel said, "You're welcome." Lida looked as if she was going to move closer but stopped a few feet away. A dark looked crossed her face. "What is it?"

"I'm still sorry about the materials."

"Oh." Hazel found that an odd thing to bring up. *Is she nervous?* Lida licked her lips, her gaze darting to the floor then back to her. Hazel shrugged. "Ain't the end of the world. We still got the library, don't we?"

Lida smiled. "We do. Once the snow starts to melt."

"I reckon that's somethin'. More than somethin'." She took a breath, then stepped forward to tug Lida by the coat sleeve, bringing her closer. She'd wanted to have Lida closer all evening. The time they'd shared on the dance floor had proved too short. "I reckon that library may be the best thing to ever happen here."

Lida leaned in, resting their foreheads together. "Hazel."

Her name sounded glorious when Lida said it. She was impressed she could think at all when Lida gently gripped her waist. Hazel closed her eyes at the sensation. She remembered how Lida's lips felt in the barn that hot July night and decided she had to taste them again.

Hazel pulled her into a slow kiss. Lida returned it, pressing forward. Like their bodies had been on the dance floor, their lips found perfect rhythm. Hazel savored the soft warmth of Lida's mouth. It was the most sensual kiss of her life, easy and slow and filling her with need.

Taking a breath, she found Lida's gaze dark with lust. Hazel took her hand. "Come with me."

She led Lida across the dining hall. The room was dimmer, the fire a dull orange crackle in the hearth. Cutting off the gas lamps as they crossed the room, Hazel started up the stairs when Lida pulled her back down.

"Wait." Hazel followed her gaze to the mistletoe hanging overhead. "I've always wanted to do this."

Hazel smiled into another kiss. Wrapping her arms around Lida, Hazel pressed herself closer, their bodies flush but still not close enough. Remembering her original thought, Hazel broke their kiss. Lida groaned, seemingly in protest. Grinning, Hazel led her upstairs.

They made it to the first room before Hazel couldn't stand another fraction of distance between them. Leading Lida backward toward the twin bed, she shed Lida's coat and undid the buttons on her vest. Her heart pounded as, in between kisses, Lida found her sash and untied it. Hazel tossed the vest aside, then made quick work of Lida's shirt.

Lida turned her, trailing kisses down her neck. "You're so beautiful," she murmured, undoing the buttons down Hazel's dress. Now only in her old silk slip, Hazel felt self-conscious. She trembled at the cool air, nervous in the moonlight that poured in the window. Though she had yearned for Lida to be the one to see her like this, she shook with the truth of their situation. Her desires were being met, her dreams unboxed and laid bare, ready and waiting for her to begin.

She faced Lida, who placed her hands on Hazel's hips, then slowly ran them higher until they framed Hazel's face. Under Lida's gaze, Hazel felt seen. She felt understood. She felt wanted, and the need that had sparked to life downstairs surged through her limbs, nesting below her stomach and creating a slick heat between her legs.

Seeming to sense her hesitation, Lida kissed her again before asking, "Are you sure?"

Hazel had been floating above the room, but the same question Lida had asked before tethered her, grounding her in the cool night made hot by their longing. She took Lida's hand, kissed her knuckles, then her fingers, leading them to her hips, then lower. She pushed Lida back so she sat on the edge of the bed. Hazel hiked up her slip, straddling Lida. "I'm sure."

Lida stirred, stretching and wondering at the soreness in her limbs. Cold morning air filled the room, and she pulled the quilt over her bare chest. Soft light broke through the half-open curtain. Hazel lay beside her. She slept on her stomach, facing the wall. Lida adjusted the quilt so it covered Hazel's perfect, bare back. She ran her fingers over the smooth skin. Hazel inhaled, waking, then turned over as Lida kissed her shoulder.

"Good morning." Hazel blinked, wiping sleep from her eyes, smiling as Lida kissed her forehead.

"Morning." Lida had slept soundly. Her night with Hazel had seemed long-awaited, and every moment had been utter bliss. She'd read about love in so many books and had imagined how it might be to make love to the one person she had feared she might never meet. But it had happened. Hazel was real, and every moment between them had been true. Lida tucked Hazel's unruly hair behind her ear. "How are you?"

Hazel's gaze had been unfocused, lingering where the quilt dipped above Lida's breasts. She smiled. "I'm wonderful." She tugged Lida closer, wrapping the blanket around them.

Lida held on to her, enveloped in the warm cocoon of the quilt that made her never want to leave. She kissed Hazel, who draped her leg over Lida's waist, pressing them close. Though the late hours had seen her satisfied by Hazel's touch more than once, a quick, hot wanting rekindled when Hazel's kisses tickled her cheek. Lida moaned and pulled Hazel against her. On the other side of the window, a morning jay trilled.

The reminder of an outside world made Lida pull back. "What time is it?"

Hazel replied, "Probably after seven." Her breath was warm on Lida's ear.

Though Lida wanted nothing more than to relive the night before, she sat up. "I need to go."

"What?" Hazel mirrored her position, the quilt loose around her waist.

"My father." She shook her head. "I didn't mean to be gone so long." Hazel quirked an eyebrow. Knowing her mind, Lida reached out. "Hazel, I'm thrilled at what happened between us. I'd hoped it would. But…" She found her bra and hooked it on, then found her pants in the far corner of the room. "He's still unstable." Awful images flew through her mind: her father passed out next to the fireplace, or worse, the house engulfed in flames after he forgot to put it out, hidden bottles of vodka made ready fuel. Worse scenarios flooded her mind until Hazel tugged Lida's chin, forcing her to look at her.

"Let's go check on him, then."

Lida exhaled. "You don't have to come. I can—"

Hazel cut her off with a fiery kiss. Lida smiled into it.

"All right, you win."

They flew back on Beth, Lida urging her home as quickly

as possible. Hazel sat behind her, her arms around Lida's waist. They had no trouble navigating the road and made good time. Lida guided them toward the paddock near the barn behind her house and dismounted.

"Go on," Hazel said, taking Beth's reins. "I'll get her settled." Lida leapt up the steps. Inside, her stomach dropped when she found her father's cot empty.

"Pa?" She checked her room, then the cot again. Fear roared in her ears. She threw open the back door. "Pa?"

"Lida."

She ran out onto the front porch at Hazel's call. God, she thought, had she found him in the yard? She'd been sure all the alcohol had been thrown out, but her father had gotten clever over time, tucking small bottles into hidden places.

"Hazel, I can't find him." Lida turned, the endless plain of white making her head spin.

"Lida." Hazel pointed to the Seagers'.

She burst through the back door, startling William, Martha, and her father. "Pa."

His mustache lifted with a smile. "Lida." He wore his undershirt over worn trousers. A cup of coffee sat on the table. William and Martha waved from their seats across from him.

"You're okay."

He frowned. "You doubted it."

She had, and for good reason, but decided against having this conversation in front of the Seagers.

William cracked his boiled egg. "Mornin', Lida," he said. Hazel stepped inside, and he tapped his forehead in a salute. "Miss Thompson."

Lida moved aside so Hazel could close the door. "Good morning, everyone," Hazel said cheerily. Rubbing her hands together, she asked, "Where's young Thomas?"

"Sleeping," Martha said, sipping her coffee. "Worn out from the festivities last night." She eyed Lida, who glanced down to find her vest's misaligned buttons.

"You didn't come home last night," her father said.

"I meant to," she said, glancing at Hazel. "I went back to the Lodge and..." She faltered, realizing she didn't have an excuse.

"Lida helped me clean up, and by the time we finished, it was far too late to ride back," Hazel explained coolly while wearing a confident smile.

Her father nodded. "Smart. Much safer."

Lida gave a tight-lipped smile, though she caught the look exchanged between William and Martha.

"Anyway, now that I've seen her safely home, I oughta be gettin' back," Hazel said. "Momma's likely to send a search party."

"How will you get back?" Lida asked, trying to keep her tone casual, though sadness seeped into her chest at Hazel leaving.

"Reckon a walk will do me good. Stretch my legs," she added, tossing Lida a look. "Bye, y'all."

"Bye," Lida said.

"Come, Lida." Her father stamped the tabletop. "Eat."

As if in response, her stomach growled. She hadn't even realized how hungry she was and joined the table, sinking into the seat, half-present, half swimming in the memories of Hazel's touch.

CHAPTER TWENTY-EIGHT

"Nicholas," Hazel's mother called from in front of the pie oven, "stir the—"

"I've got it, Momma." Hazel jumped over to the stove, grabbing the gravy ladle.

"All right. Nicholas, fetch the eggs."

Hazel replied, "Already done it."

"We need to rinse the pots."

"Did it this morning." Her mother placed a hand on her hip. Hazel grinned, still stirring. "What, Momma?"

"You done all that already? Ain't hardly nine o'clock."

"Sure have," Hazel said. "Done it all before you even got here."

"That's what you were doin' here early?"

Hazel kept her eyes on the gravy but let her smile spread. She'd met Lida just after dawn. They'd shared an hour together upstairs before Lida had returned home, and Hazel got to work after making sure the sheets were exchanged for clean ones. "Mm-hmm."

"Mm-hmm," her mother echoed, her tone skeptical.

Hazel laughed as her mother shuffled by, giving her a look before greeting Hank in the dining hall. While Nicholas kneaded dough, she stirred and fell into daydreams. For a month, she and Lida had found stolen moments to be together. Each time proved to be more magical than the last, and Hazel was falling hard. She adored Lida's thoughtful nature, her love of words, and the care she showed the people of Cedar Springs. A memory of Christmas night flashed in her mind, and Hazel forced herself to focus on the gravy, the ladle in her hand, the warm kitchen. Back in her reality, she threw a glance over her shoulder.

Her mother knew something was different. She always did, even when Hazel was certain her mother was too busy to notice anything, she somehow knew everything. It had irritated Hazel when she was younger, like when her mother had known she was the one eating the last of the peaches even though she'd tried to blame it on Nicholas. It was the same way she knew Hazel didn't care for Paul despite his years of attempted courtship.

As her mother spoke to Hank, Hazel wondered what her mother would say if she knew who was behind Hazel's new work ethic. Hazel liked to imagine a world or a time when she could be with Lida out in the open. *How wonderful that might be.* Aside from the incident with Paul at Thanksgiving, there'd never been a word about her and Lida, as far as she'd known. And most talk got to her one way or another. She was grateful for the people of her town. They didn't ask questions, and that was that. But she didn't imagine something like her feelings for Lida could make sense to most people here. Hazel was hopeful, then, since her mother wasn't most people.

The first Saturday in February, Hazel woke early and dressed. She added a dab of perfume to her pulse points and found her boots near the front door. Pulling her coat on, she was about to slip out when a voice called from the dim corner of their living room.

"Where you off to?"

"Grandpa." Hazel pressed a hand to her chest. "You scared the daylights outta me." Her smile fell as he lit a match to the end of his pipe, illuminating his stern face. "I'm headin' out."

"Too early for work."

She'd wanted to surprise Lida with a visit, but the way her grandpa was staring her down made Hazel feel like lead seeped into her throat, making any words she could come up with stick. She searched the room for inspiration, shoving one hand into her pocket to stall. Her fingers wrapped around a crumpled telegram. "I'm headin' to the school," she finally said.

"School?" He puffed a cloud of smoke. "What the devil for?"

"I'm, um…I'm working to clear it out. Hopin' to get some materials to reopen it come fall."

He eyed her, and she could see the questions hanging between them. She decided to beat him to the punch.

"Ain't got a new teacher or nothin', but who's to say once it's cleaned up with a fresh coat of red paint, someone here may look at it and take a shine to teaching." The suggestion was as unlikely as striking gold in the nearby hills, but she pressed on. "Lida's been tryin' to get school materials out here. The Havishes—you know, Mr. and Mrs. Havish of the minin' company—they may be able to help."

Her grandpa apparently only heard part of what she'd said. "Miss Jones been at the Lodge a lot lately."

Hazel pulled back her shoulders. "And?"

He lowered his pipe, his blue eyes on her. "Be careful, Hazel."

The words would have knocked her sideways if she hadn't had one hand on the chair. She braced herself against it. "I beg your pardon?"

"I told you my feelings regardin' her father."

"And they were harsh feelings," she fired back. "You think she's the same?" At his silence, she added, "Lida is one of the kindest people I've ever met. She's gracious and caring. It's not fair to place the actions of her father in her shadow."

"She cast that shadow over you, darlin'."

Hazel stepped back, taking a deep breath. "Ain't no shadow over me. Ain't nothin' but light. If you're too stuck in your smoke and your tragic memories to see that, then I can't help you." She snatched her scarf and gloves from the table and without looking back slammed the door behind her.

Hazel had wanted to run to Lida. But for some reason, she hated to admit it was because of what her grandpa had said, Hazel ended up at the school. She stood in front of the old weathered building, staring up at the sad box bell and its broken frame. The school's exterior was still intact. Inside, cobwebs stretched in thready colonies over every chair, covering the chalkboard and the old teacher's desk. She walked through the room, hardly bigger than her own living room, and kicked at a broken chair leg.

"Grandpa." She gritted her teeth, staring at the layers of dirt, leaves, and weeds poking up through the wooden planked floor. "He don't know nothin'."

"Don't know nothin' about what?"

Hazel spun around. "Momma." Her mother stood in the doorway, a broom and rag in hand. "What're you doin' here?"

"Heard you was down here with some wild notion to clean it up." She motioned to Hazel's empty hands. "Expectin' to magic this place clean?"

At her mother's smile, Hazel grabbed the broom from her, her shoulders relaxing, but her body still tight with anger. "I was in a hurry."

"Anger makes us do all sorts of things, like want to clean a whole school by ourselves."

"It ain't anger that makes me wanna do this," Hazel countered, slowly sweeping leaves into a pile. "I've been thinkin' about gettin' this school goin' for a while."

Her mother had been swiping at spiderwebs hanging from the low ceiling beams. "You have?"

"Yeah." Hazel kept her eyes on the floor as she swept. "We've talked about this, Momma. How schoolin's important. Especially in these times. Education leads to opportunity. All our folks got is the mine. The mine or leavin'. Ain't no reason to stay, otherwise." She thought briefly of Lida, then her mind shifted to Nicholas. "You seen the way Nicholas is now that he's got those books."

Her mother smiled, running the rag across a dirty windowsill.

"Imagine if he could come back here. It's better than him goin' down into those dark hills."

At this, her mother said, "Hazel. Come now."

"No, Momma." She straightened, both hands on top of the broom. "You know it's true. Our people are leavin'. Look at the Boleys. All those sisters married as far away as they could get. That's one side, the side with money and means." She took a breath.

"Then look at young Mike Evans. Hardly sixteen and down in the mine with those men, the rock doin' nothin' but crushing his lungs and his spirit."

"Mike's a strong boy. He'll be fine."

"That ain't the point, Momma."

"What then, honey?" She gestured to the grimy walls, the broken glass in the window. "You gonna spruce this place up and come Fall, what, teach the young folk yourself?"

Hazel blinked. "What if I did?"

Her mother's mouth opened, then closed.

"Momma," Hazel moved closer, stepping between overturned chairs. "Lida's tryin' to get materials, school materials. Books and things that we could use to reopen this place." Her mother's brow had raised at the word "we," but Hazel continued. "It'd be so good to have this again. Think of the Benters and little Evangeline. Young Thomas," she said, her voice growing louder with her excitement. She'd imagined a future where all those children could come and learn under a sturdy roof, in a room filled with books to help them grow and understand the world. Her mother's question had rolled the image out more, stretching it, and Hazel started to see herself in the picture.

Her mother set the rag aside. She seemed to study Hazel, a soft look in her eyes. "You really believe in all this, don't you?"

"Yes, Momma." Still excited, Hazel combed her mind for more reasons why a school was so important. "Even Paul has taken off. Who knows if he'll be back or if he'll just sell his land and move on."

Her mother said, "I didn't think that was somethin' you'd be sad about."

Hazel matched her smile.

Her mother was quiet a moment. "Sometimes, I wondered if I should have pushed that more." At Hazel's confused look, she added, "Paul. You and Paul."

"Momma—"

She raised a hand. "I know. Ultimately, I'm glad I didn't. I knew you didn't want him, not like that." She cut her gaze to Hazel, who saw a flash of understanding in it. "But I wonder if my not ever pushin' you at all is part of the issue here."

Confused, Hazel propped the broom at her side, waiting. She forced her nerves into her hand that gripped the broomstick tight. She and her mother spent every day together, and had for a long time. Despite that, they'd never talked openly about many things. Especially not things like this.

"I didn't want to push you into anything you never wanted. You seemed perfectly content, even after your daddy died, and you jumped in at the Lodge. But I fear that because of that, I ended up never pushin' you at all, toward anything."

"Momma?"

"You coulda gone somewhere, anywhere. Down to Pine City or up to Salt Lake, even."

"I never wanted to go to those places. I love it here. This is my home." At her mother's worried look, she added, "Everyone I care about is right here."

"What if they're not anymore? Honey, what if they leave?"

"I…" Hazel stepped back, her posture shifting as her mother's words came into focus. She found knowing in her mother's gaze. To Hazel's relief, it reached out tenderly, wrapping Hazel in affection.

"Honey, know this. You don't need to do anything for anyone other than yourself. I know"—she raised a hand again—"it's a far cry from how we live. And I know you'll continue to live it, but Hazel, don't forget to live for yourself, too. Don't let me or anyone stand in the way."

Hazel wiped at tears that fell onto her cheek. "By someone, you mean Grandpa?"

Her mother swiped at her own gleaming eyes before taking Hazel by the shoulders. "My daddy's a man of his time. It's up to him to catch up or fall behind."

Hazel sniffled. "Momma—" Her voice broke, unable to expel the words she longed to share. The words explaining how much she adored being her daughter. How much she loved her mother's devotion to this town, to its people. How much she loved that her mother was here, talking to her, telling Hazel that her heart's wants were valid.

Her mother pulled her into a tight hug. "I love you, Hazel. Do what makes you happy."

"I love you, too, Momma."

Chapter Twenty-Nine

The second Tuesday of March, Lida was helping William redo part of the horse fence when the sound of a motor caught her ear.

She straightened, wiping sweat from her forehead under the warm sun. "Expecting anyone?" she asked.

William didn't break the steady hammering of a post into the ground when he answered. "Nope. Don't get many shiny automobiles this way."

Lida shielded her eyes. For a moment, she thought it might be Paul, ready to berate her for coming into town and stirring things up. But he'd left, according to Hazel, hardly coming back except to check on his mother and the ranch.

The black Cadillac parked with a gasp of smoke billowing against the blue sky. Mr. Havish climbed out.

"Wonder what he wants," William said, tossing a wave at Mr. Havish, who was busy looking at his polished shoes now lined with mud and snowmelt.

"Mr. Havish," Lida said, walking over to shake his hand. "How are you?"

He used a handkerchief to swipe his shining forehead. The high collar of his starched shirt and snugness of his tie made him appear like a fearful, trapped animal, uncertain how to handle this new terrain. "Miss Jones. Good afternoon."

"How's your wife?" Lida tried not to smile as he fumbled over the back seat, seemingly searching for something. "Cynthia?" he called from the depths of the car. "Oh, she's fine. Yes, fine." He resurfaced with a stack of books and magazines tied together.

Lida stepped forward. "Are those—"

"Your library materials, yes."

Lida ran through her mental calendar. "I was planning to pick those up." She helped him, taking the top half of the bundle before it toppled. "The library resumes Monday, doesn't it?"

"Yes, Monday, yes." He followed her into the house. "I figured I'd save you a trip. Had to come up here anyway."

Lida set the materials on the table. Mr. Havish followed suit, then wiped his brow and neck. "Here on business?" she asked.

"Yes, in a way." His small eyes searched her home. "Your father?"

"At work." The mine had reopened the week before. Reading the question in Mr. Havish's gaze, she added, "William's home helpin' Martha. Little Thomas has a fever."

"Understood." He stuck his thumbs in his belt, looking at their fireplace, their fruit bowl with a pair of red apples, anywhere but at Lida.

"Mr. Havish?"

He cleared his throat. "Miss Jones—"

"Lida."

He continued. "Lida. Over the holiday, I was provided an extensive report of the employees at my mine. An extensive, detailed report."

At his pinched face, she found a chair. "I see."

"And it came to my attention that your father had, shall we say, a difficult time." He pulled a folded paper from inside his coat. "May fifteenth: late. May twenty-first: late. September ninth: disorderly conduct due to intoxication. September tenth through the eighteenth: absent due to illness." He folded the paper again. With a sigh, he met her gaze. "My dear, your father seems like a good enough man, but I fear this may not be the most suitable position for him."

"He's a hard worker, Mr. Havish."

"Yes, dear."

"My father," she started, "he's doing much better. He's been doing well since starting back last week. No tardiness. Nothing." She gestured to the paper. "Nothing like before."

Mr. Havish's gaze turned sad. Lida was ready to explain more, ready to defend her father when two realizations struck her like the ringing of a bell. First, she realized how tired she was of having to do this. She'd given this same pleading speech to foremen, managers, and mill owners all across this country on behalf of her father. It was always her speaking for him because he wouldn't. He couldn't, too consumed in his own grief and shame.

The second thing that struck her was that, even if she did say everything, beg for her father's pardon, Mr. Havish had already made up his mind. She saw it in the resolute frown on his clean-shaven face.

"Lida, I believe in second chances, but your father has abused that belief. This is the last one. One more." He held up a finger. "If I get one more note, one more call about Yaromir…it's over. My dear, the mine is hard enough. It's too hard to have any added risk." His voice softened. "Understand?"

She nodded.

"Very well." He rubbed his hands together, pocketing the paper. "I better get back." He paused, glancing at the books. "You've been a fine member of our library. We've got a girl who says she's interested in joining, but she won't be here until June. A newlywed from New Mexico." He chuckled. "Wouldn't it be great to expand the Pack Horse Initiative?"

"Yes," she said, trying to smile, but her mind was caught in a worried haze.

"And I haven't forgotten your request."

Lida looked up. "My request?"

"From last year. The strikes died down after the New Year, so shipments are coming in again on the train. Can't promise anything, but we may be able to finagle some schoolbooks here and there. I know a group in Pennsylvania willing to chip in."

Lida stood. A concerned fog had clouded her mind, but small flicks of gratitude punched at the haze, trying to clear it. "Thank you," she said. "Please let me know if you're able to send materials." *Even if I do have to leave, I can leave Hazel with something good.* Tears threatened, and she quickly shook Mr. Havish's hand.

"Well," he said, "see you then. And good luck." Outside, he added, "Tell your father I'm rooting for him." Then he climbed into his car and drove away.

❖

Hazel shook out her grandpa's quilt over the porch railing. He'd been particularly ornery lately. Ever since their heated conversation, he'd reverted to a toddler, refusing her help and turning his chin up at anything she said to him.

"He'll come around," her mother had said one night after Hazel had offered a new balm she'd been given by Mrs. Evans. It was said to help soothe aches, and her grandpa's knee always hurt him when the weather turned. But he'd ignored her, and she'd slammed the jar next to him, storming outside to clear her head.

Now, she shot a glare at her front door. "Nothin' but a cloud of gloom," she muttered. When Lida rode up over the ridge, Hazel started to feel better. She folded the quilt, resting it on the ledge when Lida pulled Beth to a stop in front of the porch.

"Hi, there." Hazel leaned against the railing.

Lida gave her a smile but dismounted quickly and snatched two magazines from her saddlebag. "Do you have the returns?"

Hazel crossed her arms at Lida's brusque demeanor. "They're inside." Lida only stood there, a pout on her lips. "You can keep my grandpa company. Misery loves it, so the saying goes."

Lida gave her a look but only held out the materials. "I'll wait here."

Hazel wasn't about to have the gloom spread. She uncrossed her arms. "Lida."

Her arm dropped to her side. "Mr. Havish paid me a visit."

"Up here? What'd he want?"

Lida fiddled with the cover of a magazine. "Well, he had good news and bad news. The good news: he's going to rekindle efforts for school materials."

Hazel's heart leapt. "Truly?"

"Truly."

"That's outstanding." Hazel stepped down and took Lida's hand and led her onto the porch. Lida gave her a small and secret smile. "What?"

"I've been dying to stand here with you."

The simple earnestness in Lida's voice threatened to break Hazel open. Her pulse quickened, so she found the railing again and held on to keep from pulling Lida into an embrace. She recalled their conversation. "You said there was bad news?"

Lida's face fell. "Mr. Havish said my father is on his final chance." She took off her hat, setting it atop the magazines on a rocking chair. "He had a list of my father's indiscretions. One more and that'll be it."

Pain throbbed in her fingers, and Hazel realized she was squeezing the railing behind her. "You mean to say…"

"If anything happens, and I mean anything," Lida said, frustration lacing her tone, "if he's late or has a bad day or…worse, he's fired." Her jaw clenched, her dark eyes scanning the western sky.

Was this how it had always been for Lida? Hazel could see it now: the relentless wheel of hope and fear driving Lida and her father across the land.

"It's like a fuse," Lida said, seeming to follow Hazel's train of thought, her gaze still on the sky. "Since my mother's death, a fuse dug its way into our lives. Each new job, each new place strikes a match, and the countdown begins." Her voice grew thick. "I try to stop it. I try to keep the match from even being struck, but…it's not mine. No matter how much I try, no matter how hard my efforts… it's not mine. It's his." Her gaze widened, a realization seeming to draw across her face.

Hazel reached out. "Lida?"

She blinked as if she'd forgotten where she was. Her voice was soft when she found Hazel's hand on the railing. "I don't know what's going to happen."

"None of us do." Hazel entwined their fingers, then pulled Lida into a hug. "It'll be all right," she said over Lida's shoulder. She closed her eyes as Lida wrapped her arms around her. Hazel willed her words to be true, willed Lida to believe them. Hazel's eyes flew open as she realized how much they had to be true because she wasn't sure, if the time came, she would be able to let Lida go.

CHAPTER THIRTY

"Pa, don't forget your lunch." Lida hurried after him down the porch steps.

Taking the lunchbox, her father smiled. "My Lida. Always to the rescue." He kissed her cheek. William stood at the end of the drive, the sunrise stretching bold pinks behind him. Her father adjusted his grip on his work helmet. "Today is a beautiful day." He stretched out his arms, inhaling deeply.

His enthusiasm proved contagious. Lida laughed. "I'm glad. Now go on or you'll be late."

He saluted, then disappeared down the ridge with William.

That day, Lida spent nearly an hour at the Evanses', listening to Evangeline read from *Mother Goose*.

"Very good," Lida said, sitting on the creaky porch floorboards. She looked up to find Mrs. Evans teary-eyed, shaking her head.

"She's gonna be readin' circles around her brother in no time."

From Lida's lap, Evangeline looked up, her curls bouncing. "Really?" she asked. "Better than Mike?"

"You bet, sweetheart," her mother said, leaning down to kiss the top of her head.

Evangeline squealed, then continued reading. Later, when Lida readied Beth to go, Mrs. Evans met her at the bottom of the stairs. She handed Lida a telegram.

"It's from my husband." Mrs. Evan's hands shook. She clasped them in front of her chest. "I can read it, but…I…I'm afraid…" Her voice broke.

Lida nodded. She unfolded the paper. Glancing over it, she smiled and read, "Love—struck it big in Tucson. Have ticket for train home in three weeks. Can't wait to see you and the kids again." She'd hardly finished before Mrs. Evans had thrown her arms around Lida.

She laughed and stepped back, wiping away tears. "He's coming home?"

Lida handed her the telegram. "He's coming home."

Mrs. Evans held the paper like a lifeline. Evangeline ran out, crashing into her mother's legs. "Come on, honey, we gotta get things ready." At Evangeline's wide gaze, her mother said, "Your daddy's comin' home."

Evangeline's excited yells echoed all the way down the mountain, following Lida to the Benters', then back home.

After a dinner of bread and Martha's soup, Lida bathed and nestled into a chair by the fire. She wrapped a blanket over her knees and lost herself in a book.

Shouts broke the peaceful spring night.

Lida stood, the blanket falling as she listened. A strange sense of automation came over her, like a lever had been pulled, setting the gears within her in motion. She was moving across the room, her mind stuck but her legs carrying her forward. She pressed a hand to the door. She closed her eyes, bracing for the inevitability on the other side.

"I said I'm fine." Her father stumbled away from William, who tried to steady him. Her father tripped, stumbling into a muddy puddle.

She flew down the steps, propping her father's arm around her shoulders, William mirroring her. "What happened?" she asked.

"Those boys from the mine." William's voice was the angriest she'd ever heard it. "I told them not to invite Yaro anymore. They seem to find it entertaining."

Lida inhaled sharply. She would never understand how joy

could be wrought from seeing a man like this. She wasn't sure if that was what stung like a thorn in her chest or the fact that her father had agreed.

Inside, they managed to lead him to his cot. He flailed his arms, nearly hitting William.

"Pa," Lida said, her face burning at William's shocked look. "Be careful."

He murmured and stood, pushing past them for the kitchen. He grabbed a cup and to Lida's relief, filled it with water.

To William she said, "Thank you."

He held her gaze. "You'll be all right?"

"I will."

"We're right over there if you need anything." He squeezed her shoulder. Tears welled in her eyes at his kindness.

When he was gone, she steeled herself, then said, "Pa."

"I do not need to hear it." He filled his cup again, his back to her.

"Pa."

He spun around, throwing the cup onto the ground. Water scattered across the floor. "Lida, I said I don't need to hear it."

She held back tears, shaken by his outburst. Both of their shoulders heaving, she said, "They fired you."

Her father stared at his shoes. "Yes. They fire me."

The same questions stormed her mind, but she only asked one. "Why?"

He picked up the cup, setting it carefully on the table. He played with the edge as if apologizing for throwing it. Finally, he said, "It's so much."

"The darkness?"

His gaze slid to her. He wobbled again. She helped him to a chair, then took a seat across from him.

"I thought things were getting better."

"Me too."

"Then—"

"The darkness. It is strong. It fills my mind, and the only way to make it stop..." He pointed to a stone on the edge of the fireplace.

Lida frowned, then went to it. Nudging it, she found it loose. A small bottle sat behind it, tucked into the stonework.

Jaw clenched, Lida took it back to her seat.

He gestured to the nearly empty bottle. "This makes it stop. When I have this, it's like I can see her again, Lida. I feel like I did when she was alive. It doesn't hurt as much."

"Pa, you know how easy it is to get hurt like this?" She hesitated, a flare of nausea rising in her gut. "Is that what you want?"

"No. No, Lida." He took her face in his hands. She swallowed, trying to fight more tears. "My Lida, I am not strong like you." His gaze shifted toward the fire. "You are always the strong one."

She reached up, gripping his wrist. "Pa."

"It's not fair, what I do. What I've done." He turned, staring out into the night. "But down there, in the mine, it is dark. Then, it's like that darkness follows me. The days become dark. Those black rocks have climbed out and followed me home. The dark is everywhere. So much dark."

She didn't have a reply. Lida could see it, the darkness. It covered her father's hands and clothes. It sat on his boots and stuck beneath his nails. And it bore into her through his blurry gaze. The darkness had rooted itself deep in him years ago, and there wasn't anything she could do about it. Not anymore.

His head fell into his hands. She rested hers gently on his messy, tangled hair. As he sobbed, Lida let her own tears fall silently.

"It'll be all right." She spoke Hazel's words, each one breaking into the fragment of hope she'd been clinging to. "It'll be all right."

CHAPTER THIRTY-ONE

"Here's your tea, Grandpa." Hazel set the teacup in front of him. He glanced at it, looking down his pipe as he drew a long breath, then coughed. His frame shook his chair in the corner by the Lodge fire. She waited until he regained his breath. "You all right?"

A few more sputtering hacks, then he grumbled, "I'm fine." He exchanged his pipe for the tea, careful as he lifted the cup and saucer. The soft clink was the only sound in the room besides the fire. The dining hall had cleared out after dinner on a slow Thursday night.

"Drink up. It'll help your throat." She turned.

"Hazel." Her grandpa's watery eyes held hers, then looked toward the kitchen where her mother helped Nicholas with the dishes. He cleared his throat, started to say something, then only lifted the tea in thanks.

Her mother was right; Henry Criley was a man of his time. She and everyone else could only help him so much. It was up to him, otherwise, to stay keen on the way life continued to change beyond what he once knew. She nodded, accepting the only form of an apology her proud grandfather was willing to give.

A half hour later, Hazel was drying a plate when her grandpa's surprised voice caught her ear. "Miss Jones?"

Hazel paused, as did her mother as she handed Nicholas a fork to polish. He frowned, took it, and looked between them as frantic steps thundered across the dining hall. Lida appeared in the doorway.

Nicholas spoke first. "Lida, why are you crying?"

The plate forgotten, Hazel stared at Lida's swollen eyes, her puffy cheeks and disheveled braid. Wherever she'd come from, she hadn't even brought her hat.

"Miss Jones." Her mother also seemed unsettled at Lida's frazzled appearance. "Lida. Are you all right?"

Lida had been staring at Hazel, hurt pouring from her eyes. She brought her hand to her mouth. In a small, shattered voice she said, "I'm afraid not."

"Lord," her mother said. "Come here, honey."

To Hazel's surprise, her mother helped Lida to a table at the edge of the dining hall, near the kitchen. She exchanged looks with Nicholas, who seemed almost afraid by Lida's behavior, and he followed at their heels.

Hazel sat beside Lida. Her mother stood nearby, concern drawn between her knit brows. Nicholas hovered close, rocking on his toes with his hands on his ears as Lida let out a cry.

"Lida," Hazel said softly, "what's going on? Has someone been hurt?"

"Your daddy okay?" her mother asked.

Sniffling, Lida looked between them. She shook her head. "He's been fired from the mine."

The air left the room. It had to have, that was the only way to explain the hollow ache ripping through her chest. "But," Hazel said, "surely Mr. Havish—"

Lida's broken look cut her off. Hazel remembered their conversation on the porch. Lida's father had run out of chances. And she and Lida had run out of time.

"Oh, sweetheart. I am sorry." Her mother's voice reached out, a comfort extending over Lida's shaking figure.

Nicholas stared at the floor near Lida's boots when he spoke. "If he's fired, he can't work."

Lida nodded. "That's right, Nicholas."

"If he can't work, where will he go?"

Hazel and Lida locked eyes. Her mother hurried forward. "That's up to Mr. Jones, honey." Hazel caught her mother's gaze. "Come on, Nicholas, we've got to get your grandpa home."

"But the dishes—"

"Will still be here in the mornin'." Over her shoulder she called, "Hear that? We're goin'."

Hazel took Lida's hand. Nicholas patted Lida gently on the back, his gaze cloudy.

She smiled through more tears. "Thank you, Nicholas."

He and her mother helped their grandpa stand. As they went by, her grandpa gave a small nod. Hazel squeezed Lida's hand. "Let me get you some water." In the kitchen, Nicholas and Grandpa were already out the back door. Her mother pulled on her coat. "Momma," she called. "Thank you."

Her mother smiled and closed the door behind her.

Lida took a long drink. Hazel moved her chair closer, pressing their knees together. Leaning forward, she said, "Tell me what happened."

Lida did. Through more tears, she told Hazel everything, including today, when her father had gotten home after collecting his paycheck and announced that they were leaving for California.

"When?" asked Hazel.

Lida shrugged. "As soon as possible, probably."

Hazel gripped Lida's knees, wondering if she could keep her in place if she tried hard enough. Her gaze flew to the Lodge door. She could bolt it shut, lock them in, stay here forever.

She tried to shake the foolishness from her thoughts. This was a time to be rational. Lida needed her to be clear-headed, to help in some way. Hazel wasn't sure if she could or even knew how, but she had to try. She used a napkin to clear away Lida's tears. She cupped her cheek, tracing her fingers from Lida's temple to her chin. Lida tilted her head into the action.

Then Hazel said what she'd known since July. "I don't want you to leave."

Lida kissed her. Unrelenting sadness poured from her, and

Hazel took it. She accepted it willingly and kissed Lida back with all of the courage she could summon.

She didn't break their kiss when Lida pulled her to stand. She didn't break their kiss as they fumbled to the stairs, nor when Lida pushed her against the wall, kissing her harder. Only when she reluctantly accepted the need for air did Hazel pull back. When Lida opened her eyes, Hazel saw the words shining back at her, the words neither of them wanted to speak when the time would come. The time that drew nearer with every passing moment. So Hazel kissed her again, unwilling to look.

Upstairs, Lida laid Hazel onto the bed. She pulled off her dress and tossed it aside. Hazel threw off Lida's shirt, then undid the button on Lida's trousers. After tugging off her pants, Hazel rolled them over, straddling her. She dove her hand toward Lida's center. Beneath her, Lida's eyes shone. Hazel found her lips, her neck, her breasts, trailing kisses across her body.

This can't be it, she thought. *This can't be all of our time.*

"I don't want this to be it," she murmured into Lida's neck. She slid her fingers inside Lida, who gasped and gripped Hazel's arm. Hazel started a rhythm, feeling Lida, loving Lida.

That was it, Hazel realized, trembling as she held Lida's gaze. That was their truth. She quickened her thrusts. Lida tightened around her fingers, her moans like music as her face softened.

When Lida cried out, Hazel kissed her. She pressed herself closer, as close as she could be to the woman she couldn't be without.

Eventually, their breathing slowed. Hazel's heart beat hard against her ribs, and she felt Lida's beating just as wildly. So wildly, Hazel feared Lida might not hear her when she said, "I love you."

Another tear slid down Lida's temple. She reached up, pulling Hazel close. Their lips brushing, she whispered, "I love you, too."

CHAPTER THIRTY-TWO

Lida sat at the foot of her bed, staring at her worn leather suitcase. The handle was so tattered, flecks of paint barely clung to the metal. All four corners were beaten, rough and faded from years of use. Lida pictured all the trains, all the crowded platforms, all the times she'd sat like this, staring at the consequences of her father's darkness.

"Knock, knock." Martha stood in the doorway. Little Thomas—who wasn't so little anymore—babbled at her hip.

"Hi, Martha." Lida swept her gaze over the stack of books at her bedside. "You want one?"

Martha rocked Thomas, his legs dangling as he gummed his hand. "I couldn't."

"Please," Lida said, "it's the least I can give. You and William have shown great care and kindness to us."

Martha looked from her to the books, then around the room at Lida's unpacked possessions. "They're yours. You keep 'em."

Hers. Lida had come to feel that way about many things while she'd lived here. This room inside the quaint cabin that shuddered in the wind, its old boards rattling in the mountain breeze had been hers. It had grown as familiar as a friend. She crossed the room, taking Thomas in her arms. She carried him into the kitchen. Martha followed. He spoke happily, his half words and jumbled sounds making them smile. He reached up to play with her hair. Pressing her forehead to his, she said, "I'm going to miss you."

"He'll miss you, too." Martha crossed her arms, a serious look on her face. For a moment, she looked as if she was going to say more but decided against it.

"I'm going to miss this place," Lida said.

"This place has that effect," replied Martha, glancing to where the window let in the warm morning sun. "When William and I first came here"—she smiled and made a waving motion—"Lord, I thought he was kiddin'. Thought surely we'd move on, especially after his momma passed." Her dark eyes glistened as she took Thomas back. She set him down, and he pulled at the hem of her dress. "This place has a way about it. Don't know whether it's that big ol' sky, them mountains like stairs to heaven, or the rocks painted like a desert. Maybe it's all of it that pulls you in, makin' you feel like you belong."

"You think that's what the Crileys had in mind when they founded Cedar Springs?" Lida asked, giving a small laugh.

Martha snorted. "Who knows. But their family sure is somethin'. They put everythin' they've got into this place. Mr. Criley, Clara… and Hazel."

Lida caught Martha's gaze. "They make it special."

Martha smiled. "That's right." She pointed to Lida's satchel by the door. "The folks will miss you deliverin' those books."

Lida kept her gaze on her empty Pack Horse satchel. She bit her cheek to hold back tears. Then she stood and dug through the bag's inner pocket. "Here." She handed Martha several lemon candies. "For when you see the Benters or little Evangeline."

Slipping the candies away in her apron, Martha scooped up Thomas at the sound of Lida's father riding up the drive. They both watched him ride around the side of the cabin to the stable.

"Well," Martha said, "don't y'all leave without a proper good-bye, now."

All Lida could do was nod. She wasn't sure what she would have done without the generous, constant presence of the Seagers. Exhaling a shaky breath, Lida wiped her eyes. She threw another glance around the room, then out the window. The wide open greeted her. Hazel was beyond those hills. She closed her eyes until she was on the Thompson front porch, side by side with the woman she'd fallen in love with. Then it was like she was being bucked off Beth as her eyes flew open. The last conversation she'd shared with Hazel on that porch struck her like the bright sun each morning. The moment she'd realized her father's sadness wasn't hers. It never had been. Though she loved him more than she could say, she couldn't do it anymore. It was his to carry and try to move forward with, not hers.

As her father's footsteps sounded outside, she busied herself by putting away the dishes.

"Got telegram from your mother's cousin, Vlad. He lives outside central valley. Lots of farming work available."

Leaning on the sink, Lida said, "That's good, Pa." She could feel his eyes on her.

"Also got our tickets. Train leaves at five this evening. Will take us south, two stops between here and San Bernardino. Vlad will meet us there, and we go up to place called Fresno."

Closing her eyes, Lida could feel the lurch of the train as its engine roared to life. She heard the piercing whistle urging them on. Another ride into the unknown, another ride carrying her away from the life she'd made here.

She turned at the sound of her father shoving things into his duffel bag. With stained hands, he found the few constant things he owned and prepared them for another journey. She looked at what the work in the mine had done to him; while his arms looked stronger, his body seemed weary. The coal had stained his hands, and faint smudges of gray lined the collar of his shirt. His shoulders hunched from being underground every day. This really hadn't been the best place for him, Lida thought. The mine wasn't a good place for someone battling his own darkness. Should she have known that before? Perhaps she could have helped save him from this latest slip into the dim cold inside his mind.

She pictured him out near the sea, in an endless open field full of citrus and clean air. She smiled. "California will be good for you, Pa."

He turned. A frown drew lines across his forehead. Standing on the other side of the room, Lida looked past him to the window. She drew a long breath, letting reality sink into her lungs, the reality that even though Cedar Springs hadn't been right for her father, it was right for her.

"I'm not going."

Her father's frown deepened. His dark eyes widened for a moment. "What?"

"I'm not going with you."

"I don't understand."

She shook her head. "I think you do."

He blinked as if trying to clear the space between them. The space that Lida knew they both needed—had needed for a long time—but had been unwilling to acknowledge.

"You go, Pa. Go to California. Go live near the ocean and green valleys and be with Mom's family. But I'm not going with you." She straightened, gesturing to the calendar on the wall, the knitted blanket by the hearth. "This is my home now."

Her father's voice was hoarse as he replied, "Lida, this is not your home."

"We haven't had a home in so long, Pa. I think…I think we've both forgotten what it can be like when it's right…when it's real." He stared, a sniffle twitching his mustache. Then she said what she knew should happen the moment she woke up that morning. "You go, but I'm staying here."

Lida wasn't sure how long they stood there, father and daughter enveloped in a lifetime of moments that seemed to wind around them. Moments that had woven their way across this country like a jagged tapestry, disjointed and unfinished. Only now did Lida realize their stories, their tapestries, didn't need to run together. She didn't need him to help write her story, and even though her heart twinged with worry and fear for this change, her father needed to mend his own heart without her.

He stepped forward, handing her a ticket. Through his bleary eyes, she met his gaze. "For when you visit."

Crying and laughing, Lida hugged him. She held on to her father, inhaled his musty smell and etched the feel of his old coat into her mind. "I love you, Pa."

He held her tight. "I love you, too, Lida."

CHAPTER THIRTY-THREE

Warm afternoon sun grazed Hazel's skin as she pushed up the sleeves of her dress. Even after opening every window of the school and keeping the door propped, the air inside was stifling.

"No wonder school's not in session come summer. Lord, how'd we learn in here?" She rested one hand on her hip, leaning against the broom. She made a mental note to see about cutting out a window on the western wall to help with air flow.

Since starting work this morning, she'd already swept out the remainder of the leaves, cleared away the cobwebs from the ceiling and corners, and scrubbed half the desks clean. Most of the chairs would need repairing or replacing, but she was pleased that most everything else was in fine shape.

She blew strands of hair from her face, wiping her brow. Satisfied with her progress, Hazel admitted, reluctantly, that her mother had been right in suggesting she come here after Hazel had woken up in a foul mood.

"Go keep yourself busy, honey. Mind can't fester if it's busy workin'."

Hazel had grumbled a protest but decided it was worth a try. Anything to keep her mind off the fact that Lida would soon be leaving Cedar Springs.

Tears stung her eyes, so Hazel returned to her work, vigorously sweeping the old floorboards some more. A little while later, she jumped at the sound of a car door slamming. For a moment, she thought Paul was back. But the pair of voices bantering were unfamiliar, and Hazel moved into the doorway to find a well-dressed, middle-aged man and woman walking to the school.

"Good afternoon," Hazel called, letting a question hang in her voice.

The man, his round, shiny face scrunched beneath a bowler hat, seemed to be concentrating on lugging a full mail sack. The woman, in a fetching green dress more suited for a night in the city than marching toward an abandoned country school, waved. Her painted silver nails glimmered under the sunlight. "Hello! Our apologies for dropping in unannounced. We stopped by the Lodge and were told we might find you here." At Hazel's silence, she added, "You are Miss Hazel Thompson?"

"I am." Hazel pulled her shoulders up at the woman's impeccable smile and makeup like a model in a magazine. But kindness shone in her gaze as she extended a gloved hand.

"I'm Cynthia Havish. This is my husband, Walter."

"Y'all own the mine," Hazel replied.

"Yes," Mr. Havish said, nearly falling sideways as the bulky bag slid to one side.

Mrs. Havish, only seeming to find this amusing, said, "We are also the proud organizers of Utah's Pack Horse Library initiative."

Hazel motioned for them to come inside. Mr. Havish placed the sack on a desk, then sighed and cleaned his gleaming forehead with a handkerchief. Mrs. Havish was saying, "I believe you are acquainted with our librarian, Miss Lida Jones?"

Hazel felt a small flush fill her cheeks. It grew at Mrs. Havish's raised brow. "Yes, I am."

"Well, here are the materials she requested on your behalf," Mrs. Havish said, a sly smile lifting her red lips.

"Quite right," Mr. Havish added. "We expect another shipment in two months' time."

Hazel reached for the bag. Inside, she found arithmetic logs, an encyclopedia, several chalkboards, two dictionaries, and a collection of children's stories.

"It's not much, I'm afraid." Mr. Havish dusted his coat. Hazel's eyes welled. "It's perfect." She met their gazes. "Thank you."

"You are quite welcome, my dear." Mrs. Havish beamed, then tossed a look around. "This is quite the undertaking."

Hazel nodded, still awestruck by the reality of Lida's efforts coming to fruition. A pang clattered in her chest. She wished, after all her hard work to make this happen, Lida could be here to see it. Hazel wished she could stay here, with her.

"Well, I always say we need more women like you in Iron County. Such good role models, don't you think so, Walter?"

"Yes, very good." He was glancing at his pocket watch. "Cynthia—"

"Yes, oh, all right. We must be off." She took Hazel's hand between hers. "So wonderful to meet you. I must say, between you and Miss Jones, Cedar Springs is on the up. I can feel it." She chuckled at her own comment, but Hazel's smile faltered.

"Lida," she said, "I mean, Miss Jones...have you any word from her?"

Cynthia frowned, glancing at her husband. "No, dear. Though we did see her father on our way up here. Said he was heading to the train station."

"Already?" Panic constricted Hazel's chest.

"Yes," Mrs. Havish said, giving a sad sigh. "I suppose he's eager to move on after everything."

Hazel felt frantic as she said, "I have to go."

"Go, dear?"

"I have to get to the station." She pushed between the Havishes. "I'm sorry," she said over her shoulder. "Please, excuse me. I can't miss her."

"Miss Thompson—"

But Hazel had grabbed her bag and was out the door. Ignoring the Havishes' calls, she winced as she realized she'd walked here. It would take her an eternity to get home and ready a horse. By then, she might be too late.

She spun around, facing the school and the Havishes standing outside. She was about to ask if they could drive her to the station when she realized Mrs. Havish wore an amused smile.

Hazel was about to ask what could possibly be funny when she registered the sound of hooves.

"Lida." Hazel's heart leapt against her chest at the sight of her riding up the hill. Her long braid flew behind her as she urged Beth closer.

Hazel was surprised she had the ability to speak as Lida pulled up beside the car. "I thought you were at the station."

Lida dismounted. "I was, but only to say good-bye to my father."

Hazel's pulse quickened. "You mean..."

Lida smiled, taking one of Hazel's hands. "I'm staying."

Hazel pulled Lida into a hug, relief and love overwhelming her. Only when Mr. Havish cleared his throat did she even remember they were still there.

"Your materials are delivered, Miss Jones," Mr. Havish announced, pointing to the school.

Hazel was crying as she clung to Lida, but she didn't care.

"Thank you," Lida said, her eyes shining. They shook hands.

"Well," Cynthia said, looking like she'd just seen a movie unfold by the way she clutched the neck of her dress, "we better get back." Pausing before them, she added, "Good luck, my dears." She winked and climbed into the car after her husband.

Once they drove away, Hazel took Lida's hand and led her into the school. Inside, she pulled Lida close, kissing her. "You're really staying?" she murmured against Lida's lips, their foreheads pressed together.

Lida smiled. "I can't very well leave now. Not when our story's only beginning."

Hazel fell into another kiss, relishing the words "our story." Her body sang with how right those words sounded. "Your father," she said, "will he..."

"Be all right?" Lida finished the question. "I can't be sure. But we finally talked, and he knows he'll have to try living without me."

Hazel nodded. "Perhaps this is the best thing for him, being on his own."

Lida hugged her, her voice soft over Hazel's shoulder. "I love you, Hazel."

She gave a tearful laugh, incredulous that this was real. Lida was here, in her arms, to stay. "You know," she said, pulling back to hold Lida's gaze, "according to those books of yours, some people look everywhere for love. Spend their whole lives searchin' for it." She stared into Lida's beautiful, dark eyes. "I was never one of those people. Never reckoned it was in the cards for me. But," she said, kissing Lida again, "love surprises us. Sometimes, it shows up, outta the blue. Sometimes, love rides right into town on the train from Cincinnati."

EPILOGUE

"That's all for today, everyone," Lida said. "Close your books and don't forget to push in your chairs."

"May I take this with me, Miss Jones?" Charlie Benter asked, waving a copy of *Doctor Dolittle* as his younger siblings found their jackets by the front door of the school. Mike Evans helped Evangeline into hers.

"I didn't assign you homework this weekend, Charlie," she replied but smiled at the earnest look on his face as the children began to file outside. The crisp fall air kicked up some of the papers on her desk. "But if you'd like to, feel free to read until chapter seven."

He nodded and scurried after everyone. Lida called after them to wait for her before they started their walks home. She picked up a few pieces of chalk that had fallen beneath seats and cleaned off some of the slates. Once everything was tidy, she joined everyone outside, locking the door of the school behind her.

Lida led the children down the hillside, Evangeline clutching her hand along the way. Eventually, the Benter clan disappeared up a ridge, all but Charlie sprinting homeward, ready for the weekend.

"Will your family be going to the Lodge tonight?" Lida asked Mike, who took Evangeline's other hand to lead her up the path to their front drive.

"Yes, ma'am," he said, careful to lead his sister around a fallen log.

Lida waved. "See you this evening, then." She shoved her hands into her coat pockets and tilted her head back to the afternoon sky. The mountains carried her down the familiar path toward home. Arriving at the Lodge, Lida found the front door open, the scent of cinnamon and nutmeg wafting out to greet her. Inside, the tables were adorned with the tablecloths from last Thanksgiving. Gourds and pumpkins were arranged in corners and on the stairs for the autumn dinner the Thompsons had been planning for the last month.

In the kitchen, she found Clara and Arthur chatting over a giant pot emitting lazy steam. Nicholas, delicately placing balls of dough on a baking sheet, noticed her first.

"Hi, Lida."

"Hi, Nicholas." Pitchers of cider were lined up on the back counter. Through the open back door, the cauldron sat over a low fire. "How's the chili coming along, Clara?"

"Oh, just fine. And it'll be the best chili this town's ever tasted, so long as Arthur leaves it alone." She nudged him with her hip, hardly moving him. He bellowed a laugh.

"Clara, I told you another tablespoon of cayenne ain't gonna hurt nobody."

"There's a time and a place for changes to a recipe, and the autumn feast ain't it."

Despite the bickering, warmth radiated between them. Lida removed her hat, glancing around. Still stirring, Clara looked up and behind a smile said, "She's upstairs."

Lida nodded, then excused herself. She snatched a candied almond from a dish in the dining room and climbed the stairs. She knocked lightly on the first door, then pressed it open.

"Hi," Hazel said, sitting in front of a small table where she'd arranged an old mirror. She dabbed a bit of rouge onto her cheeks, her gaze holding Lida's.

Crossing the room, Lida stood behind her, leaning down to place a kiss on her neck. "Good evening, Miss Thompson."

Hazel chuckled, then turned in her seat. Looking up, she asked,

"So how does it feel to have finished one full month as Cedar Springs's new teacher?"

Lida breathed deep. "It feels really great."

Standing, Hazel smoothed her dress. Lida let her gaze rove over the dark blue material. Reaching out, she ran her fingers down the sleeves, catching Hazel's hands in her own. "This dress is beautiful."

Grinning, Hazel did a turn. "You like it?"

Lida recalled the weeks Hazel had spent poring over a catalogue she'd brought up from Pine City. Finally, she'd decided on what she had dubbed "the perfect dress." It arrived last week, and Hazel had insisted on saving it for the autumn feast. The soft material clung to her figure in the best of ways, and Lida grabbed her waist, pulling her closer. "I love it."

Hazel reached up, clasping her fingers behind Lida's neck beneath her braid. They kissed, slow and easy. Lida drank Hazel in, holding her close, losing herself in the feeling of being here with Hazel, the surprise still evident in each touch that this was her life now.

Hazel reluctantly pulled back. "Suppose we oughta head downstairs soon."

"I suppose," Lida replied after one more kiss. She removed her coat and found a fresh button-down in the wardrobe they'd gotten as a gift from the Seagers. William had built it over the summer. It was another item Lida and Hazel had added to the room, which had slowly become their makeshift home since the spring.

Nearly everyone in town had seemed to accept her as another member of the Thompson clan. To Lida, it seemed a few understood what might be transpiring between them. But any whispers of gossip or snide remarks never seemed to penetrate the walls of the Lodge. Not as long as Clara stood guard, her kind arms stretched around them.

"That new librarian gonna make it tonight? I'm anxious to meet her," Hazel said, swiping at an unruly wave of hair in the mirror.

"I think so. She said as soon as she told her husband there'd be cornbread, there was no way they'd miss it."

Hazel laughed. "Good then. Momma's cornbread is legendary."

Lida had spent the summer months training the new addition to the Pack Horse Library, the young woman the Havishes had told her about in the spring. She was barely twenty, full of enthusiasm and, Lida had to admit, a much better rider than she was. She took to the paths and precarious ridges with ease and wasn't daunted by the sometimes challenging delivery routes. Having her on board had freed Lida to help Hazel prepare the school for its reopening at the beginning of September.

In a fresh shirt and dusting off her pants, Lida followed Hazel downstairs. At seven o'clock, people arrived for the Lodge's newest tradition: the autumn feast, open not only to the folks of Cedar Springs but the people of Pine City.

Cynthia strode in with Walter, both of them looking like they belonged on the red carpet of a Hollywood premiere. "Miss Jones, Miss Thompson, good evening. I cannot tell you how glad I was to receive this invitation. Weren't we thrilled, Walter?"

Mr. Havish removed his hat and was already eying his pocket watch. "Yes, thrilled, yes."

"Sit anywhere you'd like," Lida told them. Hazel took Cynthia's coat and hung it near the door. "Dinner will be served shortly."

More folks arrived. Steven Akers, the Evanses, even Dottie from Pine City showed up, looking rather frightened but smiling nonetheless. Hazel had gone into the kitchen when the Seagers arrived, so Lida greeted them at the door. Little Thomas walked in on two unsteady legs, one hand in each of his parents', who framed him on either side.

"Evening, Lida," Martha said. "I can't tell you how glad I am to be off that wagon. William could smell the chili from down the ridge, and he nearly plowed us off the road, he was in such a hurry to get here."

"Nonsense, Martha," William said, taking her coat and hanging it with his hat near the others. "Was Beth doing the hurrying, not me."

Martha rolled her eyes as Lida laughed. "I do appreciate you looking after her," Lida said.

Martha scooped up Little Thomas as more townsfolk trickled

into the Lodge. "Of course. She's the sweetest horse I ever knew," she replied. "How's your father doing?" William was shaking hands with Jerry but turned his attention back to Lida when she answered.

"His latest letter said things are going well. He's living with my mother's cousin, and work seems to be good. He's been there without incident since May." A small sense of trepidation crept up Lida's spine, but it paled in comparison to the uncertainty she'd felt upon opening her father's first letter in June. She had been pleasantly surprised at his good mood, and he continued to write each month since. Still, she couldn't resist writing her cousin, asking to be told if anything did happen, but there hadn't been any news. California seemed like a good place for her father after all. "He's planning to visit in the spring."

"That's wonderful, Lida," William said, Martha nodding in agreement.

They found a table and a steady *clomp* on the porch out front caught Lida's ear. Outside, she found Jerry helping Grandpa up the steps.

"Good evening, Henry," she said, pushing the door open wider for him to pass through.

"Miss Jones. I reckon you can tell me where my daughter is. Clara said she'd leave my tie out for me, but all I found at the house was these old suspenders."

"She's in the kitchen, but I'll be happy to let her know."

He grunted, moving past her into the Lodge. She helped him into a seat near the corner, then went into the kitchen.

"Your father's here, Clara."

"Lord, I forgot to leave his tie our, didn't I?"

Lida laughed. "He may have mentioned it."

"I'll see to him," Arthur said, squeezing Clara's shoulder and heading out into the now crowded dining room.

"Nicholas, stick those cookies in the oven, then go pour everyone some cider," Clara said, breathless over the giant pot. "I gotta start servin' here in a minute."

Nicholas grabbed a pitcher and disappeared into the dining room. Lida found another ladle and helped Hazel scoop chili into bowls. "Girls," Clara said, "I'm leaving that to y'all. I gotta go get the cornbread in the baskets out here."

"Yes, Momma," Hazel replied as Clara hurried into the busy room.

"This smells delicious," Lida said, arranging several bowls on a tray.

"Tastes good, too," Hazel replied, tossing her a wink. With a quick glance at the dining room door, she kissed Lida before carefully taking the tray and balancing it on her shoulder. "You got that one?"

Lida mimicked her, careful to keep the tray even on her shoulder. "I got it."

"Follow me, then." Hazel smiled, then carefully wove her way between everyone taking their seats. In the doorway, Lida paused. She took in the room, full of the people she'd come to know over the last year and a half. People she laughed with, people she shared stories with, people she could call home.

Utterly content, Lida followed Hazel into the dining room.

About the Author

Originally from Dallas-Fort Worth, Ledel now resides in San Antonio, Texas. She is currently working on her next novel.

Books Available From Bold Strokes Books

Always by Kris Bryant. When a pushy American private investigator shows up demanding to meet the woman in Camila's artwork, instead of introducing her to her great-grandmother, Camila decides to lead her on a wild goose chase all over Italy. (978-1-63679-027-5)

Exes and O's by Joy Argento. Ali and Madison really only have one thing in common. The girl who broke their heart may be the only one who can put it back together. (978-1-63679-017-6)

Paris Rules by Jaime Maddox. Carly Becker has been searching for the perfect woman all her life, but no one ever seems to be just right until Paige Waterford checks all her boxes, except the most important one—she's married. (978-1-63679-077-0)

Shadow Dancers by Suzie Clarke. In this third and final book in the Moon Shadow series, Rachel must find a way to become the hunter and not the hunted, and this time she will meet Ehsee Yumiko head-on. (978-1-63555-829-6)

The Kiss by C.A. Popovich. When her wife refuses their divorce and begins to stalk her, threatening her life, Kate realizes to protect her new love, Leslie, she has to let her go, even if it breaks her heart. (978-1-63679-079-4)

The Wedding Setup by Charlotte Greene. When Ryann, a big-time New York executive, goes to Colorado to help out with her best friend's wedding, she never expects to fall for the maid of honor. (978-1-63679-033-6)

Velocity by Gun Brooke. Holly and Claire work toward an uncertain future preparing for an alien space mission, and only one thing is certain—they will have to risk their lives, and their hearts, to discover the truth. (978-1-63555-983-5)

Wildflower Words by Sam Ledel. Lida Jones treks west with her father in search of a better life on the rapidly developing American frontier, but finds home when she meets Hazel Thompson. (978-1-63679-055-8)

A Fairer Tomorrow by Kathleen Knowles. For Maddie Weeks and Gerry Stern, the Second World War brought them together, but the end of the war might rip them apart. (978-1-63555-874-6)

Changing Majors by Ana Hartnett Reichardt. Beyond a love, beyond a coming-out, Bailey Sullivan discovers what lies beyond the shame and self-doubt imposed on her by traditional Southern ideals. (978-1-63679-081-7)

Highland Whirl by Anna Larner. Opposites attract in the Scottish Highlands, when feisty Alice Campbell falls for city girl about town Roxanne Barns. (978-1-63555-892-0)

Holiday Hearts by Diana Day-Admire and Lyn Cole. Opposites attract during Christmastime chaos in Kansas City. (978-1-63679-128-9)

Humbug by Amanda Radley. With the corporate Christmas party in jeopardy, CEO Rosalind Caldwell hires Christmas Girl Ellie Pearce as her personal assistant. The only problem is, Ellie isn't a PA, has never planned a party, and develops a ridiculous crush on her totally intimidating new boss. (978-1-63555-965-1)

On the Rocks by Georgia Beers. Schoolteacher Vanessa Martini makes no apologies for her dating checklist, and newly single mom Grace Chapman ticks all Vanessa's Do Not Date boxes. Of course, they're never going to fall in love. (978-1-63555-989-7)

Song of Serenity by Brey Willows. Arguing with the Muse of music and justice is complicated, falling in love with her even more so. (978-1-63679-015-2)

The Christmas Proposal by Lisa Moreau. Stranded together in a Christmas village on a snowy mountain, Grace and Bridget face their past and question their dreams for the future. (978-1-63555-648-3)

The Infinite Summer by Morgan Lee Miller. While spending the summer with her dad in a small beach town, Remi Brenner falls for Harper Hebert and accidentally finds herself tangled up in an intense restaurant rivalry between her famous stepmom and her first love. (978-1-63555-969-9)

Wisdom by Jesse J. Thoma. When Sophia and Reggie are chosen for the governor's new community design team and tasked with tackling substance abuse and mental health issues, battle lines are drawn even as sparks fly. (978-1-63555-886-9)

A Convenient Arrangement by Aurora Rey and Jaime Clevenger. Cuffing season has come for lesbians, and for Jess Archer and Cody Dawson, their convenient arrangement becomes anything but. (978-1-63555-818-0)

An Alaskan Wedding by Nance Sparks. The last thing either Andrea or Riley expects is to bump into the one who broke her heart fifteen years ago, but when they meet at the welcome party, their feelings come rushing back. (978-1-63679-053-4)

Beulah Lodge by Cathy Dunnell. It's 1874, and newly betrothed Ruth Mallowes is set on marriage and life as a missionary...until she falls in love with the housemaid at Beulah Lodge. (978-1-63679-007-7)

Gia's Gems by Toni Logan. When Lindsey Speyer discovers that popular travel columnist Gia Williams is a complete fake and threatens to expose her, blackmail has never been so sexy. (978-1-63555-917-0)

Holiday Wishes & Mistletoe Kisses by M. Ullrich. Four holidays, four couples, four chances to make their wishes come true. (978-1-63555-760-2)

Love By Proxy by Dena Blake. Tess has a secret crush on her best friend, Sophie, so the last thing she wants is to help Sophie fall in love with someone else, but how can she stand in the way of her happiness? (978-1-63555-973-6)

Marry Me by Melissa Brayden. Allison Hale attempts to plan the wedding of the century to a man who could save her family's business, if only she wasn't falling for her wedding planner, Megan Kinkaid. (978-1-63555-932-3)

Pathway to Love by Radclyffe. Courtney Valentine is looking for a woman exactly like Ben—smart, sexy, and not in the market for anything serious. All she has to do is convince Ben that sex-without-strings is the perfect pathway to pleasure. (978-1-63679-110-4)